Alex Rae

Ilea

Children of Regar: II

Copyright © 2017 by Alex Rae

Editors: Brenda Wright and
B. L. Henderson

Cover design © 2017 by P. W. Bledsoe and
Sherrie Sanchez
Special thanks to Unsplashed.com
Mountain photograph by Christian Lohner

Boat Tiger Books

ISBN 978-0-9984633-3-9

FREE BONUS CHAPTER

Visit my website

https://alexraebooks.wordpress.com/

explore other books in the

Children of Regar series and receive a

FREE BONUS CHAPTER

Contents

Prologue

In the most ancient of days, our people did not live as we do now. War and fear did not control our lives. There was peace in our land and all Regarians lived as one. The Tal and the Breen, the Benjee and the Sesti.

Each sect would send their wisest men to council at new phase of the red moon. They would pray to the life giver, Gelquin, and seek wisdom. They would resolve disputes and plan for our tomorrows.

There was order. And there was peace.

But in those ancient days there arose a prophet who could see tomorrow. A reader of dreams, a seer of visions, and the keeper of the SolStone. He brought with him a prophecy that would forever change our world. He brought a warning about the future.

> *The moons of Regar*
> *Shall future see*
> *A dark-eyed princess*
> *Come to thee*
>
> *Born of power*
> *Raised of ruin*
> *Fed by prophets*
> *Her nature turned*
>
> *Her heart to Regar*
> *Peace will bring*
> *But serve destruction*
> *To the lesser king*

The wars have come to Regar. Our world has changed just as the prophet foretold. Jaika, daughter of King Merith, is believed to be the one … the dark-eyed one who will fulfill the prophecy.

But, she cannot do it alone.

Knife

Adolphus stretched his wings wide as he flew toward the city of Palon. His mountain home was already too far away to see in the darkness, even if he had tried to look back. The red moon sat high in the night sky giving his watery-blue skin a gray hue. His long white hair, full of streaks that looked like metal, was tied back and wrapped in straps like the Tal warriors of old. Tonight, he wore thick leggings and a tight-knit, slat-backed tunic his wife had fashioned from the rough fabric of the Gogora plant, not his usual silken clothes.

As he flew, his eyes studied the sand below him, still and empty, so he was confident no one was watching. He could already see Merith's castle standing tall and fearless in the center of the city of Palon. The stone walls glistening in the red moon's light. Beyond it lay a forest of trees and a boiling river that seemed to come from nowhere.

The river marked the border between Palon and Benjee — between men with gold skin and those with white. Walls made of rock and sand enclosed most of Palon. Wise men built their houses inside those walls. Ground dwellers hiding from Kaleus and his raiders. Only reckless, fearless men worked outside those walls. Men who built tents and wooden structures that housed businesses of every kind. Especially those that were against Palon law. But tonight, Adolphus sought an honorable man whose home stood well within the walls of the city of Palon.

He tilted his shoulders to shift his flight toward the right side of the city. A merchants' district. A section of the city that housed the legitimate businesses that kept the city alive. War could ravage the land, but men would still find a way to make a profit. Harea, a sand-melter, lived here in a two-level gray house. A man who could heat sand and make clear walls and some very dangerous weapons.

Adolphus circled over the gray house three times looking for strangers. Then he thrust his shoulders back to force his wings to stand almost straight up while his legs dropped closer to the ground. He landed behind an old stone building that housed the massive ovens of the sand-melter, then closed his wings that hooked over his shoulders and clung to his back and sides. He buried himself in the darkness of the building, leaning against its outer walls where the shadows were deep enough to cover even the mightiest of men. If a blue-skinned Tal was caught meeting with a Palon, it could mean death for everyone involved.

From here he watched the clear-sand windows of the gray house. Harea would place a glower in the lower window when it was safe to meet. Then he would walk out to the stone building to talk of war. Adolphus stepped inside the house of ovens and climbed to a familiar ledge where wooden rafters met stone and sand, and the red moon's light sprayed across the ground through one of the many open spaces in the stone. Empty archways and rectangular cutouts formed random patterns in the walls to provide an exit for the heat, sand-melting heat. Here he could see the gray house and still have a clear path of escape. Here he could wait for Harea.

#

"Hello," Harea whispered into the darkness.

Adolphus jerked and chastised himself for dozing off.

"I'm here," Adolphus opened his wings just enough to slow his descent and jumped from the ledge.

Harea heard the fabric rippling of his friend's wings and smiled. "I will never get tired of that sound."

Adolphus smiled as well and stepped into the moonlight. "Someday we will fly together ... I will carry you in the sun's light and not be afraid."

"But not today," Harea whispered into the darkness. "We have more important things to talk about."

Adolphus nodded and studied his friend, then raised his hand in greeting. Harea wore a plain brown vest and rope tied, unfitted pants, more like a man from the streets than a successful merchant. He was such a small man. Adolphus felt more like he was looking at his daughter than a full-grown man. Ground dwellers seemed to be such small creatures, he thought. Small and delicate and quite without wings, even those who wore a soldier's uniform. A handful of Tal would make short work of such men, like Kaleus and his thieves. They too were only ground dwellers. Adolphus sighed, and his shoulders dropped just a little. *Why won't my people help? Why do the Tal hate the ground dwellers so?*

Adolphus stepped back to better see the gray house. "So, the crystals are still set to be collected?"

"My sources say two nights from now. The wagons are being made ready."

Adolphus restlessly stretched his neck from side to side and moved past Harea toward the edge of the building. "And you are certain you can trust your source?"

"Yes." Harea fidgeted and wrung his hands. "Now that Kaleus uses prisoners to work the mine, the crystals are coming more often. That means more weapons. Merith's men will not hold out much longer against so many weapons."

"And if *you* had some of those crystals?"

Harea stiffened his back, "We would use them to make our own weapons."

A shadow moved beyond the gray house.

"Who is in your house?" Adolphus turned to face Harea. His heart beating hard in his chest. For an instant, he thought his friend had betrayed his trust.

"Only my family… why… who…?" Harea shuddered and felt his stomach grow hollow, his eyes as big as the yellow moon.

"I see a man … a soldier. Only one …" his breath was heavy. "But there is never just one."

"They know …" Harea whispered, and then he turned and ran. Through the archway in the stones, he ran, toward the gray house. He ran toward his wife and his daughter. His arms striking at the air as he ran.

Burn rifles flared in the streets beyond Harea's home. Then a woman screamed from inside the house. A scream that could tear a man's skin from his bones.

Adolphus stood frozen for a moment, wondering if he was risking his own family as well. Then he moved. Three steps and he was at the edge of the stone building. His wings unfurled and carried him to the roof of the house. He climbed across the roof to the front and hung down from the edge to peer inside the window. The claws of his feet digging deep into the wood and thatch of the roof. He could see Harea's wife pinned against the wall by a soldier wearing the black uniform of Kaleus's army. He held her against the wall with a knife to her throat.

Two more soldiers stood on the other side of the room yelling at Harea. Probably something about killing his wife, but he did not understand all of the words. He could see the auburn hair of Harea's daughter peering down from the top of the stairway and was thankful the soldiers had not yet found her. He thought of his own daughter, Ilea, and knew he must act quickly.

Adolphus crawled across the roof to the back door. Gripping the roof with his feet, he pounded his hands against the roof. He shook the house with his fists. The soldiers started yelling, and he responded with a warrior's cry. He screeched and howled into the darkness. He wanted everyone to hear, every man and woman in the area who would come to help. The shadow of night would no longer protect Kaleus's men if everyone could see.

The voices inside the house cried out in panic, and he took a chance. Adolphus gripped the edge of the roof with his feet and dove, swinging downward, his arms covering his face. His body shattered the door. He released his grip on the roof to spin and land on his feet, shaking the house again. Before the soldiers could react, he dove for the man that held Harea's wife. He forced one hand beneath the knife, and with the other hand, his claws opened the soldier's chest from neck to stomach. Red blood sprayed up onto Adolphus's arms and open claws.

The other two soldiers pulled their swords from their scabbards and attacked. Adolphus lowered his shoulders and lunged at the two men to drive them against the wall. As he rose, he grabbed each man by the throat and dug his claws in deep. One man drew a knife from his belt and cut the Tal from below his arm down to his waist. Blue-green blood oozed from his side to crawl across his tan shirt and pants. Adolphus drew on the last of his strength to finish the soldiers and then collapsed to the floor.

Harea's wife had already climbed the stairs and was holding her daughter in her arms. Their eyes wide with fear. And Adolphus knew they were just as afraid of him as the soldiers. They stared at the dead bodies scattered about the room, the shattered door, and at him, a blue-skinned man bleeding from his side. His vision began to blur, and he was no longer sure of where he was. He watched Harea put rags on his wounds and felt the mist of sleep carry him far away.

Red Moon

Ilea studied the red moon and fluttered her restless wings, glad her mother was not here to fuss. Her mother, Seela, speaker of all languages. She could almost hear her mother's chastising voice. *I, Seela, am a proper Tal woman. A proper Tal woman stands straight with her wings hugging her body. That white sliver of bone on her wing's edge hooks over her shoulder just so. Her hair flows gracefully down her back, and the blue, swirling lifelines that edge her face, just in front of her ears, are light and delicate.*

But Ilea had never been accused of being proper or delicate, and today was no different. Instead of standing, she lay on an outcropping of rock that stuck out from a jagged cliff and let her wings drape lifelessly down the canyon wall. Their pale blue color looked gray in the red moon's light. Even her water-blue skin seemed dull, and it was hard to see her lifelines at all. The feathery-blue wisps that edged her face were much darker on her right side than her left — just like her father's. She wore her short, white hair pulled back like three tails, torn-wrapped leggings and the cropped tunic her mother hated. Her leg hung off the edge of the rock, swinging back and forth and looking nothing at all like a proper Tal woman.

Ilea had been on this craggy rock for what felt like forever, looking very improper, contemplating the moon and the meaning of life and waiting for her brother to fly over. She swung her leg and watched the red moon to see if it would move. She knew she could never fly high enough to touch it. The red moon — wise and unyielding. The red moon was always in the sky. It had witnessed countless births and deaths and joys and sorrows. When the sun was bright, the red moon grew pale, but it never left the sky. Sometimes it would sit high above the great mountains. Other times it would sink so low, that if you stood in exactly the right spot, the mountains would block out the red moon all together. But it was always there. The yellow moon would cross the sky and disappear. It would take ten or eleven suns for the yellow moon to complete its crossing, and then it would disappear completely. Ten suns later, it would reappear.

But the red moon was always there. There were stories of travelers that went to places on Regar where no one could see the red moon, but she did not believe any of them.

With the fading of each sun, the red moon would turn slightly, ever so slightly. Enough that if you cared to look closely, your eyes could see the change. There were dark shadows that mingled with the red across the surface of the moon. And as each sun ended, if you watched, you could see those moon shadows drifting across the surface. Each night the shadows would move farther across the red moon until they eventually reached its edge and disappeared. Suns and suns later, the same shadows would come back.

Ilea liked to believe that those shadows were mountains. Just like her mountains. Mountains that protected homes and families. Maybe people who could fly, just like her. Or maybe ground dwellers who climbed the rocks and risked death by falling.

Tomorrow, Ilea would see the twentieth turn of the red moon. She was no longer a child, even if her father refused to believe it. Twenty-turns was old enough. It was old enough to be able to listen to grown-up talk about war and soldiers and death. Her father, Adolphus, would speak in hushed tones as if it would protect his family if they did not know the truth. But she knew the truth. There would be war in Palon soon enough, war among the ground dwellers, and her father was mixed up in it somehow. Her brother was too. Some nights, after dark, when her brother, Dodgen, thought she was asleep, he would leave. He would sneak out of their mountain home and meet with another Tal boy and fly toward Palon.

He wasn't careful. She had been following him since she could remember. She had followed him over the sand to Palon and Devant and even to the heavy trees where he would meet with the gold-skinned Benjee. She would fly after him, up the steep cliffs that protected her home. Up the rocky walls and in and out of the smooth fingers of rocks that stuck up from the tops of the cliffs. Jagged stalks of stone that had shoved their way to the surface to be polished by the wind. No shine, no crystals, just the gray and black rock of the Great Mountain tops. If she pulled her wings close enough, she could fly in and out of the rocks like a wingaring or a buzzer, with only a slight flutter of wing to give her a push. Dodgen would never be able to see her follow. He should have been here tonight. She should have seen him fly over. The yellow moon was in the right place, so it must be the right time.

She rolled off the outcropping to drop several body lengths before her wings caught the air, reveling in their loud pop that echoed against the rocks. Making lazy, slow circles she drifted toward home, back to her city hidden within the mountain. Here the Tal were untouched by the wars of Regar. Ground dwellers could not travel to her city — to Luz. But she could travel to theirs. She could fly above the cities divided by war and hate. Cities without names. Cities that held sects that she would never know. Friends and enemies she would never meet. But in Luz, there was peace.

The blue-skinned Tal had created a sanctuary amid the stone of the Great Mountains. Water and wind had cut deep canyons into the center of the mountains, far enough away from the edges to deter any unwanted ground dwellers. Here, along the steep stone walls of these canyons, they made their homes. Using crystal powered tools, the Tal had cut deep into the sides of the cliffs to make rooms and homes for their families.

Despite the hardness of the stone walls and floors, the Tal embraced softness in their amenities. Artisans wove plant fibers with the delicate webs of the Hornhead worm into coverings for the floors or soft blankets for sleep. Hammock style beds hung from corner to corner in some rooms. Stools, backless benches, and plush pillows decorated the home to make places to sit with ample room for wing flexing. Even the Tal's clothing brought a softness to their stone world. The women draped themselves in silken fabrics wrapped around their bodies with braided straps or cutouts along the back to make room for their wings. The men wore lose fitting tops, or none at all, and what looked like strips of fabric wrapped and woven around their legs. And no shoes. The Tal used their feet as easily as their hands, gripping, holding, and especially carrying while in flight. Shoes would have only gotten in the way.

Some of the more skilled craftsmen created rooms outside the rocks. Cage-like structures anchored into the mountain, hanging free. These outside rooms were slatted and crisscrossed with slender tree limbs that allowed the sun to filter through. It was a perfect place to nap or rest while drinking in the sun's warmth.

No matter how safe, how peaceful these sun rooms might be, nothing compared to feeling the sun up close. Of course, no one could actually touch the sun. It lived in the world of the red moon, but many Tal had tried just the same. Closer to the sun the air grew cold, thin, and hard to breath, but the dizziness never daunted Ilea or any of her friends. The crystal implants in their metal bracelets were more than enough to protect them against the cold. So, on any given day, especially if the clouds were thick, the most reckless of the Tal could be seen racing toward the sun. They soared above the clouds. Their wings carrying them to the edge of the air where their vision blurred and their hearts almost burst. Then, their wings would collapse and their bodies would fall toward Regar. Limp, lifeless bodies would drop silently through the sky until their heads cleared, their breath grew strong, and their wings popped as they found the air. Reckless, risk-takers — just like the boys she should be following tonight.

She tightened her back to fully expand her wings and slow her pace as she glided silently to the mountain's edge outside her home. There, Ilea clung to the rocks, climbing across the cliff as easily as viney patch. Making her way closer to the entrance, she listened and watched for nosey neighbors. It had not taken much practice to learn to sneak away. The great negotiator, Adolphus, her father, was a heavy sleeper and snored enough to cover most accidental noises ... when he was home. The closest neighbors were older families who were seldom seen outside after sunset. And then there was her mother, her mother Seela. She was an entirely different matter. Ilea was never quite sure how many of her secrets, or her brother's secrets, were not really secrets at all, at least as far as Seela was concerned. Mothers know things.

Ilea felt for the rhythms inside her home, as she dropped down onto the sunroom floor. Her father was not home. She couldn't feel his lifesong. Her brother, who should be flying to Palon, was home, his body relaxed and heavy. She was wrong about the meeting. It must have been canceled or postponed. Maybe tomorrow or the next day would be safer. She promised herself to watch Dodgen closely for any signs that he would leave tomorrow. Maybe she had been seen. The boys would change their plans altogether if they knew she had been watching.

As Ilea entered her home, the fabric that covered her parents' room was open just enough to see her mother sleeping and the empty spot where her father should be. Her heart missed him and wondered what kept him away.

Once inside her room, she studied every pillow and stone. The crystal lamp in the corner of her room cast shadows with its yellow light. Her room looked just like it had when she left. Maybe her mother did not know she had been gone. Ilea wrapped her wings close around her body and slipped into her hanging bed. The red moon was not visible from here, but it was nice to believe she could feel its presence watching over her, watching over her family. Sleep came easily, and it seemed only moments before she could hear her mother's hushed tones from the sunroom.

It must be morning.

Seela's voice carried concern but not anger. Her words were filled with grownup talk. They must have known she was gone last night, but Adolphus had not been to her room asking for answers ... yet.

Seela was speaking with Dodgen in the sunroom. He sat with his long legs hanging outside the slatted wall, swinging them back and forth. One wing sprawled out across the floor while his other, smaller, crooked wing was tucked close to him. He tried never to let anyone see, even at home. It was bad enough that he was a darker blue than his parents, but his misshapen wing was something he tried never to share. She could tell from the wilt of her brother's shoulders, his day was not going as planned, but she certainly wasn't going to ask any questions. She did not want to risk saying something stupid that would let Seela, or her brother, know any more than they already did about her absence.

"Is there anymore ganda fruit left?" Ilea asked as she peeked around the corner. She tried to sound innocent.

Her mother sighed and nodded. Adolphus was not here, again, and the worries lined Seela's face. Ilea went into the eating room to search for something to quiet her rumbling stomach. Dodgen said the ground dwellers only fed ganda to their prisoners. That yellow fruit was not fit for Tal, but she liked it anyway. Partly just to annoy her brother.

She peeled back the rubbery skin and dug out the tangy, yellow fruit with her fingers then stuffed it into her mouth. As she wiped the juice from her mouth, she heard the *vhoom* of her father's wings as he landed in the sunroom. The wound in his side already crying out to her. She felt his warmth behind her when he entered the eating room. The weight of the worries he carried moved the air around her and Ilea could hear the pounding dissonance in his body.

"Good morning, Father." Ilea did not turn around. She tried to block out the sounds of his pain.

"Lee."

She could see the blues and grays of his voice echoing across the walls. That voice that held such wisdom and strength. His loving voice that shortened her name to Lee.

"Do you feel strong this morning?"

Her body stiffened. He never asked her that unless he needed her to do something difficult. She turned to look up into his face. He stood at least four hands taller than her. A good man, a good father who loved her dearly. She could feel it in his voice and hear it in the smallest parts of his body. But this man did not completely understand how much of the world she could see, she could hear, she could feel. How his pain became her pain as well.

"I am strong, Father," she announced and tried to feel as strong as her words.

Beneath his shirt, beneath the bandage, she could see the wound. Not the way her father or brother would see it, but the light and the colors that rose above the skin, above the wound. It started beneath his arm and wound its way down to his hip. It was a deep slash. He covered it, but she could see the gold and red glow from his side where the pieces of his body fought to make it whole again. She put the fruit down and walked over to her father. "Maybe you should lie down."

Seela watched them both from the doorway.

Adolphus nodded, "Yes, lie down." He wondered how he was standing at all.

Without thinking, she began to sing, softly. She hummed a tune without words. Her song filled with random sounds that rose and fell without pattern, shifting from high to low at unexpected moments. Yet it was pleasant to the ear. Adolphus could already feel the warmth of her voice working its way deep into his bones.

She led him back into his sleeping room, and as they walked, she sang, her song constantly changing to fill the empty places between them. In the sleeping chamber, her father laid down on several pillows in the corner of the room. The hanging bed would never have allowed her to see all of his wound, so Adolphus settled among the bedding, glad his daughter had not asked any questions.

As she approached him, her song softened again. Her eyes hazy blue that glistened with many facets like the white crystals that warmed her home. She did not remove the bandage. Instead, she brushed her fingertips across its topmost layer, adjusting the cloth, stroking the bandage with her hands, making tiny circles with her fingers. And all the while, she sang.

Adolphus began to drift in and out of consciousness. He closed his eyes and let her song wash over him. She could feel his body relax and the worries disappear. She could also feel the wound beginning to mesh. The pieces of his body were coming together, wrapping, entwining, joining together. Their songs uniting with her song. She could hear each part of him sing, the pieces that carried the song well, the pieces that cried out in fear, and the pieces that could no longer sing at all. The pieces that she could not save. The pieces that would have to die.

She felt for his rhythms as she worked. Her father's breath, his heartbeat, he was in no danger of dying. They were strong and loud and overpowered the cries of his wound. She heard them soften, just a little, as he sunk deeper into peace. With a whispered touch, Ilea began to roll back the bandage to reveal the places that were almost healed. Little by little, she exposed the wound, continuing the circles with her fingers, caressing the wound, willing it to bind.

Whatever had happened to her father, she knew it eclipsed any of her past night's rule-breaking. She no longer worried that her father would find out that she had snuck away. In fact, she had the odd sensation that he did know. Maybe he even knew where she went. Ilea was sure she would have felt him if he had followed, but he could still know where she went. Fathers can know those things. But this wound was another matter. It was smooth and clean. He had not cut it on tree or rock chasing her or Dodgen. This was a cut made by metal — a cut made by a weapon. Wherever he had been. Someone had attacked her father, and she wanted to know who.

Follow

Adolphus slept the next day. He tossed and turned and mumbled something about melting soldiers in an oven. The words never made sense, but it was not important. No one wanted to talk about his injury anyway. Dodgen left as soon the sun rose and did not return until the sky was dark. Seela spent the day busying herself with unimportant tasks and making sure to listen for her husband. Ilea wanted to stay but there was work to be done first. It would not take long, and then she would have the rest of the day to be close to her father.

Ilea flew toward the center of the city. To the place where the cliffs dropped almost straight down to end in a plateau of rock. A place where tiny pools of water would form if the sky was just the right color. She met with the others. The same three women she met with most every morning —

women like her. Women who could hear the lifesongs — Argia, Zaharra, and Tori. They would meet and sing for the city, for the people of Luz. They would sit together and join their songs to sing for those in the village who aged and those who were weak and those who fought injuries, like Adolphus. Their songs kept the people strong.

The Tal were an old people. Their lives saw many turns of the red moon and with that long life came wisdom and understanding beyond that of the ground dwellers. The elders in the village had known more lives than any Palon. Sometimes those elders would come and tell them stories of the old days, when the city was not in the mountains, but was close to Devant and Palon and the ground dwellers. How the Tal protected those who could not fly. How the Tal flew above the cities and watched for danger from the daragoons and the creatures that had long since been driven to the other side of Regar. Places so far away that you could no longer see the red moon. They fought for the Palons, the Benjee, and the Ohmar. Until those ground dwellers grew afraid of the Tal and rebelled against them forcing the Tal into the mountains.

Tori and Ilea especially enjoyed watching Zaharra and Argia quarrel with the elders. Their faces were every bit as worn and weathered. They had seen many of those same events and would tell a different version, saying the days were not as the men said. Tori was older than Ilea and had a daughter of her own, but she was not even close to the age of the elders. They would watch the arguments with wide eyes and whisper to each other about the old people, including Argia and Zaharra, and what they might have forgotten. After all, they were really old. Those giant creatures in their stories might only be the size of a Breen and the wars might have been only people yelling.

After their morning songs, Ilea returned home to spend the day sitting beside her father's bed and using her skills to persuade his body to continue healing. When her legs ached and her voice cracked and she could stand it no longer, she flew, out of the sunroom and into the open air. She wanted to forget her father and the soldiers and the coming of war. She wanted to be free. Each time she returned home, her mother would pull her close and look lovingly into her eyes and try her best to say that Adolphus would not be alive without her daughter's help. Seela lived a practical, ordered, and unemotional life. The family turned to her in times of trouble because she was always in control. So, for Ilea, to see her mother so shaken was even more terrifying than facing a thousand wars.

The next day her father awoke rested and fully healed. He ate in silence, brooding over something he would not talk about, and then left for council as if he had never even been wounded. He did not return that day. Seela did not speak of his wound or his absence. If Adolphus had shared his adventure with her, she gave no clue to its ending.

That same night, Dodgen left to meet his friends. Ilea heard the whisper of his wings as he left his room. She listened and waited, knowing she would not move until he was too far away to hear her. Ilea would be able to follow his rhythms, his colors, his body's song, but he would not see or hear her. He was a man and did not have a gifting — no man did. Only women could see the unseen, and only the special ones. Only the unlucky ones, like her and her mother, and a handful of others in the city of Luz. Dodgen would be a great warrior someday, or maybe a great councilman like their father, but he would never know the patterns and the songs and the pain of the world the way she did.

She felt the beating of her brother' heart rise as he stepped from the sunroom door to drop into the darkness and find the wind. He flew straight up the side of the mountain and within moments the rocks blocked his body's song, and he was lost to her.

Ilea pulled her wings close, slipped out of her sling bed, and moved with the shadows down the hallway to the sunroom. She paused a moment to feel. Her mother was sleeping, in her restless way. Seela's mind never stopped. Her heart always worried.

Twenty steps, soundless steps, and she entered the sunroom. Instead of dropping off the edge like her brother, she climbed. She did not want to chance a wing pop. It was awfully fun, but it could get you into trouble if you were trying to be quiet. So, she climbed the rocks, step to step, hand to hand, without thinking or planning. She made her way far enough up the cliff so that her wings would not risk waking anyone. Ilea knew just the spot. Her wings unfurled, her body dropped, and pop. She caught the air and let it lift her above the cliffs.

The red moon greeted her as she headed towards its light, soaring above the mountain. She knew where he would go. Tonight he was headed across the sand to the city and that small gray colored house that held ground dwellers.

The night was still and the sounds small. She soared above the mountains feeling the patience in the rocks. People had songs and colors but the rocks were more difficult to hear. Rocks upon rocks upon rocks made for a cold, formidable song. There was life within the rocks that you could not see with the eye. Plants that grew where they should not. Long, squirmy animals sneaking in and out of the open spaces within the mountain. Dingy and brown so that they could hide from the things that flew. These had high pitched, rhythmic songs, but the rocks themselves only moaned — moaned like an old man feeling the cold deep in his bones.

Once she cleared the highest peak on this side of the mountain, she would have to be cautious. Ilea could feel her brother and his friend up ahead. She left the mountain and headed out across the sand, staying high enough not to be seen. Dodgen was with another Tal boy. Kayz, that boy that always called her a Bartok. She would recognize his chaotic song anywhere. He was taller than her brother, and stronger too, but his body's song was jumpy and sometimes without pattern. He was never still.

Ilea matched her speed to the boys and watched the lights of Palon growing closer. It would not be long before she would see Merith's castle jutting up out of the ground. She could feel the sand passing beneath her, warm and painfully dry. Her heart ached for the ground dwellers who would never know flight or see the tops of the mountains. She tightened her shoulders and suddenly felt very glad to be a Tal.

As the lights of Palon grew close, the boys altered their course, swinging wide to the right, toward the edge of the city and one of the merchant districts. Sellers there used booths and tents for work, but they lived in real homes. Ground dweller homes, nothing like a Tal home, nothing Ilea would ever want to live in. Still, there was safety within the walls of the city. Walls that could keep out other ground dwellers.

"Fly to the gray house," Ilea whispered to the sky. "Fly to your ground dwellers."

And that is exactly where they went. The boys dropped to the ground behind a building made of rock and brick. Its walls stood so tall that even the red moon could not see them in the shadows. But Ilea could. She watched as they tiptoed through the archways of the open walls, across the dirt floor, and then dart toward the gray house, exactly as they had done the last time she had followed them. Ilea gently spread her wings and tilted her body to slow her descent, then landed in those same shadows.

She could see into the gray house, through pieces of the walls that were transparent. Dodgen had said that the ground dwellers heated the sand until it was hard and clear. Then they built it into the houses so they could see outside. Ilea thought that was silly. If they wanted to see outside, they could just walk outside. But tonight, she was glad for the hard, clear sand. They had made a way for her to see everything. The door looked different than the last time they had come. It was put together with pieces of different sizes and colors. It looked odd and out of place. And the roof had … claw marks …

A slender girl with auburn hair leaned out the doorway and pointed to a room on the second floor. Ilea had seen her before. Genoa was her name, and this was her father's house. The boys moved immediately, half climbing, half flying. They shimmied up the side of the building. The girl opened her window made of clear sand and let the boys inside. Ilea followed, but avoided the window to climb all the way to the top of the house. The roof pitched in one direction, high in front and low in back which put its back edge close to Genoa's room and the window. Ilea could see holes torn in the thatch and a sagging spot above the door.

"Sorry about your father," the girl whispered.

Dodgen's heart beat fast. "He was here last night, wasn't he?"

"Yes," the girl took a deep breath and tried to find an easy way to tell the story. "He came to meet with my father but something went wrong. Kaleus's men came. They must have known about the meeting. They had swords and guns." She stopped to find her breath. "Your dad was brave. My father would be dead if he had not..." She closed her eyes and tried not to think about the dead men.

"So, that's how he got hurt. My sister took the whole day to heal his side."

Genoa gasped, "Is your sister magic?"

Kayz laughed, "If she was, I would ask her to make me stronger, and maybe better looking."

"There is not enough magic for that," Dodgen sneered.

"I would like to meet your sister," Genoa mused. She liked having friends who could fly. They made her feel safe.

Dodgen shook his head. "I hate all of these secrets. Why won't my father share his fight with me like yours does? He thinks he is protecting me. He thinks I can't see what he really does."

"Have you told your father what you do?" Genoa replied gently. "How you fly over the sand looking for soldiers who would hurt us."

Ilea knew he had not and was surprised by the tenderness in Genoa's voice. *I think she really likes my brother.* Suddenly she felt very proud of both her father and Dodgen. She knew her brother could be reckless and a risk-taker, but she had always thought her father was quite boring. He went to long meetings and talked and argued and other unimportant stuff. It was hard to imagine him fighting or killing anyone.

"Adolphus meets with the elders," Kayz blurted. "My mother says they will listen to what he says. They will help."

"Not this time," Dodgen sighed. "The elders won't get involved. Palon won't stand a chance if we don't intervene. We don't have to go to war, just send a few Tal to make a difference. If we do nothing then we are no better than Kaleus ... just as guilty."

"Because one Tal is worth ten ground dwellers," Kayz smirked. "And how do you know all this?" He waited for the question to sink in, "Because your father told you?"

Genoa stared and again tried to block out the images of the dead men in her house. "I have seen what Kaleus does. That is no secret."

Ilea could hear Kayz moving about the room, unable to keep still any longer. "Let's go. We need to meet that wagon."

"Yes," Dodgen answered. "We will be back later with crystals for your father. He will know what to do with them."

"Yes," Genoa nodded. "You are going to the crystal mine." She wrapped her arms around her body as if trying to keep out the cold.

Ilea knew that crystals were not easy for ground dwellers to come by and that they made powerful weapons. Tal used the crystals to cut stone and make light and warmth. She had never thought about using their tools as weapons. If a crystal could cut stone, it could easily cut a man.

Dodgen nodded to Kayz and they moved to the window. Ilea backed away from the edge of the roof and flattened herself against the thatch. She could hear the girl's voice as the two boys climbed out the window.

"Dodgen," Genoa whispered, "please be careful."

They dove from the ledge and drifted into the night sky.

Ilea waited until Dodgen was only a glimmer in the darkness and then leaped from the rooftop. As her wings caught the air, she spun sideways to get a final glimpse of the gray house. Her eyes met with the red-headed girl who still watched from the window. Genoa would tell the others, she was certain. Her father maybe, or the boys. They would know Ilea had followed them. But that could not be helped right now. Ilea did not know the way to the mine. She would have to fly closer than before and worry about Genoa later. At least the journey across the sand would give her time to think, across the sand to the crystal mine.

Ilea had heard her father talk of the mine. The crystals grew in finger-like streaks across the innermost mountains, almost as if they had been driven into the rock like a giant sword. A Tal could easily pick up a few crystals with only a day's search, but ground dwellers had to rely on what they could reach. They might search for suns and suns before finding a vein of the precious rock. But Kaleus had been lucky or smart. His men had found a natural cave heavy with crystals. Her father knew that this discovery could mean the end of Palon. Kaleus could now create enough weapons to destroy that city, and anyone else who stood in his way.

The boys flew across the open sand toward the lower edges of the Great Mountains. Navigating the terrain was easy for them. The Tal knew the patterns in the mountains. Those who could fly saw the gentle curves and open spaces where the cliffs wound in and out like a river of rock. From the ground, the Great Mountains appeared solid and impenetrable. But, in fact, they rose and fell in random stature and sometimes even ended completely in pathways of rocky sand. If ground dwellers could see from above, they would find many roads that would lead them through the rocks only to find more sand on the other side. It was on one of these paths that Ilea was sure they would find the crystal mine.

She watched the mountains grow closer, rising out of the land. The change in the landscape could be abrupt at times. The desert crashing into the mountain, with its ending marked only by rocks that had fallen from the highest cliffs down into the sand below. Ilea had always thought the mountains looked like a giant had brought a bag of rocks and dropped them into the middle of the sand or maybe cut them from far below the surface and driven them upward to reveal clean, steep bluffs. Tonight, in that place where the sand and the mountains and the sky came together, there was a light. A fragile, breath of light.

Ilea didn't think there were any cities this direction, not at least as far as she had flown. So, she would stay low and close to the boys. On this night, the moon would have turned them into silhouettes if they had flown too high. The boys had been careful, as if anyone was looking for them out in the middle of this dead sand. The yellow moon made its way across the sky, and she knew they had been flying longer than they should. She began to wonder if they knew she was following and had decided to lead her on an empty chase. But the light was growing stronger. A light in a place that should have no light. A house maybe or an encampment. Maybe the light from the crystal mine.

She watched the traces of yellows and blues from Dodgen's body in the distance. Kayz was further ahead and out of her reach, so she pushed her wings to pick up speed. Dodgen's lifesong was easy to see. His smaller wing, the wing that did not grow as it should, created a distinct trace in the colors and sounds of his body. Its pieces seemed to fight just to stay alive, making a dark, dreary light and a whimper of a song. The wing drew on the strength of his back and shoulder on that side. But his heart was strong. She hated when he bossed her around and tried to be the one in charge, but she could see her father's strength in him. That was the reason she was here. Whatever Dodgen was up to, he believed it was important.

The boys suddenly slowed and dropped from the sky to land within the rocks at the edge of the cliffs. They chose a spot with an outcropping almost as big as the gray house and hid beneath it. The cause of the light they had been following was hidden by the rocks, and Ilea could see the pathway beyond that curved to lead to the source. She landed behind the boys, but chose a position above them, high on the rocky cliff. Using her claws, she crawled along the steep bluff to reach the bend in the mountain and found the light coming from a cave cut into the side of the opposing cliff. Embers from a fire and several glowers flickered at the entrance. Two men stood outside the mine, ground dwellers who guarded the contents of the mine or cave or whatever it was. They paced and chatted and even sat on one of the few wooden boxes that scattered the ground, remnants of depleted supplies. These were not strong men. Their life colors were faded as if they had not had enough to eat in a very long time. Ilea had expected more from a crystal mine. Heavy equipment, saktars, wagons, maybe even workers sleeping on the ground — she wasn't sure what a mine should look like, but it should be more than a hole in the side of a rock.

She rolled sideways and climbed back across the cliff toward the outcropping that hid the boys. Ilea wanted to get closer. She wanted to hear what they were doing. The rocks masked any life signs from Dodgen and Kayz, so she would have to risk being seen if she wanted to know what they were up to. The cliff had narrow shelves cut into the rock by the unrelenting winds that came and went during the day, so it was easy to ladder climb down the cliff to reach the rocky sand. Dropping to her knees, Ilea slithered and crawled like a child across the sand and fallen rocks and did her best not to be seen. Ready to duck down at any moment.

The boys probably had some elaborate plan like attacking the guards or creating a diversion so they could get inside. Dodgen had practice with a knife and swinging a long-handled dolo blade for harvesting grasses. Because of his wing, he had learned to use surprise and strategy when playing with the other Tal boys. He had to be quick, and he had to be sneaky. More than once, Ilea had seen him tackle a much larger boy and win by dropping from above him. Maybe Kayz could just scare them to death with his wild flying or endless chatter. Either way, Ilea wanted to see it happen.

She could see Kayz now. He had crawled out from beneath the rock ledge, and he was watching the cave, watching the guards, waiting for his chance. He crouched there among the rocks and sand like a Breen ready to devour his prey. But Dodgen was not beside him. She could feel him, his song. He was not too far away, probably working his way toward the entrance of the mine.

Ilea scanned the parts of the cliff she could see, watching the shadows for the gray and yellows that would be his song. The guards sat beside each other now. Their faces bored and weary and totally unaware they were being watched. Maybe if she could get closer to them, she could find Dodgen.

Ilea hooked her fingers around the sharp edges of the rocks and lifted her body up and over, her wings pulled close. She slithered between and across the fallen stones and continued to watch the shadows and Kayz and the light from the mine. Her body twisted and rose, and then she felt it — a claw digging deep into her ankle. It jerked her body backward and she braced to hit the jagged teeth of the rocks. But instead, her head hit flesh. She immediately recognized those wiry legs that wrapped around her and rolled her to the ground.

Dodgen pinned her hard against the ground and stared down into her face. "Why are you here?" he hissed.

Ilea could feel the anger crawling up the back of his neck.

Dodgen growled, "This is dangerous, and no place for you."

Her eyes were wide, and she smiled at his cleverness. She had not expected him to double back or to catch her. Maybe Dodgen was even smarter than she had believed. Ilea did not answer, so he released his grip on her shoulders, unlaced his legs, and sat back amid the rocks.

"I want to help," she whispered in her most sincere voice. She did want to help but mostly she just wanted to know what he was doing.

He took a deep breath and studied his sister. "I know," he nodded. "But it is hard to … do what I need to do when I have so many others to take care of."

Ilea watched his wings relax. Even his crooked wing was fully exposed. And for the first time, she realized just how much she loved him. She felt his sadness and knew she had hurt him deeply. "I will protect myself," she said. "So do not worry. We will be brave together."

Dodgen smiled at his sister. He knew she could see things that he couldn't. He knew she could do things that he couldn't. Somehow that had always made him feel small next to her. Ilea could be mean sometimes, scaring him in the dark or taking his last piece of sweet bread, but she had never made fun of his size or his wing. She had always believed he could do whatever he tried. She treated him like … a brother. So, he would trust her now.

"Come," he said and motioned toward Kayz.

They crawled over and around the rocks toward the mine and the open spot. When they arrived, Kayz did not seem surprised to see her and she wondered how long they had known she was following. Ilea thought she could detect a sense of relief in Kayz. He did know that if they got hurt, she could make repairs. Which made it a little easier to be brave.

"It's a mine," Kayz directed. "They cut crystals out of the rock in there. They break up the big rocks to find the smaller crystals inside them."

Ilea sneered. "Yes … I know."

"It's full of prisoners," Dodgen shuttered at the life they must live in that dark place.

"And full of really big crystals. Way bigger than in our mountain" Kayz reminded them. "We only need one or two."

"One or two … prisoners or crystals?" Dodgen smirked and Kayz slugged him in the shoulder.

"Crystals, you Bartok. We need to use them against Kaleus's army."

"Shut up!" Dodgen barked, trying to plan. "We don't need to talk about that."

"We only need a few large ones," Kayz rambled. "Genoa's father can cut them and make lots of weapons. He knows how to do those things. Even small weapons can do a lot of damage. We just need a few, just a few."

"And maybe save a prisoner or two?" Ilea questioned. "That would be nice."

"And where would they go?" Kayz mocked. "They would just wander around in the sand. We would have to carry them someplace. We can't carry crystals and ground dwellers."

Ilea did see his logic and hated it at the same time. "So why doesn't someone come and rescue these people?"

Kayz shook his head and looked at Dodgen. "She's such a girl, isn't she? She really is a girl." Then he turned to face Ilea. "Soooooldierssss." He made the word sound long and stupid. "They're on the outside. They're on the inside. They could be in the rocks. We can't fight them all. We are not grown-ups."

"Speak for yourself," snapped Dodgen, still planning his attack. "I don't think many people know this place is here. At least not the kind of people who would help."

Ilea nodded and fought a tiny wave of hopelessness for those who worked in the mines.

Kayz settled down among the rocks, twisting his wings this way and that to get comfortable. "So, we wait. They should be here soon."

Ilea tried not to look as naive as she felt. "Wait for what?"

Dodgen closed his eyes, shook his head just a little, and sighed his heaviest sigh of annoyance. "The delivery. Isn't that why you are here?"

"I was just following you."

"So, you have no idea what is going on, do you?" Kayz smiled and widened his eyes in know-it-all fashion. "You came all this way and you don't even know why. There are lives at stake. Secrets to be hidden."

Dodgen swallowed the words he wanted to say. "We … will … wait … for the delivery."

Ilea looked at Kayz who was now pretending to be asleep. "So, what are they delivering?"

"Supplies," Dodgen studied the men in front of the mine and tried to ignore Ilea. He wanted to know everything about them, especially if they had friends inside. There would be no room for surprises.

"The moon," Ilea tried again. "The yellow moon tells you when they are coming. Right?"

Dodgen suddenly realized his sister had been watching him for a long time. She would have needed to follow them at least two or three times to figure out the timing of the deliveries. He turned his gaze away from the soldiers and stared in disbelief at his sister.

"How long?" Dodgen asked, knowing he wouldn't get a clear answer.

"How long for what?" Ilea mumbled and pulled at the bottom of her tunic. "Nobody knows I'm here," Ilea stalled. "I haven't told anybody."

Dodgen gave her his best I-mean-business look. That look that older brothers give little sisters to let them know they will be murdered brutally if they do not comply. "How looong have you been following me?"

She knew this was not the time for games, but the truth might not be the best idea either. It had been almost ten turns since the first time Ilea had followed her brother out past Palon into the woods to meet with the golden-skinned Benjee and the other ground dwellers that he should never have known. She took a chance that Dodgen was distracted enough by the crystal mine not to get mad.

"Since the Benjee," she confessed.

Dodgen's eyes grew wide. "What?"

Ilea waited for Dodgen to continue. She waited for him to yell, to ask questions, or even grab her, but he just shook his head and stared past her at nothing.

"The Benjee," he whispered. He had almost forgotten.

His shoulders relaxed, and he leaned back against the rocks, and for a moment he forgot about the guards and the crystal mine. Instead he thought of a heavy forest that grew just beyond Palon where he had dared to meet young Richard whose father led the army for King Merith of Palon. Richard, the son of the Captain of the Guard, and Dak, and two Benjee boys whose father also served as a soldier in their city. They were going to steal weapons and fight alongside the troops to stop Kaleus. But Dak had been caught by his father, they stopped going to the meetings. It seemed like such a long time ago.

Now to find out that Ilea, just a child, had been hiding in those trees, watching him, all that time. It took his breath to think of all the places he had been since that night — the places he should not have gone. The secrets, the dangers he had led her into never knowing she was there. He felt embarrassed that he had not known. How could he have not seen her? Was she that good at hiding?

Ilea stared at her brother, wide-eyed, still waiting for his anger.

Dodgen growled, "You should not have come."

Then he shook his head and laughed, just a little. Just enough so that Ilea knew there would be no anger, but she didn't understand why. The colors that shimmered around his body were warm yellows and blues and Ilea knew that she was forgiven.

"I think I am gonna be sick," Kayz snorted. "She followed you, all this time. You mean you're not gonna punch her in the face? If she was my sister, I would make sure she never followed me again. I would …"

Dodgen shot him a look that would have chilled the heart of even a grown Tal. Kayz froze.

Ilea tried to remember ever seeing Kayz speechless before.

"I'm glad we are on the same side," she whispered to her brother. Then she slid down low amid the rocks and shifted her weight back and forth until she found a comfortable spot. The delivery might never come, she thought, imagining the empty sand and the disappointed looks of Dodgen and Kayz.

Ilea fought to keep her eyes open, and finally laid her head against one of the taller rocks. She tried to remember at what point in her life she had learned to sleep among the boulders and feel comfortable. Rocks were not too bad for sleeping. You just had to find the nooks and crevices where your bones would fit. Her wings were especially sensitive, so she curled those toward the front of her body. That way most of her wing didn't touch the rock. Wings were sensitive and needed special protection: frosted, sheer flesh stretched across a spindly bone frame. The wings of every Tal sang louder songs than the rest of their body, full of light and humming sounds. Wings could feel the air just like your fingers could feel the sand. If you brushed against something, ever so slightly, your wing would feel it almost before you touched it. But that sensitivity also made them vulnerable. A cut or scratch on a wing could hurt as much as any wound.

Ilea felt her mind drift as the haziness of sleep crept across her body, winding its way along her neck and back. Only to be broken by the jolt of her brother's claw against her shoulder.

Again, the claws! What is it with him and the claws? Could he not be so rough? Now I have scratches on my ankle and my arm!

"I see the wagon," Dodgen whispered.

Ilea wondered why he bothered to whisper after he had whacked her arm. Maybe he just enjoyed it.

"Why do they come in the dark?" she questioned. "Wouldn't it be easier to see what you are doing in the day time?"

"Only if you want to be seeeeen," Kayz pretended to whine.

Ilea closed her eyes. *I had almost forgotten about you.*

Dodgen sighed, "In the morning, the winds will come and the tracks will disappear."

Dodgen's voice was like that of a Guardian or maybe a prophet. Kayz thought that somehow his friend seemed much older than he was when they began this adventure.

"So how did you find this place?" Ilea pretended that Kayz wasn't there.

"The wagon," Dodgen said, never taking his eyes away from the sands. "On our way to Devant, we saw the wagon and followed it."

"You went all the way to Devant?" Ilea knew that Devant was twice as far as Palon. She had never been there, but she knew it was in the other direction from her home. The stories said that it was full of crystals, and water, and beautiful flowers … and soldiers … and Kaleus.

"We never made it that far. We saw the wagon and followed it to Palon. The next night they finished the trip to the mines."

"We had heard stories, but never believed them," Kayz stammered, painfully aware that Ilea did not want him there. "We kept coming back until we saw the wagon again. They make the trip every ten suns. We flew high so that they could not see us. I don't think they were even looking for us."

Ilea chided herself for missing the pattern that the wagon followed. She had been watching the yellow moon, not the sun.

"The ground dwellers wouldn't look for you," Ilea agreed. The Tal had always kept to themselves, away from those species that walked on the ground. So, no one was afraid of the Tal.

She thought about what would happen if they got caught. Would the soldiers come to their home? It was not easy for a ground dweller to scale a wall, but there were stories. Stories of Kaleus and those who served him … of magic … of people disappearing, of explosions, of fires. Stories of a blue stone that could do all of this and more. Ilea did not want the blue stone to come to Luz.

The three of them watched the wagon and the saktars that pulled it. Strong, thick healthy animals with fur that shagged heavy around their feet and hung in tangled strings from their back and neck. The wagon was built from solid wood with long slender planks extended from poles beneath it. The sand dipped in the two trails that the curved wood beneath the wagon left behind. Two men rode on the platform at the front — ground dwellers. One with a beard so heavy, even the Tal hiding in the rocks could see it in the moonlight.

Close to the opening in the rock and the guards, it stopped. The guards stared at their visitors as if they did not care one way or the other what happened next. Others came out of the mines. Frail people with clothes that hung from their bones. Ground dwellers with quiet, faded lifesongs. Some with songs no louder than a soft breeze. A few had stronger colors, yellows and greens, but gray and black smoky lights surrounded most of their flesh. Ilea's heart ached. These people were dying. They walked and talked and worked, but they could not continue this way for long.

They unloaded bags from the back of the wagon. Small bags, not much bigger than a man's head, but it would take two or sometimes three of the faded workers to carry them. Bags of supplies … bags of food that the prisoners would never get to eat. They filed out of the cave. A death march that replayed every ten suns. Even Ilea's skills might not be enough to save some of these ghosts.

The two drivers spoke with the guards, laughing heavy and loud like men who had worked together for a long time. They did nothing to help the procession of workers who unloaded the small, sand colored bags. Neither did they try to stop them from escaping. No one held up a weapon or blocked the way. They just laughed and talked and drank some kind of liquid in dark bottles that the drivers had brought.

Dodgen hoped the dark liquid was the same as what the Tal men drank when they laughed just like the guards. The same liquid that made them sleepy and slow and walk with a stagger. The liquid that made them dull and allowed the small things to go unnoticed. Tonight, he must be one of the small things.

Kayz fidgeted among the rocks, wiggled his wings, and sighed an eternal, noisy sigh of boredom. His fingers drew circles in the sand that had sifted between the stones. He watched the stars and then the guards and then Dodgen, restless for action.

Ilea kept thinking about what Kayz had said before — where *would* the workers go if they ran away? Where could the workers go? This mine was a horrible place. Whatever was happening in there, it had to stop. The anger billowed inside her. She wondered if the Tal elders … if her father … knew about this place. They must know. The elders knew everything. Why don't they come? Why don't they save these people? A handful of Tal men could stop this.

Dodgen fired off a warning look at both Kayz and his sister. No gifting was needed to feel the anxiousness in his partners. Neither was good at being quiet, and tonight, they must be quiet. They could easily betray their hiding spot.

The men's voices shifted, and Dodgen knew they were starting to say goodbye. One of the drivers walked over to the wagon and pulled down the cloth that covered the back. The supplies were gone and only two bags of crystals had been put in their place. The saktars would have a much easier journey going home. The wagon would slide along the sand as if it were empty.

The drivers climbed onboard. One of them shook the straps that ran to the saktars' necks and then started to sing. The other man joined in the song as the wagon moved forward into the darkness carrying the crystals and its intoxicated drivers. Their loud, bellowing voices echoed against the high cliffs.

Dodgen nodded to Kayz.

Ilea shoved her brother hard. "I'm coming too," she whispered as loud as she dared.

"No," Dodgen commanded. "Not yet."

Ilea could see the heavy blue light that surrounded her brother's chest and heart, just like the light that surrounded their father when he would not be questioned.

"One at a time," Dodgen explained. "Follow the plan." He pulled a soft bag from the rocks and handed it to his partner.

Kayz looked at Ilea. "We will each take a crystal … one at a time … from under the tarp on the wagon … careful … quiet … one at a time."

"No one gets caught," Dodgen commanded.

Ilea glared at both boys. "I am too fast for them. I will never get caught."

Kayz grinned so wide that his back, spiked teeth showed. "I wonder how many people in that mine thought exactly the same thing?"

"Silent!" Dodgen barked.

Ilea nodded. "Silent as the sand," she breathed. Her wings quivered with the danger. She could feel the air beginning to stir. It would be morning soon and the winds would come. When the sun was high, there was always wind. Sometimes gentle, like a mother's touch, and other times like the angry claws of a Breen tearing into your flesh.

Kayz tied the straps of the bag around his waist, stretched his wings, climbed over the rocks, and flew off toward the wagon. His wings whispered against the air, and there was no pop. He kept his wings tight and flew low to the ground, not more than waist high to a grown man. Kayz tilted his left shoulder to cause a quick spin around, just once, just because he could. Swift, sharp turns, Kayz darted across the sand to the back of the wagon. Lowering his head, he landed in the trails of the wagon. Three short steps and Kayz jumped up to hook the claws on his feet into the wagon's back boards. One of the saktars raised his head and shook it hard to voice his concern about the trespasser. The drivers just kept singing.

Kayz held fast with his feet and extended the claws in his fingertips. Two sharp swipes and the rope that held the tarp fell in shreds. He pushed his hand into the belly of the wagon and pulled out two crystals. Then slipped them straight into his bag, just in case they tried to sparkle. Kayz opened his wings and let go of the wagon. For a heartbeat, his body floated, frozen in the darkness. The wagon and the voices moving past. Then he dropped into the sand and ran so that his wings could catch the air. But this time, there was a pop. He flew up into the darkness away from the red moon knowing that its light would expose him.

Ilea admired his stealth and wondered what else he might have stolen over his lifetime that no one would ever know about.

Dodgen was next. While the drivers were looking for the cause of Kayz's wing pop, her brother crawled out of the rocks and started running. But he overestimated his skill. The air filled his wings and he rose from the ground with a resounding pop, just like Kayz. The sound caught the driver's attention, and Dodgen had no choice but to retreat to the cliffs. The drivers studied the back of the wagon, watching the tarp and listening for more sounds. Then the bearded driver sputtered and waved his hand backward, dismissing the mystery and yelling something that Ilea was sure meant that he didn't care. The other driver spurred on the saktars with a shake of their straps.

Kayz finally returned to their hiding place among the rocks and studied the cliffs to find his friend. When he could see nothing, he pulled another hidden bag from the rubble and began to remove the crystals from his waist-tied sack. Ilea knew he was preparing for another try. It would take time for her brother to plan his next move, but not Kayz. He did not plan. He would not think before he flew. So, she decided to take a chance. While Kayz busied himself with the crystals, Ilea climbed. Over the scattered rocks, working her way to the cliffs and the pillars of stone along the edge. Ilea climbed, hand and foot and claw, she climbed until she reached the height of at least two men. And then she dropped. Silently, with only a whisper of wings, she dropped, and flew toward the still moving wagon.

As she got closer, she could feel the song of the crystals. She could feel their warmth, see their whites and yellows beneath the covered tail of the wagon. Ilea tried not to hear the sound. She tried to close her ears and her mind to their song. She gritted her teeth and landed in the sand behind the wagon. Her heart pounded in her chest, and she knew she could not stop the music. The crystals began to glow. All of the crystals, in both bags, matching her lifesong. This was a mistake the drivers could not miss. They both turned, and the glow from the crystals exposed Ilea.

The bearded driver yelled, pulled a burn gun from beside his seat, and fired. Ilea felt the scorching heat in her shoulder and the warm blood ooze down her arm. She ran, away from the wagon, toward the cliffs that could hide her. Ilea opened her wings and lifted from the sand. The blood dripping as she rose. Another burn hit the back of her leg and she spun to the left. The driver fired still again, and the flesh charred at the tip of her wing. Ilea screamed. The long wailing scream of an injured animal. The lights in the crystals shuddered with her pain.

Her wings fought the air as she fell. Claws open and slashing at the sky. As she collapsed in the sand, her body folded in pain and her hand clutched at the blood that covered her shoulder. Then she heard the sound — the *phoom* of wings. Not Dodgen or Kayz, but the fury of a full-grown Tal splitting the air.

The drivers shrieked and a Tal drove them from their seats. Heavy claws tore into their shoulders and chests and then tossed them to the ground. Ilea watched the flailing of pale blue wings, thick arms slashing up and back, and then the ground dwellers grew still. The Tal man stood straight, closed his wings, and turned to look at Ilea. She didn't move.

She could hear Dodgen behind her, the unbalanced rhythm of his wings, growing louder as he came closer. He could see the same things she saw. He could see the motionless wagon, the lifeless, bloody ground dwellers on the sand, and their father standing beside all of them. Their father, who had never seemed brave or ready to fight. Adolphus, a man she hardly recognized, walked toward her and her brother. Long, purposeful strides, a man filled with fear and anger and hate and love — a storm of colors and songs mixing together.

The sound of shots fired echoed from the mines then five guards rushed toward the wagon. Four more came riding out of the darkness on saktars. They had been too far out for Ilea to see, but they had been there this whole time, waiting to protect the wagon. Waiting to kill anyone who tried to take the crystals.

She could see the flash of their weapons as they fired, one after another, into the Tal man … into her father. As he turned to flee, she could see the warm blood dripping from his chest and the line of darkness from beneath his arm to his waist. The scar from the wound she had healed only days before.

In an instant, Dodgen hit the sky and headed toward the guards. Screaming, weaving in and out, falling and rising to draw their fire. The burns from their guns sprayed across the darkness, missing their mark to explode in the empty air.

And Ilea could be still no longer. As she willed her body to stand, the fire in her wing and leg took her breath. Her eyes watered and blurred. Nausea rose in her throat as she walked and crawled toward her father now laying on the ground. His blood turning the golden sand to blue.

Ilea knelt beside Adolphus and tried to lift his head. She pulled at his shoulders and lifted his heavy arms. With her help, he rose to his knees, blood dripping from his hands. And then, to Ilea's amazement, he stood. Bent, staggering, weaving, leaning against each other, they walked. Blood oozed from Ilea's shoulder, but she didn't notice. She just sang — her song of healing. Erratic, distorted, moans of music broken by whimpers of pain from every step. She pushed her song into his chest and arms, willing the wounds to close, trying to save the last of his strength. If they could just make it to the rocks, there would be a chance.

Ilea pulled and lifted and dragged Adolphus, but he stumbled in the sand and fell to his knees. The sound of weapons shattered the darkness and Ilea knew that Dodgen was still alive, still helping them to escape.

"Nooo!" she screamed at her father. It wasn't supposed to happen like this. "We didn't know you were coming," she pleaded. "We couldn't know."

Ilea wrapped her arms completely around her father's bloody chest to keep him from collapsing to the sand. His eyes dark and almost empty. The song from his body drifting from this world to the next.

"No!" she screamed. "No, no, no! You can't leave me!"

Adolphus made one more attempt to stand. Ilea pulled and lifted and dragged him the length of a man's body. He crawled forward, lurching toward the rocks, only to melt again to the ground. Her song became a scream. Her father's body jerked with the pain and Ilea was making it worse, but there was no time to coax. The lights of his body were fading. She could feel the pull of the mist that rose above his body. Soon all that made him who he was would be gone. Ilea had seen death before. The mist would eventually turn white and then disappear altogether. She never knew where it went. She could never see any further than this world.

Ilea shook his body to force the life to stay, to give him the will to fight. She couldn't focus enough to use her gifts. She tried to sing, but the sounds were choked and filled with tears and whimpers. She clung to his body. His blood covered her hands and arms as she lay across his chest. Ilea pulled at the mist that would leave her, trying to anchor it in place, inside Adolphus.

Strong arms jerked her backward. She could smell sweat and burned flesh. A voice yelled something about causing her pain, and then covered her head with a black cloth. The butt of a gun smashed into her skull. And everything went black.

Oberon

Oberon stared at the blue puzzle pieces spread across the long wooden table in front of him. There were pieces as small as a grain of sand and some as long as a man's finger. Apathetic, unfeeling shards that had the power to change his life forever. And beside the shards … lay the unfinished SolStone. A jagged, blue stone that had once formed a perfect circle no bigger than the palm of his hand, etched with faded symbols along its outer edge. Oberon used one finger to push one of the puzzle pieces closer to the SolStone and its many jagged holes. He waited — waited for the glow, but nothing happened. He picked up the piece and cast it out the uncovered window. The only window in the tiny room. Then repeated the ritual with the next shard.

The red moon had made at least ten turns since Galimar had shattered the SolStone. Oberon had lost count of the days, but it seemed like forever. He could still see that giant of a man holding his sword above his head in triumph and bringing it down upon the SolStone, shattering it into oblivion.

Galimar should not have been chosen to wield the powers of the SolStone. That should have been my right. I gave my life in service. I am a true Guardian. I deserve the power.

Oberon growled and paced the stone floor of his room wondering if Galimar would even recognize him anymore. He still wore the robes of a Guardian just as he had for the past twenty-three turns of the red moon. He still wore his black beard short, but his hair was longer, the top was almost to his ears. He did slick it back, though, just like in those days with Galimar. How he hated Galimar.

He stopped again in front of the table and tried another shard. He knew the SolStone would never be complete. Even when Galimar used it, pieces were missing from its edge. One piece he had given to Jaika and that scrawny excuse for a caregiver, Inita, before he had sent them away. He remembered the bright watery light Galimar had created from the SolStone. He remembered watching Jaika and Inita walk through the light.

And he remembered Galimar destroying the SolStone and their home, their place of study, the Guardian's temple. Yes, how he hated Galimar.

It had been easy enough to start over here in Devant. Galimar wasn't going to tell anyone about the SolStone, and the story of the temple fire had grown with every telling. The people of Devant believed it was a great explosion with wild animals and armies and creatures that did not even exist. So they were eager to accept him as Guardian in their city. A man who worshipped the creator Gelquin. A Guardian who had escaped certain death because of his faith and purity. They were more than happy to provide him a tiny stone room in the Guardian Temple of Devant.

He made another try with a shard a little larger than a grain of sand. As he slid the piece close to the amulet, it glowed. The stone and the shard glowed the same blue-white light that Oberon so desperately wanted to see. He moved them closer together and the SolStone pulled the tiny piece into place. In an instant, they were one. No line or crack existed where the two had joined.

Even though the stone was only half way formed, it still had powers, but he needed practice. These powers were difficult to control and were unpredictable at best. Oberon studied the tiny, stone room, the only room he had known since Galimar's betrayal. The table, the chairs, the bookshelf, the open window. His eyes focused on several glowers beneath the window that had withered and faded. These plants were supposed to provide light for his room, but water was precious ... more precious than light ... so the plants had not been cared for the way they should. He picked up a fading yellow glower and placed it on the table in the center of the room. The edges of its leaves were brown and crisp, and it gave off a soft, tired glow.

Oberon picked up the SolStone, turning it over and over in his hands. His thoughts reliving the night of its destruction. He pictured the stone in Galimar's hand. He thought of his face and the mental concentration he had used to create the wall of light. He tried to copy those mannerisms, to behave exactly as Galimar had when he used the SolStone. The symbols must be on top, and his fingers should grip the edges with white-knuckled strength. He extended his arm forward and turned the stone to face the glower on the table, just as Galimar had done the night of the fire, the night he had sent Jaika away.

He aimed the disc at the dying plant and focused his gaze on the withering leaves and the tiny bulbs that should have grown into flowers but remained dark and unopened. Flowers that would have illuminated his entire room. The SolStone began to glow with the blue-white light that he knew would come. Rays of light shot out from the amulet and covered the flower. Oberon gritted his teeth and tightened his shoulders to hold the light in place. If it passed the flower, it would destroy the stone wall and anything else beyond. He felt the heat of the stone and the power that fought to escape.

Oberon took a deep breath and relaxed his grip. The light receded into the SolStone and drove him backward against the stone wall. The glower stood on the table, charred and disintegrating. The clay pot that held it was melted and black.

He fought the urge to slam the SolStone down on the wooden table and yell to the sky, "Why? Why won't you work for me?" He thought of the dozen times before that he had done just that. The dozen times that the SolStone had been damaged. He tried so hard to clear his mind. Galimar was so loving and forgiving. The idiot forgave everything that had happened to him. His face and arms were covered in burns from Kaleus's soldiers and even those men he did not hate. Oberon was sure that was the reason the stone worked for Galimar, because he could forgive.

With a heavy sigh, he stepped away from the wall. His heart full of dark hatred. He knew he would never forgive Galimar or Merith, the king he followed. The king they had both served. The king who sent his daughter, Jaika, through the light of the SolStone. The king who had chosen to trust Galimar with the power of this amulet and not him, Oberon, the leader of the Guardians. If forgiveness was required to work the SolStone then he was doomed. The few times it had worked for him, the results had been chaotic, but it had worked. It had healed and destroyed and removed whatever objects Oberon had placed within its path. He just needed to find the pattern.

Oberon dismissed the idea of forgiveness and laid the SolStone down on the table. Once again, he focused his attention on the shards. Maybe the stone was just not complete enough to be controlled. If he could fill a few more gaps and spaces, they would meld together. He was convinced that with each new piece the stone would grow stronger. Each piece of the puzzle brought him closer to the power that he deserved.

He continued the search, one shard after another, dragging each piece closer to the SolStone to wait for the glow that did not come. Piece after piece went through the open window. Piece after piece refused to join.

Oberon bit his lip and looked up to the ceiling, throwing his hands out in anguish. "Oh mighty Gelquin, I have been a faithful Guardian!" he shouted. "I have confessed my crimes and my anger … my mistakes. Why have you not allowed me to prosper?" He fell to his knees. His head bowed and his Guardian's robes cascading around him on the stone floor. "I have lived my life for you," he whispered. "I have helped others to prosper and you have denied me everything."

He blew out his breath and thought about his life. The years spent in service. The days alone. The hours in prayer … the fear, the loneliness, the regret. Oberon raised his head, his face to the ceiling, but this time his eyes flash in anger. His mouth tightened with resolve. "If you will not help me, I will take it myself."

He waited for pain, or for the fire from the sky. He held his breath for the ground to open up and swallow him, but nothing happened. He had defied the creator, and the creator had done nothing. And for the first moment in his life, he doubted. *If the creator was all powerful, why would he tolerate such insolence? Why would he not strike me down?*

Oberon's stomach twisted, his neck was red with heat, and he smelled of sweat from the heavy robes. He stood and looked around the room as if someone might be watching. There could be eyes in the shadows or beneath the chair who studied him. He could feel the eyes from everywhere.

In slow motion, Oberon reached down to grab the bottom of his Guardian's robe and lifted it up over his head to reveal a plain white tunic and pants with animal hide strapped to his feet. He kicked his robes into the corner of the room and again waited for the ground to shake. But nothing happened. He looked around the room knowing that if he renounced his Guardianship, he would lose everything and have no place to stay. He looked from wall to wall. His eyes danced across the books on the shelf, then to the dying glowers, and the brown satchel that hung on the door handle. There was nothing here, nothing dear to his heart ... except the SolStone. He lifted it from the table and then slipped it into the satchel that hung on the handle of the door. With his hand on the door, he took one more look around the cold, stone room. He focused on the handful of books stacked on the shelf. One book, more tattered than the rest, stuck out from the bottom of the stack. Oberon crossed the room to pull it from the stack and study the blank cover. The inside pages held a child's scribbles: drawings of indiscernible creatures and words written in scrawling, craggy letters. This book he would take.

Oberon thought about the boy who had drawn the pictures. He wondered where he was now and if he was safe. His heart still held the memory of the last time they were together. The tiny boy in rags with deep eyes who had fought the tears so bravely. Now he would be a young man. A man who probably would not even remember the old Guardian who had abandoned him. Oberon had feared Gelquin then. He had feared what would happen when the others learned he had a son. But he would live in fear no longer. It was time to find the boy. Oberon had been given no choices in his own life. His fate had been decided by the Guardians. At seven turns, he had been completely abandoned by his father, given in service to the Temple. Oberon dropped the book into his satchel, and he walked out the door of his cell. He would find his son and give him the choices he deserved.

His cell opened into a common room where three more doors led to other Guardian cells. When he had come to Devant, no one had known his story. No one knew about Merith or Jaika or Galimar. There had been no need for explanations when he arrived, and there would be none now. Clutching the satchel to his heart, he opened the final door and walked out into the sunlight. Out onto the same street that he had walked almost every day for the last ten turns of the red moon, but this time, there would be no Guardian's robes to slow him down.

Oberon smiled up at the sun and breathed in the air of his new-found freedom. Then he looked out across the dirt road into the icy faces of two black-tuniced soldiers, uniformed men of Kaleus's army. They came toward him. Their boots stomping in the dirt. One raised his hand to his sword.

"Are you Oberon?" the older soldier growled in such a forceful voice that there was no possibility of questions.

Oberon nodded with a wide-eyed stare, and his arms quivered beneath his thin, white shirt.

"You will come with us," the soldier announced as if a crowd were listening to every word.

Oberon wilted as the soldier grabbed his arm and shook it hard. He offered no resistance but kept a death grip on the satchel that held his most prized possessions. He pulled it hard against his chest as they led him away.

The guards laughed. "We are not here to take your things. Just to take you to Kaleus." They laughed again. "He needs your … services."

Oberon's mind raced with questions about Kaleus and what he could possibly need. He had no skills save that of Guardian knowledge. Did Kaleus wish him to pray?

The soldier dug his fingers into Oberon's arm and pulled him forward. Unlike the Guardian temple of Palon that Galimar had destroyed, Devant's temple was within the city. But it was in an older part of the city, quiet, peaceful, and less traveled. The soldiers led Oberon through that quiet street to a pair of bored saktars tied to a pile of rocks stacked outside an empty house that leaned heavily to the right.

"Can you ride?" the soldiers asked, as if it would have mattered if Oberon had said no.

Oberon was quite familiar with saktars. Not an especially skilled rider, but he knew which end smelled the worst. The guards climbed on their mounts, and one guard grabbed Oberon and half dragged, half lifted him up to sit behind the saddle. Together, they rode toward Kaleus and the palace.

At first, Oberon was afraid, clutching his satchel and watching the empty houses. His heart pounded in his chest and the warm sun felt like fire on the back of his neck. The saktars lumbered along in no hurry to get anyway. The soldiers chatted about things that didn't matter: food they would like to eat or women they would like to see and a soldier they both agreed would be better off dead than in their army.

They rode around the edge of Devant, and Oberon could see the changing landscape in the city he had walked through so many times in the last ten turns, taking food to the hungry or meeting with those starved for companionship. Always focused, always on a mission, he had turned a blind eye to the streets and the people he passed, not caring for anything outside the task at hand. But today, there was no goal, no job to complete, so he watched as the city unfolded before his eyes. Homes and business that looked as if a strong wind would take them to the ground, tents, wooden shacks, stone and sand piled upon stone and sand to make a home or a place to sell wares or to sell things that should never be sold at all. As they rode, these places transformed into homes with glowers growing outside polished, heavy doors. Heated glass windows that brought in the light and made the stone walls glow. Shimmering rocks that could have been mistaken for crystals. Those rocks that miners cursed when they dug them up. But they made wonderful houses. The sun made them sparkle just like a king's castle, just like Merith's castle.

The homes became even more lavish as they rode. The golden sand becoming moist, dark earth and eventually hand cut stone. Even a tree grew here and there among the scattered flowers. Until inevitably, just beyond the thickest foliage, they reached the Palace of Devant. The home of the king of Devant. The young king who had allied with Kaleus only to have everything taken away. So, Kaleus was now the king of Devant and any other city that his men had taken. He left his soldiers scattered here and there among the people of his cities. Soldiers who brought discipline as they saw fit. Collecting taxes and offerings for the king.

Oberon had been spared much of that danger as a Guardian. Even the vilest of men respected the temple. Murder and theft was acceptable, but defying Gelquin, defying the creator, was something else altogether. He sat a little taller in the saddle, believing himself to be braver than Kaleus. Oberon had defied Gelquin and still lived. He had done what Kaleus was afraid to do. Perhaps this was his chance. Kaleus was a man of power, even more powerful than Merith. Kaleus could be the chance he had waited for — the chance for revenge. Kaleus wanted Merith dead and to take the city of Palon. Oberon would be more than happy to help.

He stared down at the precisely placed stones beneath the saktar's feet that led through the garden. The winding path was encompassed on each side by flowers. Pink, yellow, knee-high flowers that bristled up out of the ground giving way to tall, draping canopies of lush greens and blues as the saktars carried them forward. He knew if they rode past the castle that the sands would return. These flowers grew by the magic of the crystals that lay beneath the ground. The crystals brought life. They brought water. And where the crystals ended, there was only sand.

As the saktars followed the stone pathway, Oberon could no longer see past the wall of flowers. He swayed back and forth on the saktar as the walkway curved, swinging right and then left to finally emerge at a circular courtyard and the entrance to the castle.

The courtyard held a stone basin the width of two grown men laid head to foot. It brimmed with water and tiny animals swimming to and fro in aimless directions. The bottom was covered with stone that looked burned and once used for target practice. The stone was barely stone it was pierced with so many holes. Burned, charred stones that came from somewhere Oberon has never been. Water bubbled up through those stones. And past the basin, beyond the carved steps, were the archways that led into the palace.

The guard reached back and slapped Oberon on his leg, hard, and made a kind of grunting sound. Both soldiers laughed. They dismounted and pulled Oberon to the ground. He kept a death grip on his satchel, pulling it beneath his arm away and from the guard. The guards laughed again.

Together, they walked beneath archway after archway, through an open metal gate and a set of towering, wooden doors, then down an endless hallway to a grand hall with a sky painted ceiling and white pillars to hold up that sky. Oberon could only guess at what the inside of this room had seen. The music, the dancing, or perhaps the king's council ending with the condemnation of the guilty. They walked past an elevated platform which filled the back wall and held a mammoth, silver throne. It was covered with shining stones. There were only four deep steps leading up to the platform, but even those sparkled and gleamed. Two narrow, black banners hung behind the throne covered in odd writings and crossed swords.

Still more doors at the back of the hall led to a short hallway with at least five guards posted along the walls. Two stood in front of a single wooden door with metal bars across the front. Cold-eyed, black uniformed soldiers from Kaleus's army, ready to follow orders. One moved aside, and the other threw his body against the door to push it open. There was no squeak or groan from the metal hinges. The guard took several steps into the room and then knelt.

Oberon stood in the doorway, clutching his satchel, his arm still gripped by the bearded soldier. The room before him could easily have held six or seven of the cells used by the Guardians. The walls were filled with heavy tapestries woven into patterns and pictures. Each corner of the bed was decorated with an engraved post, spirals twisting in and out of the wood, rising almost to the ceiling. The posts were joined together at the top with still another post to give the illusion of a separate ceiling over the bed. Sheer fabrics hung from the tops of each post. Billowing fabric draped over the top of the bedposts then cascaded to the ground. Two were half pulled closed, but even in the shadowy light, Oberon could see a man lying in the bed.

A small, slender woman with straight, black hair emerged from the shadows and stepped toward the bed. She bowed toward the resting man and then looked at the soldiers. They seemed to understand what to do though no one spoke. Oberon felt his heart sliding down inside his chest and his feet dragging as the soldier pulled him forward. He recognized the smells in the room. The smells of sweat and blood and urine and someone waiting to die. Oberon swallowed hard. He thought he was coming to see Kaleus, the mighty king, but instead he was here only to speak a death prayer. He decided that if that is what they wanted, he would do it. If they wanted prayer, he would pray. Gelquin wouldn't listen anyway. He had denounced his Guardianship and Gelquin hadn't even heard that. Why would he listen now?

The soldiers left him at the bedside with the tiny woman with long, dark hair, so straight it looked as if it had been cut from straw. She put her hand on her stomach and pointed to the man in the bed. Oberon could not help but understand. Blankets stitched with gold and water blue thread lay across the man's legs, but his stomach was covered with blood soaked bandages. The woman did not need to point.

Oberon took a small step forward, wondering how this man had been hurt and how he could still be alive. This man must be very important to Kaleus. To bring a Guardian in for prayer was an act of desperation. Oberon took two more steps and quietly slipped to his knees. He still held the cloth bag in his hand as he bowed his head. He laid his hand and the bag on the ground and began to whisper the prayers of a Guardian.

The man on the bed growled, "no." He lifted his head and shoulders up as if he could climb out of that bed by sheer will and then dropped back to the pillows. "Use ... your ... power," he whispered. "Magic."

Oberon's heart quivered and almost stopped. Sweat dripped down his back and his skin prickled. *How does he know about the stone?*

The young woman moved closer to Oberon and held out her hand. He stood but did not take her hand. He did not trust her any more than he trusted the man in the bed.

Oberon stared. "What do you want?"

She said, "He knows. He knows you possess magic."

Oberon took a deep breath. "I don't understand."

"Stories have been brought to our kingdom. Stories of your magic. You escaped a great fire. You used your light to heal a soldier and stop your enemies."

Without thinking, Oberon looked down at the bag. "My powers are new and I am still learning." He tried to explain that he could not control the magic and that people get hurt. "This man could die," he rambled. "He could die and then what would happen to me?"

The young woman touched his arm. "If you do not … you will die." Her stare was certain and clear and without hesitation. She was simply stating a fact.

Oberon nodded, knowing that he would rather die than give up the SolStone. But if there was a chance he could heal this man, then Kaleus would be in his debt. He turned back to the bed. The woman and the guards stepped back against the wall as if they expected an explosion or huge fire to take the room. Oberon stooped and picked up the satchel, then bowed his head and again began to recite his Guardian's prayers. If he was to die here, then he would make his peace with Gelquin before it happened. He laid the cloth bag on the bed and lifted the flap. He slid his right hand into the bag and felt for the SolStone. His fingers danced across its surface to find the etchings and then turned them to face the man in the bed. He tightened his fingers around its edge and gripped with all his strength. He knew the bag would not hinder the light. It might even destroy it and the book he held so dear, but that was a chance he had to take. If he removed the stone from the bag, they would know the true source of his power.

His eyes focused on the man and the wound beneath the bandages. He thought about the light that would come from the SolStone and imagined it bathing the wound, softly, gently, caressing the wound, moving across the man's body into his chest and legs, filling him with strength and life. He saw all of this in his mind as he held the SolStone.

And then the light came.

The blue-white light he feared. It rose from the bottom of the bag. Not with the force that had destroyed the glower in his Guardian's cell, but with a gentle breath of blue-white smoke. The light floated upward from the bag reaching out to the man on the bed, caressing his wound with the whitest light Oberon had ever seen from the SolStone. The light widened and stretched out its fingers until it covered the entire bed. He heard a gasp behind him from the black-haired woman, and he could feel her pulling backward, closer to the wall. The soldiers' boots scuffed against the stone floor as they too moved farther away from the bed.

Oberon felt his strength flowing into the SolStone. His body shaking with the strain. He dropped to his knees beside the bed, relaxing his fingers around the stone. The light quivered and receded as slowly and delicately as it had entered, floating, twisting back into the bag. Oberon dropped his head onto the bed and breathed deeply, slowing his breath and heart, just like had done for most of his life, his life of practiced meditation. He waited for the woman to scream or the guards to yell. He waited for the sword to take his head or pierce his back. But all he could hear was the breathing, the steady, rhythmic breathing of the man in the bed.

Oberon pushed himself to stand. He released the SolStone and pulled his hand from the bag. There was no hole on the bottom. In fact, the bag looked new and refreshed. The stitching was strong and the dirt and dust that scared its surface had vanished. He closed the flap and again pulled the bag to his chest. With slow fluttering lashes, the man in the bed opened his eyes. He turned his head to look at Oberon, and he smiled. Tenderly and without fear, he smiled.

Oberon met his gaze, thankful that they were both alive and not charred into a pile of dust like the glower. Then he turned his focus to the bandages. He stared at the bandages as if he could see through them if he just looked hard enough. The man in the bed shifted and sighed much like a child waking from a peaceful nap. His face was no longer ashen and pale, but instead was covered in a pinkish glow.

Oberon stepped away from the bed. No one in the room spoke. The soldiers, the small woman, no one moved to stop him. He took two more steps backward, and then turned toward the door of the room. Always watching the guards. Everything and everyone in the room stood frozen as if time had stopped moving. He continued toward the door, sliding his feet across the ground. Maybe if they didn't hear his feet they wouldn't wake up. And no one would stop him. He heard a low moan from the man in the bed, and then he cleared his throat. Without even looking, Oberon knew the man was sitting up. He could feel his eyes boring in the back of his head, but he didn't want to turn around. He didn't want to face the man in the bed. He wasn't dead. That was a good sign, but there are worse things than death. What if he had something growing out of his stomach, or an extra arm. Oberon stopped at the door.

One of the guards pointed toward the bed. "My Lord Kaleus lives!"

The guards fell to their knees and Oberon's heart rose into his throat. *Kaleus? The man in the bed is Kaleus?*

He closed his eyes and swallowed hard and felt grateful that he had not known the man's identity when he used the SolStone. He would never have been able to stop the fear and Kaleus surely would have been burned beyond recognition.

"You have saved me." The voice came from the man in the bed. "You," he said it again, louder this time.

Oberon forced his feet to turn his body around to see the mighty Kaleus. His shoulders were broad and he pulled loose the bandages across his stomach to reveal sinewy muscle without any trace of the wound. He was whole. Oberon had done it. He had saved Kaleus. He looked toward the ceiling and tried to feel for Gelquin. Was he listening? Was this part of some unforeseen plan? Either way, he would take his chance. Kaleus was alive because of his skill. So when his chance came, he would convince Kaleus to march on Merith and to destroy all the people he hated.

"What would you have me do for you?" Kaleus spoke, catching Oberon off guard.

Maybe that was his way of saying thank you. Oberon measured his words. His request must come at the right time. He must be careful to keep Kaleus in his debt. "Must I decide now, your Majesty?"

Kaleus offered a thin-lipped smile. "Of course not. There is plenty of time for that."

"I *am* hungry," Oberon said remembering the piece of stale bread he had eaten for breakfast.

"Then we shall have a banquet," Kaleus nodded and pointed to the guards at the door." Make it so! We will have a grand meal to celebrate Oberon and his magic."

The soldiers did not hesitate. They bolted out the door and left Oberon standing in the middle of the room.

"With your permission," Oberon continued his journey out the door, taking several small steps backward.

"You may go wherever you wish," Kaleus gestured toward the door with his palm up. "You are welcome in my kingdom anywhere. Whatever you would like to see, Nela will make it so."

Oberon studied this tiny woman with the dark hair. "Nela," he nodded, "Nela, I would very much like to change clothes."

Kaleus clapped his hands. "Oberon wishes to be refreshed!" His voice echoed against the walls. He swung his legs from the bed onto the floor and then stood. He said something to Nela about a room that Oberon couldn't understand.

"Shouldn't you rest?" Oberon questioned.

Kaleus's brow wrinkled and his eyes clouded with confusion. "I feel ... good," he said, hesitating, as though he was not sure how he felt. "Perhaps you are right." He nodded and laid back down on the bed.

"I am sure you will be rested by meal time," Oberon assured the king.

Kaleus nodded and looked up at the ceiling. "Meal time ... yes ... rest ... until it is time to eat." Then he closed his eyes.

Nela scampered to the door. Such a tiny woman. Oberon considered the vast number of times she had to move her legs just to cross the room. She bowed slightly and then hurried down the hallway. Oberon followed, thankful to be away from Kaleus.

They returned to the grand hall with the sky-painted ceiling, past the stage and throne, and past the white, stone pillars. At the back of the room, they turned away from the main entrance and journeyed into the maze of hallways within the castle. Endless corridors of wooden doors. He couldn't believe she even knew where she was going. It all began to look the same. Oberon found himself disoriented and almost dizzy with confusion. Nela scurried so quickly that he dared not linger for fear he would lose her.

Some of the doors were open. Empty rooms, storage rooms, bedrooms, even another kitchen. The rooms were smaller than Kaleus's bedroom. The colors were simplistic, but the tapestries and furnishings were finer than anything Oberon had expected. There was more luxury in one of these rooms than he had known in his lifetime. At the end of one hallway, Nela led him up a short flight of stairs to a small landing with three open doors.

Nela stopped at one of the rooms and motioned for him to enter. "For you," she said.

Oberon guessed this room could only be a place for the king's closest friends. He entered only a few steps and stood frozen just past the doorway. There was a melted-sand window high in the wall that let the light in. From the top of his head to the ceiling, the glass let the sunlight into the room to give the stones in the far wall their shine. And beneath that window was still another glass with a silvery backing that reflected everything in the room. He couldn't remember ever seeing himself so clearly. He looked faded and worn like the stone roads of the city. His clothes were dirty and his eyes dull. His hair hung in ratted strips and his beard was longer on one side.

Nela continued to tell him about the room but her words sounded far away. She pointed to his left at a bed that would easily fit three people. Massive, carved legs held it off the ground. On his right stood a cabinet, taller than a man, with metal handles and wooden doors the color of the sand.

Nela lifted the latch on those doors and pulled them open as if they weighed nothing at all. "Clothes," she said, pointing into the cabinet. She said something else about Kaleus offering him the best, but Oberon still wasn't listening. Then she turned and motioned to a table beside the cabinet that held a stone basin of water and a white cloth. "To clean," she said. Then she walked back toward the doorway, weaving around Oberon still frozen in disbelief. "I will bring you food and drink." She said and closed the bedroom door.

Oberon nodded even though she could no longer see him. He had no words. No words for this room or for this palace or for the lost soul standing before him.

Oberon sat on the bed, and for the first time since leaving Kaleus's room, he loosened his grip on the satchel. He opened the bag and took out the SolStone and turned it over and over in his hands still not sure why it had worked so well. The stone was cool and looked just the same as it had when he left the Guardian temple.

He looked up toward the ceiling. "So is this your work, or mine?" *Gelquin is probably not even listening.*

From the bed, he had a clear view of the cabinet and the clothes within. The bottom of the cabinet held tall black boots, brown boots, and some the color of the sand. The door had hooks that held belts and straps. Hanging within the cabinet were pants that looked like they were made from animal hide. Bright colored tunics of purples and reds were covered in embroidered flowers and swirling designs.

Oberon stood and drew a heavy breath. "I don't know if this is your doing or mine … either way … I will no longer live in fear." His words echoed against the stone walls.

He laid the SolStone on the bed and went to the wash table beside the cabinet. He took off his dirt stained undergarments and dropped them to the floor. With a ceremonial kick, he sent them flying under the table. Then he used the water in the basin and the rag to wash his face. He washed his shoulders and his arms and chest. The smell of sweat and dirt began to disappear as he finished his legs and feet. Two bottles of oil stood beside the basin on the table and a flat blade with a bone handle. He used the blade to even out his beard, trimming it short and removing the unruly hair high on his checks. Then he tested the bottles. The first smelled of flowers but the second had the musky odor of a leader. He poured several drops onto his fingers and then rubbed them through his hair and his beard. Oberon watched himself in the glass as he worked, pleased with the lanky muscles that rippled along his arms and chest. Years of walking and working and serving others had kept his body strong.

He stepped to the cabinet and pulled one of the leather straps off the door, then he tied his hair back, wrapping it multiple times. He remembered hearing a story once about a warrior who had worn his hair this way. And today, he felt like a warrior. Oberon ran his fingers along the clothes hanging in the closet. The tunics were of various sizes and he found himself wondering if Kaleus's body had changed over the years or if this room had seen many guests. It felt odd to think that other men had worn these clothes … and were they still alive?

Oberon found a pair of black animal-hide pants that fit nicely. Then he tried the sandy-colored boots, but they were too big. Instead he found a black pair in the back of the cabinet with silver tips on the toe. He didn't know where even a king could get such shiny metal. Next, he tried on the purple tunic, but it draped from his shoulders and made him look like a half-starved creature that might scurry away under the bed. So he traded it for a smaller, simpler black one from the back. He synched it up at the waist with a belt. He was finished with flowing, draping Guardian robes. He was now a leader, and he would dress like one.

On the inside of the door, next to the belts, he found a strap with a tiny bag that tied at the top. A necklace that someone would wear to hold his valuables or coins to keep them out of sight. He opened the tiny satchel, took the SolStone from the bed and slipped it inside. He tied it tight. Then he put the strap around his neck and dropped it inside the tunic. He would never be without it again. Later, maybe, there would be something stronger to carry it in, but this would do nicely for now.

Nela's soft knock on the door sent a quiver down his back. "Enter," he said in his best leader voice.

He watched her teetering and balancing the tray as she pushed the door open with her back. Without thinking, he moved toward the door to help her. The surprised look on her face told him this behavior was inappropriate for his rank.

He took two steps backward and pointed to the washing table. "Put it there. I will eat when I am ready."

She nodded and did exactly as he commanded. It felt delicious to tell someone what to do … to watch them obey. She nodded again and left the room. Oberon stood in front of the melted-glass window, the one with a silvery back, the one that showed his reflection. This was the true Oberon. Not the man in the flailing robes and disheveled hair. This man in the glass was the Oberon he was meant to be.

Nela's tray held some thinly sliced meat with brown sauce, some kind of red, round fruit that he had never seen before, some bread, and a clear flask filled with liquid the color of sand. He tried to eat like a king, like a man who had never known hunger, tasting one item and then the next, never rushing. He opened the flask and the fermented odor bathed his face. He knew if he drank very much of this, he would not make it to dinner with Kaleus. He lifted the flask to his mouth and drank, heavy gulps, letting the liquid run down his chin. He could taste the power in the meal. The power to have whatever he wanted. He was no longer a slave to anyone. He was ally to Kaleus, treated like a king, and he wanted more.

In the reflection in the glass, he could see the bed and the open satchel. And suddenly he remembered the book — that crumpled book of pictures that held so many memories. Oberon crossed to the bed and pulled the book from the bag. "Everything is different now," he said, speaking to the book as if it were alive. "I will come for you, and you will know a better life. You will have food and drink and a safe place to sleep. You will know power and strength and you will never be afraid." He ran his fingers across the torn cover of the book. "I will find you, and I will make things better."

That delicate knock came again and Nela was back. This time he opened the door himself. "What?" he barked, tasting the force of the word.

Nela bowed her head, "Kaleus wishes to see you."

He glanced over his shoulder at the empty room where the Guardian Oberon had been completely washed away, and then he turned and followed Nela to what he hoped was a new beginning. As they walked, he studied the hallway. He studied the stone on the wall and the high-cut windows that allowed only enough sunlight in to shine the top half of the far walls. *Why did I not notice this before? Why did I let fear cloud my eyes? The light, the walls, even the ceiling doesn't feel as high.*

Oberon studied each door as he passed. Some held heavy gouges which could have been from simple clumsiness … or someone trying to escape. Perhaps there had been skirmishes in this very hallway: soldiers, weapons, swords. He studied the stone floor for signs of old blood. The pillars, the turns, the twists, he took each one into his heart. Remembering details, he wanted to learn everything about this palace. He would never be lost again — not like the Guardian Oberon.

As they entered Kaleus's chambers, Oberon stood by the door with his right wrist in his left hand, across his stomach, just like the soldiers that guarded the outer doors. He stood, admiring the room, the softness of the fabrics, and the ornately carved furniture. Kaleus knew how to live as a king. He was nothing like Merith. He closed his eyes for a moment and he was back in that castle, counseling King Merith and his wife, sitting on worn chairs, and eating stale bread.

Kaleus sat up and beckoned him to sit on the bed. "I see that Nela has taken care of you. You will be staying … won't you?"

Oberon stepped closer to the bed. He wasn't sure if Kaleus meant to stay for the meal or for the night. Either way, he really didn't have anywhere else to go. "If that is what you wish." He spoke almost in a question.

"If you found the room suitable, you should stay."

Oberon was surprised that his comfort mattered at all. Why was he asking these questions? Maybe healing him had softened his spirit or at least made him grateful to be alive. "I would like that … perhaps … even more than one night." He held his breath and waited for his boldness to be reprimanded.

Kaleus considered his words and nodded, "That would be acceptable." Then he motioned to Nela. "Now, I would like to dress and attend my banquet, if that is acceptable." Kaleus stared at Oberon as if waiting for an answer.

Oberon's face burned with irritation. "That … is a … good … idea." His words were measured as though talking to someone who could not understand. Whatever rapport he had with Kaleus, he intended to keep it. "I will wait in the grand hall with the painted sky … if that is acceptable?" When Kaleus did not respond, Oberon left and closed the door behind him.

He stood in the hallway for a moment considered what had just happened. Kaleus must still be feeling weak. He certainly did not seem like a man who could murder children and destroy cities. He more closely resembled one of those quiet tenants in the dirt and stone houses living close to the Guardian temple. While he was in this gentle mood, maybe it would be a good time to ask for his help with Merith.

Oberon walked down the hallway into the great hall and out into the middle of the room, his boots clonking on the stone floor. They were starting to feel heavy after the sandals he was used to, but he was enjoying them too much to even consider taking them off. He studied the ceiling, wondering who had painted that sky and how they could ever have reached that height. It would have taken days upon days to paint the sky. Even the colors would have been difficult to find. He thought about the world above that ceiling and if Gelquin was truly watching. And how he might feel about what was happening. Even though he had denied the creator and taken up his own life, he felt that there would surely be a moment of accounting. A day when he would be held responsible for his choices — but it wasn't going to be today.

He crossed the floor and stepped up on the platform at the front of the room. Four stone steps and he was on the king's level. He stood beside the throne, looking left and right around the room. He squinted to look deep into the shadowy corners and out the doorways. Once he was completely satisfied that he was alone, he sat down. He sat down on Kaleus's throne, crossing his feet at the ankles, and settling against its pillow covered back. He felt deliciously tall and powerful. Even if the room had been filled with people, he would float above them, giving orders that would be obeyed without hesitation. He knew the chair itself held no power, and that Kaleus had won this with violence. But if Oberon were king, he would not be like Kaleus. He would be benevolent and caring. He would make sure that everyone was taken care of. He would take from those that had too much. Those with the beautiful houses with the polished doors and the glowers in pots on the lawn. They would be forced to share with those who lived in the rock and sand houses beside the Guardian's temple. His soldiers would make sure that everyone had enough.

The latch rattled on the hallway door and he scrambled down the steps and out into the room. Kaleus entered in black pants and a pale red tunic, the color of the sky as the sun sets, colors that highlighted his red-brown hair. Stitching covered the front of the tunic. Black swirls and twists, giving the illusion of a flower here and there. An artisan had spent suns and suns working on that design for this one man. That shirt alone told everyone in the castle that he was the king.

"You like my sky?" Kaleus spoke with assurance and clarity. His voice was heavier than in the bedroom.

He continued walking and Oberon fell in step beside him, beginning to see the real king. "Yes, did you commission the work?" He glanced back to see Nela following a few steps behind.

"No," Kaleus shook his head. "It was here before me. I know nothing about that sky except that it pleases me and it pleases you. So it shall remain? Would you like to eat?" He continued walking as if the answer would not change a thing.

"Yes," Oberon answered just to make himself feel better.

Kaleus's jaw hardened and his eyes grew cloudy. "Nela," he snarled over his shoulder, "is the meal prepared?"

"I ... I ... was ... will ... find out," she stuttered and scampered ahead of them to warn the kitchen staff.

Kaleus continued walking and resumed their pointless conversation. His mood once again becoming complacent. "I hope the food will be to your satisfaction. I am told that Guardians eat only the simplest of food."

Oberon wanted to explain that he was no longer a Guardian, but thought better of it. "I am sure the food will be ... fine." He found it difficult not to say acceptable. "It will be nice to have something with more flavor."

"Mmm ..." Kaleus nodded. "I suppose there are rules for Guardians and what they should eat."

Oberon thought about the vast number of rules that he knew better than his own name.

"You don't really look like a Guardian," Kaleus laughed. "Before … you looked more like a wild man from the streets."

"I don't feel like a Guardian," Oberon gritted his teeth and cursed his thoughtless words. He did not want to remind Kaleus that he was a Guardian.

Kaleus stopped, turned and looked straight into Oberon's face. "Then perhaps it is time you became something else."

Oberon couldn't help but smile. This was truly his chance. Kaleus was inviting him into his home, into his world. Together they would show Merith and Galimar what happens to those who betray them. They would know his pain, the pain of becoming nothing, the pain of losing everything. Kaleus was truly the ultimate weapon.

"You have so many soldiers," Oberon changed the conversation, but Kaleus did not seem to mind. He just continued walking.

"Yes. Some are here by choice and some … not." Kaleus smiled just a little, pleased with himself. "I inspect my soldiers every morning. You may join me if you wish."

They passed through the outer doors of the great hall. Oberon could see Nela standing at the end of the corridor. The ceilings were taller here, and the hallways much wider. The doors were arched and some were engraved with symbols. The double doors at the end of the hallway were open, and Nela looked like a child standing beside them.

As the two men entered the room, they were bathed in evening sunlight from the melted-glass windows across the top of the outer wall and three sets of double doors that stood open out into the garden. Beyond the doors grew the same draping blue flowers that Oberon had seen in the courtyard entrance. Hand-cut bricks made a terrace and another walkway. He assumed that if they walked out the doors and down that path, they would end up at the front of the palace. The center of the room was almost filled with tables. Long tables made from stone and wood with benches along each side. Except for the one at the front. That table was covered with a white cloth and less than half the size of the others. The chairs were covered in deep green fabric across the seats and backs and lined with pillow fluff at least four fingers thick. Oberon smiled, thinking a man could sink into one of those and be lost forever.

The room was designed to be filled with people, eating and drinking, but instead it held only a row of servants behind the covered table. Some servants held clear pitchers with brown and yellow ale. Others held platters filled with yellow and purple fruits, cooked meats, and foods Oberon had never seen. The smells were intoxicating. It had been so very long since he had felt the warmth of fresh bread or the tartness of halpa fruit on his tongue. The people stood in rows behind the table, waiting for Kaleus to tell them what to do, waiting for Oberon to sit down in the chair at the end of the table.

Nela hurried past the two men to bow and hold out her hands in greeting.

Kaleus laughed, "Isn't it wonderful to be king ... king of all you see." Then held out his arms in a grand gesture as if to say look at all I have.

Oberon breathed deeply, taking in the charred wood and grease smell from the meats and the sultry smell of the sweet breads afforded by only the richest of men. He straightened his shoulders. *This is truly what I was meant for. I deserve more than the life of a Guardian.* He fought the instinct to look up to Gelquin. He was finished with all of that. A part of him wanted to yell to the sky, "Do you see what I have done? I never needed you! Look what I have done without you!"

One of the servants pulled out the main chair, and Kaleus sat down at the end of the table. It looked more like a throne than a chair, with its tall back, wooden carvings, and lush pillows. Kaleus motioned to the other end of the table and for Oberon to sit down. The distance between the chairs would make it difficult to talk, but he would not be daunted by this king. His chair was smaller … simpler … less important, but it was still grander than the rough-cut chairs in the temple.

Two servants brought empty plates and a chalice, made from the same silver metal on Oberon's boots, was placed in front of Kaleus. Oberon's cup was of simple hardened clay. A young girl placed a small loaf of warm bread next to each of them while still another brought a platter of small birds smothered in a brown sauce. They filed through one by one, ladling and skewering, fruits and meats and plants to fill the empty plates. The mugs were never empty, with Kaleus taking more drink than food. While they ate, the servants stood ready to serve.

Oberon watched them work in unison without a word. Each dressed in plain white, untinted tunics and pants much like Oberon had worn beneath his Guardian's robes. Some wore tunics that draped all the way to the ground as though two people could have fit inside. One looked like he had simply cut a hole in a large cloth for his neck to push through. No expense or time had been wasted on their clothes. But they were clean and bright-eyed, not like the empty souls that lived near the temple. He could understand why a person would serve a man they hated if it meant giving their family food to eat and a place to sleep.

Much of the food was new to Oberon. The red fruit was tart and sweet at the same time and the juice ran down the corner of his mouth. Kaleus laughed at Oberon's messiness and bit into one of the same juicy fruits, not bothering to wipe away the juice. Then he began to tear the birds apart — like a ravenous Bartok. The days spent wounded had left him hungry, or at least that was what Oberon assumed. He watched him empty plate after plate, tearing apart at least ten of the small birds and three loaves of bread along with endless cups of ale.

Oberon ate slowly, choosing one piece at a time to allow himself to experience each new taste. Meals had simply been a ritual for a Guardian. Eating and reciting prayers for what Gelquin had provided. Somehow it made him feel superior to

Kaleus to eat with grace and reverence instead of like a wild animal. This king would never know such patience. Perhaps this could be a weapon against him.

"How long ago were you injured?" Oberon almost yelled the question and his words echoed across the hall.

"You do not need to shout, my friend," Kaleus smiled. "I was cut four suns ago."

"You must be very strong to stay alive so long with such a wound," Oberon nodded. "Perhaps you should not drink so much ale if you want to stay healthy. Your body needs water and plant juice." He looked at Kaleus and swallowed hard. The ale was making him careless with his words.

Kaleus's face grew calm, and his eyes glassy. He clapped his hands twice. "Bring me some water and some nectar from the halpa fruit."

Oberon stopped eating and watched a servant, with a long braid down her back, follow his orders. Wide eyes and tiny hands, she seemed more child than woman. He was surprised Kaleus would take his suggestion so seriously. Perhaps he was still disoriented from the injury or lack of food. This was not the Kaleus he had expected to dine with.

"This will be better for my health," Kaleus assured the staff, then turned to Oberon with a dark look in his eyes. "How long have you been a Guardian? You don't look like a Guardian. You looked like a wild man from the streets when my men brought you ... like an idiot." Then he stabbed one of the birds.

Oberon swallowed hard, beginning to see the real Kaleus. But why was he using the same words he had spoken in the great hall? "I would rather not speak of it." Oberon answered softly and closed his eyes to brace for an angry response. He could never tell Kaleus that he was no longer a Guardian.

"Hmmm," Kaleus huffed. "Very well, we will not speak of it."

Oberon opened his eyes and looked at Kaleus, who just continued eating as if no words had been spoken at all. They sat in silence for a few moments, then the servant girl returned with two melted-glass mugs with symbols etched on the sides: one of water and one of fruit juice. She sat them both on the table in front of Kaleus being careful not to get in his way.

He picked up the cup of nectar and sniffed its contents. "What in Gelquin's name is this mandu?"

"It is what you commanded, my lord." The girl quivered and stepped back from the table.

Kaleus kicked back his chair, stood, and hurled the mug over her head to smash against the wall behind her. Blood-colored juice splattered across the shimmering stone wall. Immediately the young girl's hands went up, and she cringed beneath his glare. Oberon knew what was coming, but he didn't understand why. Kaleus had agreed to the water and juice. He had even ordered it willingly. Why was he so angry?

The girl dropped to her knees and cowered against the stone floor. Kaleus growled and raised his arm to strike.

Oberon stood, thrusting his plate forward across the table. "No!" he yelled.

Kaleus straightened his shoulders and lowered his arm. His eyes became cold and empty, and Oberon watched a blank look pass over his face. The same emotionless look as when he had ordered the juice and water.

"Very well," he said and sat down in his throne of a chair.

Oberon felt his heart beating in his throat. His arms trembled as he gripped the edge of the table. Everyone stood frozen, watching Kaleus begin to eat. Oberon took a chance. "So," he breathed, "the servant girl can go?"

Kaleus looked over at the girl on the floor as she peered up at him through her fingers. "The servant girl can go," he repeated. Then he returned to his meal.

Oberon's breath came faster as he tried to sort through what he had just seen. Why would Kaleus follow his command? Could it have been the SolStone? Could the stone have changed him in some way? Forcing him to listen to the man who had wielded the SolStone to save his life. He wanted to know the truth. He wanted to know just how far this change would lead.

Oberon took his seat and tried to decide how to proceed. He looked at Kaleus and his eyes had brightened again. The empty look had vanished, and the snarl had returned to his face. Oberon licked his lips, took a deep breath, and mustered his most demanding voice. The voice he had never been allowed to use as a Guardian.

"Give me your drink," he said, staring straight at Kaleus.

The blank stare returned. Kaleus stood and picked up the mug of water. Then he walked to the end of the table and placed it in front of Oberon. Oberon nodded, and the king returned to his seat.

Oberon could not believe what he had seen. This was a power he could use. This was his means to destroy Merith and Galimar and anyone else who got in his way. But if he ordered Kaleus to deploy his soldiers, would he simply agree and then not remember later as he had with the juice? Could he order him to remember? And what about tomorrow? Would this gift still be here? This would take some time to dissect. Time that Oberon was more than willing to put in. He tried not to laugh. Having Regar's strongest leader on a string would make him unstoppable. The people in the city, the army, the soldiers, they would do anything Kaleus told them to do ... for today anyway.

Oberon pushed back his excitement and focused on the moment. "Thank you for my room," he said to Kaleus.

"You are very welcome. You did save my life … you Bartok." Kaleus's face was clear. There had been no question, no command.

He thought about telling Kaleus he was going to live in this palace with him forever, but that could wait. If Kaleus came out from under the spell of the SolStone, he would have Oberon thrown out. And for now, not everyone should see this power. The servants might be grateful if he could eliminate their beatings, but the soldiers were another matter. The soldiers would expect a clear-headed commander.

The questions spun in his head, and he knew that whatever happened he would have to be on guard constantly. He looked up at the ceiling and tried to drive away the thought that Gelquin had planned this. He must have known how it would be used … used against Merith. Maybe this was not Gelquin's work, but some other dark being that enjoyed tormenting others.

Kaleus asked for more food in his customary growling voice. The big-eyed servant girl brought Oberon a glass mug with etching on its side just like the cup of juice Kaleus had smashed against the wall. This one was filled with white ale that had a strong smell and tiny bubbles at the surface. She set the drink in front of him, then placed hands on her knees to bow. He knew she could not thank him with words, so as she lifted her delicate face, Oberon met her gaze with one of understanding. They exchanged a look that gave him more than thanks. He had recruited his first follower. The next step to controlling the palace of Devant had been taken.

She slipped away, and Oberon ate in silence. Kaleus continued to bark orders to the servants, but every few moments he would look to Oberon as if he expected something to happen. But Oberon said nothing. All he could think about was the SolStone and what could be accomplished with practice. If he could master its power, perhaps he could control all men, or at least the right men — armies of men who would do his bidding without question.

Eventually the servants took away the empty plates. An older man brought warm, wet towels to clean their hands and face. As he took the towels away, Oberon stood and stretched his arms up over his head, feeling the weariness of the day settle into his bones. In less than one crossing of the sun, he had left Gelquin, been kidnapped, taken to a palace, healed a king, and become one. All of that in less than one crossing of the sun.

Kaleus stood, just as Oberon had and stretched in the same manner, mimicking his movements. "I think I would like to rest," Oberon said.

Kaleus nodded and motioned to the far wall. Oberon turned to see Nela standing quietly. She heard his soft gasp and knew he had forgotten she was even in the room. She had been watching when he stopped Kaleus from hitting the servant girl and when he had ordered the king to bring him the drink. She may have even seen the passing look of gratitude from the servant girl and her gift of ale. But then, the servant girl would have seen Nela. The servant girl brought the ale to Oberon even though she was being watched. Maybe Nela was not an enemy but an ally. If she had been mistreated, maybe she would be quick to follow a man she believed to be just — *justice in Devant, what does that really mean?* Fairness, justice, wisdom, he thought he possessed all those qualities until Merith betrayed him. The anger and hatred that replaced them had taken root so deeply that he did not even feel like the same man.

Oberon stared into Nela's cold eyes. She wore the same emotionless look she had worn since the moment he met her.

"Come, come," she said, then simply turned and walked away.

Oberon followed her with the occasional glance over his shoulder toward Kaleus half asleep in the chair. The servants were smart to keep him drunk. He was much easier to handle that way. Oberon felt a kinship with the servants in the palace. They followed a man they believed would protect them, but when tested, at best, he would probably serve only his own interests. A man who could be cruel at times, and who kept the luxuries of life just beyond their grasp.

Oberon followed Nela back to his room, but this time Oberon could predict their path. Every turn and shadow was held fast in his memory. With a little more study, it would be rather easy to navigate the hallways. He wondered if Nela could feel the change in his confidence.

When they arrived at his room, Nela opened the door and allowed him to pass through.

As he entered, Oberon turned to face Nela and study her face. He was hoping to find a clue as to how she felt about what had taken place in the banquet hall. "Will I speak with Kaleus in the morning?"

Alex Rae

Nela shrugged and gave no sign of what she might be thinking. "He rises when he rises, and he does what he does." She nodded and then walked away.

Oberon listened to the heavy click of the latch, and tried to decide if he had been told that knowledge of Kaleus was not to be shared or simply that his daily routine was too chaotic and unpredictable to explain. He hoped it was the latter. Unpredictability would help to hide the changes he planned to make.

In the room, he removed the silver tipped boots. He slipped off the ornamental shirt and heavy pants and folded them neatly on the chair. The ways of a Guardian were simple and never made more work for others and were so deeply engrained into his soul that even now, in this palace, he could not escape them.

He laid down on the bed and stared at the empty ceiling … wooden beams mixed with stone and mortar. He considered who might have built that ceiling, laid those stones, and poured the mortar. The backs that ached from cutting the timber and honing it into shape. Those men who worked and served a greater master. He felt the softness of the mattress beneath his body and the whispered light of the glower that had been placed in the corner. He was not like them anymore. He would no longer serve anyone. As sleep came, he remembered the worn book of drawings and breathed a promise to find his son and bring him to this place.

Jail

Ilea groaned against the darkness and heard the metal chains rattle that tugged at the shackles on her right foot. She shifted on the cold, stone floor, and then cried out in pain as she moved her head. Her neck burned like fire and the whispers in the room echoed and pounded against the inside of her skull. She rolled sideways and tried to flex her wings only to cry out again as metal spike-filled shackles dug into her flesh. Metal bands that kept her wings folded and useless. She could feel the dried blood sticking her clothes to her leg and chest.

"Lee."

She heard a voice in the darkness.

"Are you alright?"

It was Dodgen. She could see his faded light in the shadows, and knew he had been hurt.

"I thought you were dead," Dodgen moved closer and put his hand on her shoulder. The chains rattled as he moved.

"No," she breathed. "I'm not dead."

Dodgen tried to stand, but the chain linked his leg to one wall of their cell, and his wings bore the same metal cuffs as hers. She could feel the pain from his body without even trying.

"I have been working on the door," he said. "My claws can't get through it. I did a lot of damage but I can't get it open." He flexed his claws open and shut as he spoke. "And there is some Bartok standing outside in a black uniform holding a burn gun. He looks through that hole in the door sometimes and glares at us."

Ilea's eyes were getting used to the gray light, and she could see the stone blocks that formed the walls of their room and the massive door that blocked their way out. A small rectangular window was cut in the top of that door and it made a swath of light across the floor. She couldn't help wondering if this would be their lives from now on, or would they eventually be moved to an even darker place.

"Lee," he whispered. "I don't even know where we are. They put that bag over my head and then I woke up here. Where is here?"

Ilea was trying hard to think and fight the sleep that pulled at her body. She needed time to heal, to rest and heal her pounding head. She pushed herself up to sit and felt the room spin above her. The nausea rose in her throat. The floor was cold to her hands, and she was thankful for her bracelet and the tiny crystal inside that kept her warm. Ilea lifted her hand to the back of head.

"They hit you. I saw them put the bag over your head. The bags they put the crystals in." Dodgen spoke with regret. "I'm sorry I wasn't fast enough."

Ilea tried to smile and didn't say that she would have hit her head sooner if that was all it took to make him be nice to her. She could still feel finger marks in her arms from the soldiers pulling her backward, and the dusty smell of that black bag. And then her heart stopped … and she remembered.

"Father."

"I know," whispered Dodgen. "I know. I could see you with him. What happened?"

She could feel the emotions boiling inside Dodgen. He had been awake long enough to start thinking about what might happen next. He had already made the transition from disorientation to fear to anger and frustration. Ilea would need to catch up.

"He was hurt." She didn't want to talk about it. She didn't even want to remember it. "Why was he even there?" Ilea fought against the pain in her head to think.

"I don't know … I know he was part of a plan to stop Kaleus," Dodgen explained. "He had been sneaking off, flying to Palon to meet with the man in the gray house. I followed him night after night … til one night I caught Genoa in the back. She was sooo scared. She had been told terrible things about us … that the Tal were murderers and child stealers."

"The red-haired girl…" Ilea had seen her in the gray house.

"She had never spoken to a Tal … not even our father. She wouldn't let me stand close to her." Dodgen snickered. "But I won her over with my charm."

Ilea smiled but it made her head ache worse. She watched the ribbon of light on the floor as he talked. The patch of light through the hole in the door. The light that never moved. "There is no sunlight here."

Dodgen wasn't listening. "I would hide outside the house and try to listen. Everyone was afraid of Kaleus and his soldiers. They were building weapons for war but they needed crystals for power. They had found the cave in the mountains … the cave that led to the mine of crystals. Kaleus's soldiers stopped killing … they would take people to the cave instead. Women, children, old people … it didn't matter. They would take them to dig in the mine. I know our father was trying to save them. But the crystals … he wanted to stop the crystals … they would make Kaleus unstoppable." He paused, remembering the scene outside the mine. "I just didn't know he would be there …"

Ilea thought about the wound she had healed across her father's chest and side and all the nights he was gone from home.

"He was alone, Lee. No one would listen to him. The council didn't want to get involved. I had to follow him. I just wanted to protect him."

"I understand," Ilea soothed, ready to talk about anything but Adolphus. So why bring us here? Why not just kill us?"

"Maybe they have something worse planned." Dodgen muttered and she could feel the anxiousness in him rise. "Maybe they want to make an example ... to scare away the other Tal. Once they find out our father's been hurt, the elders will come. They will rise against Kaleus. He could use us to stop them ... at least, that's what I would do."

"I am sure he thinks just like you," Ilea tried to make a joke. She was glad he didn't know their father was dead. It was hard to think of his empty body lying in the sand with no one to watch over him. She would not allow herself the luxury of grief. She needed to focus on getting out of this place.

"If I could get the guard to open the door, do you think you could take that Bartok down?" She could tell by the wilt in Dodgen's shoulders that he didn't think he could. *That must be some giant of a man out there*. "Maybe if you weren't chained up," Ilea nodded, not wanting Dodgen to feel discouraged.

"Yes," Dodgen agreed. "Without the chains … I could take him."

Ilea laid back down on the ground and tried to think. If they could just get out of this room, out of this building, the ground dwellers could never catch them. "I don't suppose they gave us something to eat?"

"You and your stomach," Dodgen shook his head hard and his chains rattled. "You should be as big as a mountain as much as you eat."

Ilea closed her eyes and reached out into the room with her thoughts. She could feel Dodgen fidgeting. Except for a few tiny crawling creatures, there was nothing else in the room, only her brother. The same brother who had teased and antagonized and fought with her … and saved her life. Having him close made her feel stronger, made her able to think more clearly. Maybe, together, they would get through this. She thought about the red-haired girl in the gray house and wondered if the soldiers would look for her. Her family probably wasn't safe now. If they got out of this place, she would go back and warn them, tell them to leave. If … the word felt heavy and hard to face.

Ilea stared into the shadows on the ceiling and felt for the Bartok outside, the ground dweller who guarded the door. She was drifting. She welcomed the darkness that pulled her away, but then her brother's voice pulled her back.

"I don't think you are supposed to sleep when your head hurts. Isn't that what you always told me?" Dodgen scooted closer and tugged at her elbow. "Make them move around, right, no sleeping?"

"That's for other people," Ilea said. "It works different for me. Everything works different for me." She sighed, "I need to repair the damage. It's just harder when it's mine."

"I wish I could help you," Dodgen murmured. He slipped his hand up to that curve where her neck became her shoulder. She could draw strength from him sometimes. He had done it before when she was sick. He didn't understand quite how it worked, but he would try to give her whatever she needed. He used his other hand to stroke her upper arm and focused his thoughts on peaceful places: the forests that grew between some of the cities, the sky above their mountain home, and the red moon. He tried to focus, but it was hard not to feel hatred for the men at the mine — for this man Kaleus and his soldiers who killed and imprisoned whomever they wished, for the men in the darkness who had wounded his father. He was slowly beginning to understand how men could fight wars. If others hurt the people you love, all you can feel is hate. And hate can devour everything.

He could feel Ilea pulling on his light, and tried harder to quiet his thoughts. He wondered if there were others who could share their strength like this. He focused his thoughts on the women who sang with her in the mornings and other faceless Tal who might share their light. Maybe someday she would find a husband who would know her thoughts and give her strength from far away. A man would care for her ... always ... better than ... His heart suddenly ached for his father. He remembered seeing him fall, and watching as the soldiers dragged Ilea's body across the sand. His anger was replaced with an emptiness as he remembered the last time they were together. How quiet and withdrawn his father had been. Maybe, even then, Adolphus already knew he would be visiting the mine. And now ... who would care for him when no one even knew he was there ... outside the mine ... alone in the sand.

"Kayz," he breathed.

Ilea's eyes fluttered open. "Yes," she smiled. "Kayz was still there."

Dodgen could feel their hope rising.

Rescue

Everything happened so fast. The shooting and the yelling. Kayz's legs felt heavy and his hands wouldn't work at all. He watched as the soldiers pulled Ilea from her father, and Dodgen drew their fire in the night sky. He wanted to help. He wanted to fly from behind the rocks to stop them, but he knew they would kill him and then he couldn't help anyone. He just couldn't make his wings move.

The soldiers threw Dodgen and Ilea across the back of a saktar and led them away. Then the others began to disperse with some of the men returning to the mine and others leaving on their mounts. The bodies were left to be eaten by Breen or covered by the sand.

As the last soldier entered the mine, Kayz crawled out from the rocks toward Adolphus. He slithered across the sand, staring at his weakening body … Adolphus's body … caked with blood … his breathing jerky and forced. Kayz knew he couldn't lift him so he started dragging his body across the sand. First, he slipped his hands beneath the shoulders of the dying man and pulled. But, after a few steps, Kayz collapsed to the ground, panting. Adolphus was just too heavy.

Kayz pushed down the fear that threatened to choke his thoughts. Thinking about the soldiers and what might happen to Dodgen wasn't helping. He looked toward the rocks for ideas and remembered the crystals still hiding in his satchel. The crystals he had stolen from the wagon. The crystals that held so much power that was completely useless to him. But the bag, that might be of help. Kayz scrambled back to the rocks and pulled the crystals from the satchel. He also untied the bag from around his waist and then returned to Adolphus. Using the straps, he tied the man's feet together and hooked the bags across his own chest. He felt like a saktar pulling a wagon. Slowly he dragged Adolphus, across the sand, his wings sprawling behind him.

Every three or four steps, Kayz would stop and breathe. "It's okay, sir. I'll hide you. It's okay." Five more steps and he stopped again. "I can do this. I can do this." He pushed himself forward until his muscles screamed and felt like they would tear into pieces. Until, finally, they reached the edge of the rocks, and Kayz collapsed. He glanced up at the red moon and asked it for more light.

Lying on his back, he studied the places where the sand and rocks came together to find an opening wide enough for Adolphus. Kayz forced himself to stand. Then, using his makeshift harness, he pulled Adolphus behind the rocks. His lifeless arms scraped against the jagged edges, but it was the best Kayz could do.

He sat there beside this man, watching him fight to breath and wishing Ilea was here. She would know what to do. She could save her father. Kayz knew there was little chance that Adolphus could survive without her — here, among the rocks and the sand and the sun. He found some water Dodgen had left in his supplies and tried to make Adolphus drink. He swallowed a few drops but just breathing was hard enough.

Kayz pulled the crystals from their hiding place in the rocks. "Ilea could make them sing. I know she could." But she wasn't here, so Kayz decided he would try anyway. He placed one in each of the dying man's hands and tried to find their power. "Think about Ilea," he instructed.

"Find her in your thoughts. Find the parts of her that live in you. The parts of you in her. She can save you. I know she can."

The crystals were silent.

"Again. I am not giving up. You can do this. Find her. I will find her too. She tells me I can if I just focus. We can find her." Except for the darkness, the glow would have gone unnoticed. The crystals hummed with a pale green light, just for a moment, and then it faded away.

Kayz felt Adolphus breathe, a deep easy breath. "You can do this," he said. "You can't give up. They need you … I need you." Kayz tried one more time to find strength in the empty night, and once more the crystals fluttered in the darkness.

He hoped it was enough. "I have to get help. It takes a full crossing of the sun, but we can be back by night." That sounded like a such a long time.

And for the first time, Adolphus opened his eyes. Kayz pushed Adolphus a little deeper into the rocks. The sun would come to this place eventually, and it would be blindingly hot for a healing man. He pushed him beneath an outcropping for partial shade and placed the water container between his chest and arm. He piled a few more rocks around the man to protect him against anything that would come to attack: Breen and Sojar ... and man. He left the crystals in Adolphus's hands and piled sand around them to hide the glow and keep them in place.

"I will be back," he whispered knowing there might be no one to come back to.

Kayz climbed the rocks and the side of the cliff. The winds of the day were already starting to shift, and their tracks were being swept away. There were three dead bodies out in the open and even those were spattered with sand. He launched himself from the rocks and headed home. He circled once to make sure he would be able to find this place again. Then he flew. He flew hard and fast and without fear. It would take time to get home and even more time to convince someone to help.

The rising sun welcomed him with its warmth as he flew, and he worried that he should have changed the rocks ... piled more or maybe less around Adolphus. The winds will help to cool him, but the sun could still be hot. He had to stop thinking. It was slowing him down. He focused on the mountain and the path that would take him home.

It felt like suns and suns since he had left Adolphus when he finally saw the cliffs of Luz. Kayz could hardly stand when he landed in the sunroom of Dodgen's house. His wings tore at the walls as he collapsed onto the floor. "Seela!" he yelled as he struggled to stand.

"What's happened?" Seela rushed out of her home, her wings quivering.

"Adolphus is hurt and they took Dodgen and Ilea." Kayz poured out his words.

"Who did?" Seela knelt beside Kayz.

"Kaleus's men. We went to find the mine and the crystals. We were supposed to stop them. And then Adolphus showed up and everything fell apart." Kayz chattered endlessly with the story of the soldiers and the guns and his missing friends.

Seela tried to follow his tale of wounded men, but parts of his story did not make sense. Her husband had told her about the gray house in Palon and the kind glass maker there. He had talked about the mine that held the crystals Kaleus so desperately needed to overtake the other ground dwellers.

Seela spoke slowly and enunciated each word. "Where are my children?" She held Kayz by the shoulders and tried to control his chaos.

"They took them." Kayz's body shook from exhaustion. "To Devant, I think. To the prisons there. It was my fault … I should have been braver."

Seela forced herself not to panic, using her logic to hold back the tears. "Is Adolphus still alive?"

"Yes," Kayz gasped, "but not for long."

"Then we need help." Seela's mind filled with the names of any Tal in the city who might be brave enough to fly to Devant or able to carry her husband. "We will go to the council. Surely they will not dismiss us when one of their own is in need."

Kayz shook his head.

Seela lifted the boy to his feet. "They will go to Devant to bargain for my children. They will go get Adolphus. They must help us."

"Can I have some water?" Kayz began to melt in her arms.

Seela cursed herself for not taking care of this boy. He had flown such a great distance to try and save her family, and she had only pushed him to do more. "Of course." Seela left Kayz in the sunroom and went back into her home to get water and some meat from yesterday's meal. She watched him eat and listened to more of his scattered story about the wagon and the soldiers. The bags of crystals and the capture of Ilea and Dodgen. When his words had run out, Seela left him to rest.

She flew to the level space deep in the cliffs where the healers sang, and the Tal councilmen met. Sofos and Ramon met there almost every day and today was no exception. They did not even look up when Seela landed. They wore the formal capes of the council and sat along stone steps that edged the back parts of the landing, growling back and forth at each other about water and its beginnings.

"Water is created by the mountains. There can be no other explanation," Sofos pointed his boney finger at Ramon and shook his pale wings.

"Water comes from the crystals. It is plentiful in those areas." Sofos was the oldest member of the council, and Ramon was one of the few who was willing to argue with him, even

139

though he was half his age. "The crystals provide sustenance for the plants as well as water. Surely you can see this."

"You are mad, Ramon. The mountains are the life blood of Regar." Sofos stood on shaky legs, straightened his cape across his shoulders, and turned to look at Seela, "Yes … yes … what is it?"

Seela knew Sofos would not be interested in Adolphus and the plight of Palon, but Ramon might listen. Either way she had to try. This was the only way to save her family. She gathered her courage and knelt in front of the two men. Ramon stood alongside Sofos, staring wide-eyed. Seela had never been known for humility or fear, but Ramon could see both of these emotions boiling within her. Whatever had happened, it must be serious.

"Stand up, wife of Adolphus," Ramon encouraged. "Tell us what troubles you."

"Yes," mumbled Sofos with a heavy sigh, "tell us everything."

Ramon held out his hand and helped Seela to her feet. He was taller than Adolphus and his hair was much darker. The two men had been allies in the council and standing so close to her husband's memory completely swept away her resolve. Her knees buckled and the tears dripped down her checks. Ramon caught her in his arms and carried her to the stone steps.

Sofos puffed his air and walked out into the center of the landing.

"What has happened?" Ramon looked deep into Seela's eyes to try to help her stay calm.

"Kaleus has my children," Seela whispered through her tears. "And my husband lies dying … waiting for help."

Before Seela could continue, Kayz burst onto the landing, rolling across the rock as his legs crumpled from exhaustion. "There is a mine in the mountains … a crystal mine. Kaleus will use it for weapons. His men will come here …" He took a deep breath and recounted the story of Adolphus's injury and the capture of his friends, never once giving Ramon or Sofos a chance to speak.

Sofos shook his head, "This is something Adolphus took on himself. The council will not help bring war to Luz." Sofos turned to glare at Seela. "Your husband brought this on your family."

Ramon left Seela on the steps and met Sofos head on. "We are not leaving Adolphus there. I agree there should be some discussion, but we are not leaving him to die."

"The council's decision was to exile any Tal involved in the war with Kaleus. You voted the same as the other council members. I stand by that decision." Sofos spread his arms out wide. "Those who make war are not welcome in the city of Luz."

"That decision was made long ago," Ramon shook his head. "But things are changing. It is inevitable. War will come to Luz."

Sofos refused to answer.

"I know you think we are protected here among the rocks," Seela had found her strength and could be silent no longer. "But the ground dwellers … they will find a way. With new weapons or machines … somehow they will find us and then you will have to decide what you are willing to fighting for."

"I'm coming too!"

Kayz looked up to see Tori fly out from one of the many crags of rock that covered the walls of their city.

"I'm not as skilled as Ilea, but I can heal Adolphus, at least enough so that he can fly home."

Seela wanted to object. Tori was so young and had a child of her own, but she was a healer like Ilea. They sang together each day to heal the city. If anyone could save Adolphus, she could.

Kayz looked at the councilmen and Seela … all of these adults trying to decide what to do. "We need to go now!" he shouted. "The more time we waste the more time Adolphus loses!"

"We need water," Tori blurted out her plan and then flew from the landing.

"You will be removed from the council if you become involved in this war with Kaleus," Sofos glared at Ramon and his open defiance. "I will see to it personally."

Ramon did not flinch, "I will save my friend and then we can discuss this war. If we are not careful, my friend, there will be no city to council." He looked at Seela and then back to Kayz. "Take her home. Gather supplies … just like Tori. I will find a carry harness." He would also bring the burn gun he kept hidden in his sleeping room, but he wasn't going to announce that to Sofos. "I will meet you both at the top of the cliffs."

Seela lifted from the platform and Kayz followed. As they landed in her home, Seela again felt the tears. "I cannot go with you. I have to find Ilea and Dodgen."

"I know … I know," Kayz soothed, feeling that same knot in his stomach as when he had watched the soldiers drag Ilea away. *I should have been braver … everything would be different now.* "I will go with you."

Seela tried to push her worry to the back of her thoughts. The worry that she could be too late, that Adolphus and Ilea and Dodgen could already be dead.

"First you must find Adolphus. You are the only one who knows where he is." Seela knew if she found her husband dead, it would be even more difficult to face Devant. She would need the hope of his return to keep her strong. Seela straightened her shoulders. "We are going to save my family."

Kayz touched her shoulder, "… *our* family."

Seela smiled, "Yes, our family. But now … now we need supplies."

She went into the eating room and gathered two soft water flasks. "Go to the fountain and get water. I will gather some food and we will meet at the cliff tops."

Kayz shook his head, not knowing what else to say. So he flew. He flew down to the lower levels of the city. Past the flat rock where the councilmen spoke, down into the caves where the water comes up from the ground to be cleaned by the mountain rock. The water here was clear as the night sky. Tori was already there, filling her flask as well. She could feel the worry in Kayz, so she didn't ask any questions. The answers wouldn't have mattered anyway. Adolphus was in trouble and so were Dodgen and Ilea. They needed her help. It was the right thing to do. They would have come for her if the situation was different.

With full water bags, they flew to the clifftops. Seela was there with small bags of supplies. Bread chips, fruit … just enough, with extra for Adolphus.

It took much too long for Ramon to find the carry harness and to explain to his wife that he must leave. It was more difficult than facing Sofos to walk out of his home with Lara so angry. He could feel her eyes as he lifted off from the edge of their home. You are endangering our family, she had said. *When had the Tal become so afraid?*

He found the others waiting at the top of the cliffs, each wearing a shoulder flask of water. Ramon also wore a flask but had removed his councilman garb and now wore a commoner's tunic. The council would not be a part of this endeavor.

Seela met him at the edge of the cliff. "You must take care of Adolphus," she fought to find the words. "He may not even be …"

"Stop thinking like that. He is strong. He needs you."

"No," Seela argued. "He needs Tori. She can help him more than I can. But Ilea and Dodgen, they cannot wait. I can't take the chance that they will be …"

Ramon was beginning to understand.

Seela steadied her shoulders. "I will break with the group … I will continue on to Devant."

"You believe Kaleus plans to kill them?" Ramon didn't like her plan one bit.

Seela just nodded and focused on the moment instead of the possibilities.

"I know Adolphus would want you to protect your children," Ramon hated the idea of

Seela facing the city of Devant alone, and he made himself a promise to find her once Adolphus was safe.

She thanked him for his help. Then they joined the others and a *vhoom* of wings echoed across the cliffs as the four Tal took the sky.

"Do you know where you are going?" Ramon yelled as they lifted off.

"Just be sure to keep up!" Kayz found it exhilarating to give a command to a councilman. "I will get us there."

They flew beneath the setting of the sun, feeling the warmth on their backs. Spinning and diving to find the fastest air currents. Kayz constantly pushing them to fly faster. Tori focused her thoughts on Kayz and Seela to try and give them the strength they needed and once in a while, she would reach out for Adolphus … just in case.

It was more than dark when Kayz broke away from the group. He waved Seela on as he led the others down toward the mine and Adolphus. She tried her best not to imagine what they might find. Her lifesong ached for her husband. She asked the creator Gelquin to protect him … to protect them all. In her heart she knew he would

forgive her for not stopping to say goodbye. Now
… the red moon would be her only companion.

#

Oberon walked the hand-cut stone pathway
through the palace gardens. It was beginning to
feel more like his garden, even though Kaleus
walked beside him down that same pathway. He
had only to ask and it would be changed to fit his
desires.

Their walks had become routine. Each
morning they would eat and then spend time in
the gardens. Sometimes they would walk until the
sun had moved into the center of the sky. It was
safe here, in the garden. No one listened except
the flowers, and Oberon could practice asking
Kaleus to obey without looking foolish.

Their walks had also provided time to learn
the palace schedules and its past. After suns of
painstaking questions, he learned that Kaleus had
once been a soldier himself. In Regar's past, most
fighting among the cities had been scattered and
unorganized. Kaleus had taken control of a few
men and began to change that. Men who were

unhappy with their place in life and willing to take what they thought they deserved.

Kaleus had led his men to the outer cities. Places without castles and kings, places where they could take what they wanted: money and saktars and women … and power. Each time they ravaged a village, some of the soldiers would stay behind, often becoming kings themselves. But that was not enough for Kaleus. He wanted to be king of all the cities. He wanted a grand place to live and make his grand plans. He spoke of the prophecy and the dark-eyed princess who would change the balance of power. He spoke of Jaika.

Oberon knew that part of the story all too well. Jaika, the daughter of Merith, and how Kaleus wanted to use her to take power. It was just a prophecy that so many wanted to believe. But no one seemed to believe enough to leave its fulfillment to fate. He remembered how Merith and Galimar had used the SolStone to send her away, away from Kaleus. What he did not know was just how much of an illusion Kaleus had been. To disguise his limited resources, he had sent small groups of men into Palon, over and over, to cause chaos and make it appear that he had legions of men under his control. One such raid had even taken the life of the queen. But the palace of

Devant had been an easier target. The king was young and foolish and had been easily caught off guard. So, when Kaleus had sent word that he was coming from Devant to take Jaika, he would have lost. Merith sent his daughter away for nothing.

Oberon had not thought about her in such a long time. His hatred for Merith and Galimar had overshadowed any feeling he might have had for this child. Now, with the SolStone, he could search for her. He could use her to fulfill the prophecy and bring peace to the land, under his rule of course. It would be much simpler than war.

Each time they were in the garden, Oberon became more skilled at controlling Kaleus, but it could be hard work. The more suggestions he made to Kaleus, the more docile he became. But, there were moments when Oberon lost control and Kaleus found his way out of the stupor, barking orders and demands that Oberon would have to undo without drawing any attention or unwelcome questions. But these were becoming more and more infrequent. When the two soldiers burst through the palace door and out into the gardens, that is exactly what happened.

"Lord Kaleus!" The two men shouted as they ran, then stopped on the pathway and dropped to kneel before their king.

"What it is?" Kaleus barked and Oberon knew he was losing control.

"We bring you news from your captain, my Lord. Two Tal conspirators have been arrested. They are murderers and thieves. They killed soldiers in the mountains."

"Then they will be executed," Kaleus growled. "An example must be made. I will not look weak in the eyes of the Tal. Tell the captain to take care of it." Then he quieted and turned to walk further into the gardens as if nothing out of the ordinary had taken place.

"Why would your soldiers be in the mountains?" Oberon questioned. The messengers were leaving and no one else was listening, so he could ask any question he wished.

"They are guarding the prisoners in the mine." Kaleus's eyes had returned to their glassy state as he continued to walk.

"What mine?"

"The crystal mine."

Oberon huffed. Kaleus answered only what was asked. It was difficult to get him to provide any details. That would have meant he had to think on his own. Oberon was still navigating the fine line between obedience and an empty stupor. "Tell me everything about the crystal mine."

Kaleus stopped walking and stood frozen, just staring at the garden. Oberon knew he had asked too much of the man, so he tried again. "When was the mine discovered?"

Kaleus continued to stare out at the flowers. "A little more than one turn of the red moon."

"That's good," Oberon encouraged. "And you have prisoners who work in the mines."

Kaleus just stared.

Oberon growled as he realized he had made a statement and not asked a question. "How far is the mine?"

"Not far."

Oberon shook his head and paced up and down the walkway muttering to himself, trying to choose a better tactic. He stopped and looked into the empty face of the king. "You do not want to kill the Tal prisoners. You will change your command. The prisoners will be caught and their release will be negotiated."

Kaleus just stared.

Oberon knew it was pointless to explain to this man that they needed the Tal on their side. If they decided to fight, the Tal would be a formidable enemy. One that Kaleus's men might not defeat. If they were no longer neutral, if they had decided to fight in the existing wars, Oberon wanted them to fight for him.

"You will go back into the castle, find your soldiers, and tell them not to kill the Tal."

Kaleus nodded and continued his stroll.

Sunlight

Dodgen watched over Ilea as she slept. It felt like suns and suns had passed since they had arrived in this place. The patch of light on the floor never moved, so it was impossible to tell just how long they had been captives. He heard the guard change places with another at least twice, and food was offered through a partially open door a few times. But other than that, time seemed to go on forever. Ilea slept and healed, and he watched.

Dodgen didn't remember falling asleep, but the stiffness in his legs meant it had been quite a while. There was a plate by the door and some half eaten ganda fruit. Ilea was sitting up, digging at the shackle on her leg.

"So, you finally got something to eat," Dodgen smirked and sat up to stretch his legs.

"I saved you some. I know it is your favorite."

He could tell by her sharp response that his sister was feeling better. "I was right about the prison food. You do have to give me that."

"If my claw wasn't so curved, I would have this stupid thing open already," Ilea snarled and threw up her hands in defeat. She stared at her brother in the shadows. "Yes, you were right about the food … feel better?

Dodgen nodded, "Yes, I do."

Ilea couldn't help but smile. The wounds in her body had healed. Thinking was easier. Her thoughts were clearer … more connected. She felt like herself again. "Any ideas on getting out of here?"

"Actually …" Dodgen slid over to the door to finish off the fruit. "While you were sleeping, I was thinking."

Ilea prepared herself for some crazy scheme that might get them killed. Still, she preferred crazy to doing nothing at all, and it would keep Dodgen from asking about father. "Yeees?" she tried to sound interested.

"When you heal someone …"

"*Yes.*"

"You talk to the small parts in their body … right?"

Ilea rolled her eyes. They had had this conversation many times. "Living things have a lifesong. It is a sort of vibration. I can join with their song and help them."

"Even rocks … right?" Dodgen was not sure his idea would work, but he wasn't giving up.

"Yes, even rocks. The song of the stones is faint but I can still hear it. Their pieces still have life."

Dodgen considered his next words. "If you can make things heal … if you can make things get better … can you also break them?"

Ilea had never considered using her gift to destroy. She didn't think she could take a life that way. "I will not kill that man behind the door."

Dodgen held his breath. He had forgotten about the guard. If he was listening, he might … "Come," he whispered and motioned with his hand toward the center of the room.

Together they slid across the stone floor holding their chains to keep them as quiet as possible. Ilea was beginning to hate this plan already.

"I don't want you to kill anyone, just damage some things. I've seen what you do with the rocks, the way you torture them to make patterns for your bracelets."

"That's not the same." Ilea snapped. "I don't kill the rocks. I just … rearrange their parts."

She thought about the stones and crystals that she had changed over her lifetime. The patterns and songs she had forced to the surface to make jewelry or decorations. She had a lot of trouble controlling the patterns. Even the stones had a rhythm to keep, and they resisted change. But they were not destroyed, just changed. She used to give them as gifts. Once even to a princess she found hiding in a viney patch. She wondered where Jaika was right now and what she would do if she were locked in a prison cell.

"Do you think you can do that with our cuffs?

Ilea studied the shackle on her brother's leg. This was not a plan she would have even considered. Maybe it could work. This metal was burned and shaped by ground dwellers so there was not much life inside, but maybe there was still some patterns to be found.

Gently she placed her fingers on her brother's leg and began to caress the pieces of his shackle. Her fingers danced along each edge and joint until she had a clear image of the device. She closed her eyes and began to sing. Soft, gentle sounds, weaving their way into the metal. Then suddenly her voice trembled and pushed at the air. Her song became jagged and sharp, dropping and rising in pitch and intensity to settle into a deep guttural sound ... a monotonous irritating sound. The side of the cuff became warm and tiny sparks bit at Dodgen's leg. He reached down and pushed the shackle sideways to move the hot metal away from his skin. He didn't want his leg melted along with the cuff.

Ilea squinted in the misty light, watching Dodgen's cuff refuse to move. "Grrr," she clenched her teeth and growled with frustration, and the metal shackles beneath her fingers shook.

Dodgen jerked his leg backwards. "Did you feel that?"

Ilea huffed and dropped her hands to the floor. "It's hard ... it's so hard."

The guard outside slammed his fist against the door and yelled something about being quiet.

They just sat there … brother and sister waiting for something to happen. Waiting for the guard to burst through the door and take away any chance of escape.

"I can't do it," Ilea whispered and then looked at the small window in the door. "It's easier to help than to hurt." She watched her brother in the shadows, knowing that she had failed. Her strength would not be enough to free them.

Dodgen moved closer so that only she could hear. "Maybe that's wrong. Don't destroy the metal, just push it or bend it or change it. Coax it the way you do the parts of the body that are hurt."

Ilea nodded. She hadn't thought of it that way.

"Take a deep breath," he soothed. "Don't focus on the whole thing. Just the place where the metal comes together … the joints … the connections. That one tiny piece … then the whole thing will fall apart."

Instinctively Dodgen put his hand on her hers and Ilea understood. "I will try." She quieted her mind and began to sing. Not the melodious song used for healing a wound, and not the erratic song from before, but a gentle humming sound. A song the guard would never hear. Almost like a wing-a-ring that flies close to your ears. She focused her thoughts on the tiny piece where the edges joined. Some of the metal was cold and dead, but deep inside there were the muffled, delicate songs of life.

There were no sparks this time, no heat. Dodgen watched the metal joint shutter and shift and then tiny grains of what looked like sand sifted out from between the larger pieces. He reached down and shook the cuff and the hinge broke free.

"Whooooooooooo," Ilea's breath trembled as she relaxed. "Better," she said. "That was easier. The metal is not all the same. There are parts inside that are different … softer. Their song is different. I can change them, shift them closer to the surface …"

"Then the rest falls apart," Dodgen said. He moved the open shackle into the shadows, holding the chain to keep it quiet.

"Yes …yes. That's right," Ilea agreed. "Now your wing … your wing."

She knew from her own wings, that these shackles had spikes inside. Otherwise they would slip right off. It would be easy to hate the man that designed these. He must have known how they would be used.

She smiled, and Dodgen turned his back to her. Ilea placed her fingers on the edge of the shackle that held his wing. Dodgen slid a little closer and placed his hand on her leg to keep their connection. It was quicker this time. Her breathing did not even change. And then the dust began to fall from the metal joint.

She reached up and pulled it open. "Careful," she warned. "It won't open all the way." She wriggled his wing from between the spikes. Tiny bits of blood dripped from the puncture wounds on his wing. She knew the pain … it was the same as her own. But they could be healed now. He opened his wing and she touched the torn places with her song. The light danced across his wing and the wounds vanished. The dried blood was all that remained to show that they had even existed.

"The other one will be even easier," Dodgen nodded.

Ilea had barely touched the shackle when the dust came and it fell apart. Because this wing was much smaller, it came loose with ease leaving only one or two places to heal. Dodgen carried each piece of the metal into the shadows.

"Now you," her brother commanded. "Your wings. I'll help you."

Ilea couldn't reach the shackles on her own wings, so she must rely on her brother. He moved behind her, keeping one hand on her shoulder and the other on her restraint. Within moments, he could see the joint dust.

"I am going to open it," he whispered. "Hold on."

He used his fingers to pry it apart. Dodgen was stronger than her, and he could force it open wider and even twist it slightly to free her wing.

"Now the other," she said.

In less than a heartbeat, her wings were free. "I need a moment," she breathed and bowed her head. Slowly she opened her wings, and he could see the light shimmer across her skin and the puncture wounds disappear.

She suddenly closed her wings and looked at her brother, wide-eyed. "Hide," she breathed.

Dodgen buried himself deep into the shadows. Ilea bowed her head and hugged her knees to make it hard to see that her wings were free. She could feel the man at the door turn and look through the hole. His eyes searched the room but the broken shackles were well hidden in the shadows, and Dodgen was only a hazy outline in the gray light. Ilea was thankful for the darkness and pulled her knees in even tighter. Then, she heard the man grunt with dissatisfaction and look away.

They both held their breath and waited for him to rattle his keys or open the door. If he came in now, Dodgen could escape but Ilea's leg was still bound. She would be trapped in this cell with that giant of a man. Dodgen knew he would die protecting her.

As their hearts quieted, Dodgen watched a flicker of light spark from Ilea's final shackle. Without a sound, she pulled the metal cuff from her leg.

Dodgen emerged from the shadows and crawled to Ilea's side. Her eyes were bright, but he could see the weariness in her face.

"I want to try something," she said. "I think it will work, but it may take some time." She slid across the stone floor. With the chains gone, she did not make a sound. Ilea put her hand and cheek against the rough wood door and closed her eyes. She could feel the man on the other side and the same sadness as before. She reached out with her mind through the door to find all of him.

She cooed, almost bird-like. No song this time. "hooooo …. hoocooo …" Her voice was soft and hypnotic.

Dodgen backed away. He could already feel the weight in her song and did not want to listen. Soft and slow, "sleep," she whispered through the door, and caressed the guard's lifesong to quiet his light. She could feel the parts of his body relaxing. She felt it when he put his hand against the wall and when he slipped to his knees on the stone floor. He shook his head hard to clear the dizziness but Ilea would not let it leave. The peacefulness beckoned and called, and he could not resist.

Dodgen heard the thud when the guard hit the floor.

She could feel Dodgen's heart beating faster. "The door," he chattered. "Now the door."

He forced himself to whisper … to stay calm and not throw himself against the door. "Just the lock … just one piece. Find the place where the latch meets the hook."

The latch was anchored to the wood facing around the door and connected with the metal hook that held it in place. That connection … that point was the only part she had to sing to. "Not the whole thing," she whispered to herself. "Coax, not destroy," she repeated the words Dodgen had spoken earlier.

It was not quite the same metal as their shackles. It was harder, darker, colder, but it too was not pure. There were tiny parts inside that did not belong. Even air was trapped here and there. Tiny bubbles of air that weakened the metal. Ilea sang to the air and to the tiny grains of sand. She sang to the flecks of rock and vapors of water that lived within the metal. Their song joined with hers and they shifted deep within the latch. Like tiny bugs they quivered and moved and weakened the metal until the place on the lock, no bigger than a man's finger, was full of holes.

Ilea swallowed hard and looked at Dodgen. "Softly," she said. "No sound."

Dodgen reached up beside her and pushed against the wood. The lock gave and the door swung open.

Ilea peered down the dusky hallway reaching out her light to find others who might try to stop them. "There is no one else in the hall," she whispered and turned back to her brother. "All of the other cells are empty. There's no one here."

Dodgen nodded. "Because they are all in the mine. That's probably where we would be going next, if we still had those stupid things on our wings."

Ilea turned and pushed the door further open and it bumped against the guard's body. They both held their breath, but he didn't move. They stepped out into the hallway and Ilea continued her search for people.

"Which way?" Dodgen asked.

"There are more people that way," she pointed. "I think the other way is closed … it feels closed."

"Then we will take our chances with the people," Dodgen made his decision as certain as any military leader. And he led the way toward the end of the hallway.

"I wish we had something to cover us … to hide our wings."

"Sure," Dodgen sneered, not caring who might hear. "I will keep an eye out for some new clothes.

Ilea didn't answer, feeling as stupid as her suggestion must have sounded. Then Dodgen started running. They both ran as fast as their legs would carry them, wishing they could fly. If they could just get out of this place, they would be safe. Ilea had been right. At the end of the hallway was a set of stairs and a way out.

"There is sunlight up there," Ilea panted. "The sun comes into that room somehow. Windows or holes … some way to escape."

Dodgen nodded and headed up the stairs. He intended to go first. He had failed at protecting his sister in the past and it wasn't going to happen again. Thick stone steps led up to still another wooden door. Dodgen turned the latch and looked out into a hallway. At the end of that hallway, he could see a grand room filled with tables and people milling here and there. Ilea had been right about the light too. There was sunlight splattered across the walls and floor. Behind those people, there had to be a way to get out.

He turned to Ilea, put his hand over his mouth and then started out the door. Ilea followed in his shadow, knowing that if they had to fly, he would start running and she would be left behind. As they cleared the door, Ilea looked over her shoulder to see an endless hallway with no escape, so she prepared herself to face the giant of a room filled with people.

Together they tiptoed toward the open spaces of the grand hall, waiting for someone to scream and point at their intrusion. As they entered the room, Dodgen could see the lofty ceiling painted with blue sky, sunlight dripping from the stone walls and the windows across the far wall ... and the doors. The arched, double, doors that stood open to the garden beyond.

They stood frozen for a moment, watching the people walking in and out of the tables lined up across the room. The tables were filled with soldiers and people dressed in fine clothes. No one seemed to notice them yet. These people were too busy eating and laughing and serving.

Dodgen weighed their chances of flying out those doors or using the windows above them. He had seen the glass at Genoa's house, and it could be too thick for him to break. Then a woman in the room screamed and pointed, and their moment of indecision was gone. Another woman yelled and then a soldier. One by one, the soldiers began to stand, scattered about the room, from table to table they rose to fight.

Ilea's heart pounded in her chest.

"Come on," Dodgen said and started running.

He opened his wings and headed toward the painted sky ceiling of that grand hall. Ilea followed. Three steps and she rose above the crowd. Then they dove for the doors. No one seemed to remember the open doors. They just screamed and pointed and shouted vile threats. Dodgen flew low and pulled in his wings as he dove through the doors, double doors, grand, arched double doors. More than wide enough for a young Tal. Ilea was right on his heels. As they cleared the doors, Dodgen and Ilea twisted sideways to miss the bearded man dressed in black and the red-haired ruddy faced man emerging from the garden.

"No!" Oberon shrieked as he saw his chance for an alliance escaping. Without thought, he pulled the SolStone from beneath his shirt. Still in its bag, he aimed it at the two young Tal. He focused his thoughts on stopping them, but he didn't have a clear idea of just what that would look like. Still, the SolStone responded.

Light burst from the bag. Waves of watery light, just like the light that Galimar had used to send Jaika away. The light shot skyward and poured over one of the Tal, and in a heartbeat, Ilea was gone.

Dodgen flew into the sun, alone, spinning and twisting, and trying to find his sister. But she had vanished. His body felt empty and cold as if it had been completely ripped apart. He closed his wings … and dropped. Like a stone dropped from the highest cliff, he fell. The sun blinding him from above and the wind rushing past his face, rushing into his ears, tearing at his wings to open and stop his descent. The sound of the wind grew thick as he neared the ground, and he spun, flipping over, opening his wings to dive into the garden and destroy whomever had taken his sister. But he was stopped by the wings of a full-grown Tal. The *vhoom* of her wings pushed him sideways and he rose above the flowers, hovering, staring in disbelief. Seela screamed as she dove. Her claws were open and her arms spread wide, she raked her claws along the stomach of the red-haired man and hit the man in black full force, driving him to the ground beneath her. She screeched again and raised her arms to tear this man apart.

"No!" he begged. "I can bring her back! I can save her!"

Seela wavered for an instant and then plunged her claws deep into Oberon's chest. "Do it!" She screamed, "Do it now!"

He gasped with the pain. "If you kill me, she is lost."

Seela swept her wings backward and the thrust lifted her upward and she relaxed her claws. Dodgen stared in disbelief at his mother standing before the ground dwellers, claws dripping with blood. A warrior he had never seen before.

"Bring her back or I will kill you," Seela spoke slowly, matching the language of the man in front of her.

"I need time to heal," Oberon lied. "I am too weak."

Deep in her heart Seela knew he lied, but she couldn't take that chance. He had sent her daughter away, and only he could bring her back. Dodgen landed behind his mother and watched to see what would happen next.

Soldiers flooded the courtyard and grabbed the two Tal by their shoulders and arms, pulling them toward the ground.

"No!" commanded Oberon. "Let her go!"

The soldiers hesitated and looked to Kaleus who had fallen to his knees and held his hands over the bloody wounds across his stomach.

Oberon sat up and crawled toward Kaleus. "Remember what we talked about in the garden. Tell your men to let them go."

The king's eyes were closed, but Oberon was certain they were cold and lifeless. "Let them go." Kaleus's words were more a plea than an order, but the men responded anyway.

"Take them to the council chambers so that the king may speak with them," Oberon had to be careful or the soldiers would see through his charade.

Kaleus made no move to challenge Oberon, so the soldiers obeyed. Dodgen kept waiting for his mother to attack, to cut down these men with her claws, but she followed them without resistance. She tucked her wings behind her in cape-like fashion and followed the black-uniformed soldiers, holding her head high and her rage buried deep in her heart. Down the stone hallways of this grand palace they walked, not knowing if Ilea was even still alive.

Three soldiers led them down a maze of stone hallways and stairs to a meeting room. A lonely place where one might go to make plans that no one else should hear. Seela raised a claw and hissed at the men as they led them inside, so the soldiers decided to stand guard in the hallway. The lock clicked as they removed the key.

The room held one massive round table surrounded by straight-backed wooden chairs. The table was round, but the elaborate chair at the far end indicated exactly where the leader would sit. There were no windows here, but glowers lined the gray stone walls and cast golden shadows about the room. Dodgen paced the back wall and tried to make sense of what had happened. Seela turned one of the chairs around and sat down backwards, with her arms and chin resting on the back of the chair. Her wings trailed out behind her.

"She is still alive," Seela assured her son. "There have been stories about a blue light and a doorway. King Merith sent his daughter through such a doorway … a great many turns ago."

Dodgen stopped and stared at his mother. How could she change from a savage warrior into this complacent, calculating, helpless …? He fought back the words he wanted to say. "You should have killed him."

Seela looked at her son with a stranger's eyes. "There will always be time for that." She was angry at her family, angry at Dodgen and Ilea and Adolphus for risking their lives over shiny stones. "We are going to make a bargain to get your sister back."

Dodgen shook his head, "I saw him destroy her."

"No!" Seela slammed her hands down on the table. "She is still alive … somewhere." Seela stood beside the backwards chair.

"How can you say that? If you only knew …"

"I do know," Seela studied her son in the glowers' light. "I know the things you saw while you were following your father."

"You knew … I followed him?"

"Of course I knew. Your father would leave, and then you … and then your sister would chase after the both of you."

Dodgen started pacing the room again, refusing to look at his mother.

"Adolphus told me about the glass-melter in Palon and their meetings. He was trying to help the ground dwellers … to save them from Kaleus."

"Isn't there a king in Palon … and an army?"

"Yes," Seela nodded. "Yes, but they will not be enough. Kaleus's men fight like wild beasts. Attacking with no pattern, with no mercy."

"And this man … this man that you are willing to make a bargain with? What about him?"

Seela sat back down in the chair, "Because … it is the only way I can breathe. If I think about her being gone, my insides twist and my heart …" Her words grew soft and her shoulders sank. "She is alive. She has to be … she just has to be. The others can take care of your father. We need to help Ilea."

"He's alive?" Dodgen gasped. "I knew she was wrong. Ilea said he was dead, but I told her ... I knew it."

So much had happened since Dodgen and Ilea had been imprisoned. "I don't know if he is alive." Seela's voice quivered. "He was when Kayz flew home. He took Tori and Ramon to find him."

"Ramon ... in the council?" Dodgen sounded impressed. "And Tori?"

He couldn't think of anything else to say. His sister was gone and his father may be dead. There was just nothing else to do or say. Dodgen pulled out one of the chairs, and they sat in silence. It wasn't until the door began to rattle that they looked to each other for hope.

When Oberon entered, he wore the same blood-soaked shirt as he had in the garden courtyard, but his wounds were closed. The dried blood and the missing wounds sent a clear message of power. This man in black dismissed the guards and walked with such confidence that the altercation in the courtyard seemed almost a dream.

"I am Oberon," he announced his name as though they should have already known.

Dodgen shot him an angry look.

"I am second only to Kaleus," he continued. "I lead in his absence." The guards weren't listening, so it didn't matter what he said.

Dodgen looked at his mother, unable to understand the words. This was not a language spoken by the Palons or the Tal.

"The other man in the garden, the one you injured," Oberon spoke directly to Seela, "was the king." Then he repeated the words in the language of Palon, and this time Dodgen understood.

Seela stood and kicked back her chair. "Oberon ... I am Seela. Where is my daughter?" she demanded, using the first language spoken by Oberon. The language Dodgen could not understand.

Oberon was caught off guard. "You speak the language of the temple?" he said, realizing he had not made this woman as uncomfortable as he had hoped.

"I speak all languages," Seela stared into Oberon's steel blue eyes and fought the urge to rip him apart. "So again, I will ask you, where is my daughter?"

Oberon took a step back, surprised at her skill. If this woman could speak multiple languages, she could be useful. "She is safe. In another place." He chose his words carefully with complete understanding that this creature could easily destroy him. "I do not know the name of this place, only that the light is the doorway."

Dodgen growled. He could see by anger in his mother's eyes that this man was making excuses for not bringing his sister back.

"I will not leave without her," Seela again spoke in the secret language of the temple. "I will stay here … with you … in this horrible place."

This new language made it difficult for Dodgen to follow the conversation, but he knew the tone of his mother's voice. She was telling this man exactly what she wanted.

The thought of Seela staying was appealing to Oberon. He had heard stories of the many giftings the Tal women possessed, and a translator could be quite useful. "I agree," he said, but this time he spoke so that Dodgen could understand. If he was to forge an alliance with these creatures, even this boy must be included. "You should stay. It will take time for me to locate your daughter, and I welcome your assistance."

Seela and Dodgen looked at each other and tried to decide why this man was being so nice.

"I am not leaving you here alone," Dodgen cautioned his mother. "I will stay here with you until he finds Ilea." He lowered his voice, "It is not safe here."

"Mmmmm … Ilea … so that is her name." Oberon wanted to learn more. "And she has a gifting as well." He waited for Seela or Dodgen to deny the charge, but they offered nothing. "I saw what she did to the shackles … and the lock on the cell door. Or was that you, my young friend?"

Dodgen was uncertain whether to argue or agree, but Seela took full advantage of the question. "That is why it is so important to find her. No one else can do what she can."

It was a lie, of course. There were other healers in Luz, but Oberon needed to believe she was the only one.

"Yes," Oberon agreed. "It is important that I find your daughter … but while I look for her, I need your help with another task. A task that requires your gifting with languages."

Seela nodded in agreement.

"Before your children escaped, Kaleus and I were on our way to release them. We do not wish to fight the Tal. In fact, we would like to become their ally. I understand that we need to prove our intentions. If we work together, perhaps that would be a beginning."

"What is the task you require?" Seela cared nothing for an alliance, but she was prepared to do what was necessary to find her daughter.

Oberon licked his lips and continued. "I am searching for a young man of great importance, but even within a single city, the dialects can change. A skilled linguist is difficult to find. I will provide accommodations for you if you will stay and translate for me."

"And my son will go free?"

"No!" Dodgen shrieked. "I will not leave you here with this man." He growled low in his throat.

Seela grabbed her son by the shoulders. "You must find the others. You must take care of your father. You can come back. You know where to find me." She released her son and turned to Oberon. "Can he come and go as he pleases?"

Oberon smiled, "If he returns to Devant, he will be allowed to see you. I will make sure the guards understand that your son is not to be fired upon … you have my word."

Dodgen looked at his mother. "I don't trust him."

Seela glanced at Oberon, "I don't either, but we have to start somewhere. If nothing else, he can send me to her."

Dodgen's heart ached. There was a good chance he had already lost his father, and he did not want to face losing his mother.

"We will walk out together," Seela said.

Oberon stepped out into the hall and instructed the guards to leave. Then he motioned for Seela and Dodgen to follow. Down the hallways they walked, each knowing that this may be the last time they will ever be together. Seela held on to Dodgen's hand so tightly that it hurt almost as much as his heart. The three of them walked back out into the garden where Seela had attacked. There was still traces of blood on the hand-cut stone, and somehow that was comforting to Dodgen to know that his mother was capable of such strength.

"Go find your father," Seela nodded and tried very hard to look unconcerned, but Dodgen knew better.

He hugged his mother close. "I love you … and I will find him. And then I will come back here … and make him bring Ilea home." Dodgen let go and looked away from the tears that formed in her eyes. He took a step back and glared at Oberon, "I will find you if you hurt her. There will be no place you can hide."

Oberon just nodded his understanding. This boy's threat was insignificant, but angering the entire Tal clan was another matter. Three steps and Dodgen was in the air. He lifted off toward the mine and his father. Oberon could not help but envy those powerful wings.

As her son became a tiny speck in the sky, Seela turned to Oberon. "Now what happens?"

"Let me tell you about this young man I seek. I have not seen him since he was a child but he is very important to me. I will tell you what I know so far." Then they turned and walked together back into the palace.

What Dodgen and Seela could not see was a guard at the top of one of Devant's highest towers. A soldier in the black uniform of Kaleus's army who held the wings of a Talec bird as he attached a message to its neck. A Talec trained to carry messages to the guards of the crystal mine. A message that read: *The Tal is our enemy. Death or imprisonment are the only options.*

Switch

Officially, the side of the truck read 'C & J Power', but a craggy 'wash me' had been carved into its mud coated tailgate. It had once been white, this International truck, dirty and scratched and carrying a bucket designed to lift a lineman to the dizzying heights of a broken transformer or power line.

The radio crackled inside the truck, "Earth to Sam. Earth to Sam. You guys still there?"

Burt picked up the mic and winked at his partner, "So, all you care about is Sam? I'm here too ya know."

"That you Burt?"

"In the flesh." Burt wasn't his real name, but he could hardly work a line with a name like Bartholomew Judson. It had been Bart for a while.

Eventually it became Burt, and he got tired of correcting people. So, Burt it was.

"How far are you guys from the tower?"

"Mmmm … bout a mile out in the truck. Then we gotta walk. And ol' Sam here may not make it if there's any wind."

Sam just shook his head without saying a word. He had already heard almost every tall or thin joke in existence.

The voice on the radio sneered, "Yeah, yeah, yeah … just get that line repaired. The power has been cut to both towers. I double checked just to be sure. Don't want my Sam to get fried."

"Don't worry … I'll have your prize engineer home for supper."

Burt hung up the mic but kept talking anyway. "Yep … all the guys at the station think you are the cat's meow."

"It's just because I fixed those turbines last year." Sam's voice was deeper than expected for such a frail looking man. Deep and buried in an indeterminable accent. A shaved head and skin the color of morning coffee had left him open to jokes most of his life.

"And the generator ... and Frank's TV. Those guys think you can fix anything."

"I like to try." Sam stared out the window at the trees that passed as they worked their way up the edge of the mountain. This was as good as any place to stay for a while. His father had moved them so many times, staying in one place could feel uncomfortable after a while.

"You got any family, Sam?"

"Just my brother, but I don't see him very much." He should have added that he lived in California and had an amazing job designing cars.

"Is he a fixer like you?"

"Yeah." Sam thought about the hours spent tearing down motors with his brother and his dad. "He fixes things ... it's in his blood."

Burt slowed the truck and pulled off onto what looked like a road and parked beside some fallen rocks. "We have to walk from here. Some controls are at the base of the second tower, but to fix that line, we have to climb. Been up there three times this month. But I guess you already knew that."

Sam nodded, "I have been studying the weather patterns. I want to try a different type of anchor."

"And that fancy wrapped line you got back there. That won't be fun to hang."

"I know, but maybe it will be the last time it breaks."

"Be careful there mister. You'll have me believing you really can fix anything." And then Burt laughed that big-hearted laugh that made any problem seem fixable.

Both men climbed out of the truck and began collecting their gear. Burt lifted a dirt-stained panel on the side of the truck bed and pulled out backpacks full of tools and a set of harnesses and carabiner type hooks for climbing. Burt picked up a roll of blue electrical wire and draped it over his right shoulder much like a cowboy carrying his lasso.

The trail to the steel lattice towers was not treacherous or steep. But it was lined with heavy rocks that made it too narrow for the truck.

"The rest of the towers have nice roads, but not this one," Burt mused. "And of course, it's the one that breaks all the time."

Sam wasn't listening anymore. He was studying the landscape and reviewing possible scenarios for repairing the tower. Further up the trail, he could see the cliffs of the narrow passageway to the next tower. This section had been cut with explosives, but the rock already showed signs of smoothing in long ruts along the walls. He tried to imagine the path and speed of a wind current that could do so much work. Sam could see the ladder up the middle of the tower as they came closer. A hundred feet in the air with catwalks out to each tree-branch that held the electrical wires. None of the cables were snapped, so finding the problem could take a while.

Burt took out his keys and opened the man-sized metal box at the base of the tower. Dials and wires and digital readouts covered the instrument panel within. Part of the lower panel showed scorch marks. Sam pulled a screwdriver from his pack and squatted down to take a look.

"I have to go up there," he said without turning away from the panel.

"I know," said Burt in that lackadaisical manner that never seemed to change. He scratched his chin for a moment. "You have climbed one of these before, right?"

"Of course," Sam replied. He didn't exactly lie. He had climbed towers like these on two occasions. They weren't quite as tall as this one, but he knew the drill. And couldn't remember the last time in his life he had truly been afraid. Maybe when his mother died. Everything after that seemed so easy.

"Put your gear on," Burt said. "Wonder boy is not getting hurt on my shift."

"I know, I know." Sam dropped his backpack and pulled out a harness and hooks. He felt in his pocket to make sure his phone was still there. A few pictures would be nice for later.

Burt pulled another bag out of his pack and added a few tools. "These might come in handy when you get up there. If you can find the problem, go ahead and fix it, and then I won't have to go up there."

Sam nodded. Burt was always joking, but he was there when you needed him. He was a tough man on the line and everybody enjoyed working with him.

"I'm gonna finish taking apart this burned section to see where the fire started. Who knows … it might be helpful to know that."

Sam just nodded and smiled and buckled the harness around his waist. Carrying his backpack, he made his way to the ladder and started to climb. After the first ten steps the ladder became surrounded by a cage. Sam connected his carabiner hook to a pole that ran along the side of the cage. Every eight feet it would meet a connecting pole, and he would have to unhook it and move it to the next pole. Then he could begin to climb the next eight feet. It was a slow process, but he was not a man to skip details. People get hurt that way.

"Eight … sixteen …" He counted. "Next set is twenty-four." He counted the spaces as he climbed, stopping each set to look around him and feel the wind.

At forty feet, he felt the shift. The air around him seemed to solidify and move in gentle waves. Burt must have seen it too because he yelled something from the ground that Sam couldn't understand. The air turned to blue water, and then the water filled with light. He could feel the watery air closing around him, and he reached up to push it back. A light flashed, and he was gone.

Burt watched as a massive bird fell from within the light and hit the tower to careen into the rocks below. Flailing and screeching it fell. *The light must have taken it down and where the hell was Sam.* He rubbed his eyes to clear away the spots from the light and then studied the tower again. There was no Sam. He could see a single carabiner hooked to the tower and part of a strap swinging in the wind. And then his stomach twisted. *What if that was Sam I saw flying toward the rocks?* Burt started running. His heavy boots crunched on the gravel as he half slid half ran toward the heavy rocks that marked the edges of the cliffs. A bluish-green liquid streaked the tops of the rocks where he climbed. Then there it was, wedged between the rocks, twitching and gasping … a girl. A girl with blue skin and white hair and wings. Wings sprawled across the rocks bleeding here and there from the fall.

Burt shook his head, climbed down from the rocks and walked back to the truck. His heart racing in his chest and his face ashen. He opened the door and pulled the mic off the radio. "This is Burt … station 12 … anybody there?"

A familiar voice crackled over the speaker. "Are you guys at the tower?"

"You gotta get some people up here," Burt said. "There's a fairy up here … a blue fairy … and she took Sam."

He dropped the mic and held on to the side of the truck as he slid to the ground. Burt could hear the voice on the microphone yelling for more information but he didn't want to answer. He just stared out at the road and tried to breathe.

#

Ilea could hear muffled voices, and a light burned her eyes as bright as any sun. But this sun was so close she could almost touch it, if she could just make her body move. Her head pounded, and she could feel open, weeping wounds on her back and shoulders. The bones in her left wing trembled while they fought to mesh and heal. Ilea lay upon a high table that kept her close to the blinding sun that stabbed into her eyes each time she tried to open them. Within the light, three warriors covered in glistening yellow armor moved about the room. Their arms, their chests, their legs … their entire bodies were covered in the yellow suits. Their faces were protected behind clear shields much like the melted-sand windows of the gray house. These masks hid both their face and voice.

Ilea could feel their lifesongs beneath the armor. Agitated and nervous, but their bodies sang just like any ground dweller from Palon. But this place, this place was not Palon. Everything felt wrong. The room felt white and slick with silver shining metal here and there. Heat coursed through the walls in streams of fire bringing power to the sun above her and some of the other parts of the room. Ilea had never felt anything like this. Maybe she had been taken by a prophet or a man with giftings beyond her own.

Ilea closed her eyes and focused on the wounds in her wing, knitting the bones and flesh together. If there was any way to escape this horrible place, her wings could carry her to safety. She thought about Dodgen and the shackles and the prison. And the light … they had flown together through the open doors and above the garden. She remembered the man in black and the blue-watery light that had covered her in the sky. She could see a metal tower in her memory … but now she was here, wherever here was.

Ilea's heart pounded as she started to shake, and her lifesong began to scream. She shrieked against the walls and they shuddered. She shrieked against the warriors in yellow and pushed them sideways. As she tried to leave the platform, Ilea felt the pull of the straps that tied her hands and chest down. Her body went limp against the pallet, she closed her eyes, and focused on the straps. They were softer than the metal shackles of Kaleus's prison. So with an easy push, her light intertwined with the fabric of the straps and began to search for its weakest part. The yellow warriors stood at the edge of the room, waiting and watching, unable to see the light that would soon unravel the straps. Whispering, circling, her lifesong found the sticky substance that bonded the strap to itself as it wrapped around the metal buckles. She moaned and growled and threw her strength into the bindings. The sticky substance dissolved, and she was free.

Ilea sat up and tore the straps from her chest and arms, wadding them into a tangled mass. One of the warriors came toward the bed. Ilea swung an open claw and tore through his chest plate. It hung in shreds like a woman's dress. The warrior panicked and backed away. The other two advanced. Yellow hands grabbed at her arms and shoulders to push her back down on the bed. Ilea kicked out with her feet and tore the side of the second warrior's uniform, ripping it open to expose the ground dweller beneath. A voice shouted from the ceiling in words she did not recognize, and all three warriors retreated. A door slid open in the wall and they passed through.

Ilea sat up on the table, focusing her breath, fighting the pain in her wing and back. A panel opened in the ceiling to reveal a slatted gate. From between those slats, a white mist floated into the room, washing over her to fill every corner of the room. She could not resist its power. Her thoughts spun and she settled back onto the table, understanding that the yellow warriors had won.

Chasers

Nick Powell pushed his glasses back up on his nose and stared in disbelief at Jack. Jack sat sprawled on the concrete floor of the lab cuddling a pink, hairless dog that might have been a yellow Labrador in another life. It was tucked under Jack's arm and looked small against his muscled frame. The poor thing had been shaved, dyed pink, and probably injected with jelly fish DNA. That was the only rational explanation Nick could come up with at that moment. He remembered reading about cats that had been made to glow in the dark using the DNA of a phosphorescent jelly fish. Whatever they had used, this thing was just a dog. It had never seen any place other than Earth. This was just another dead end.

Jack had removed the fin that had been attached by a harness to Pinky's back, but that did not make him any more attractive. He was still pink and bald. And Pinky was a terrible name, but it did seem to fit the situation.

"There ya go, big fellow," Jack cooed and rubbed Pinky's belly. He proceeded to feed his new friend some stale crackers from a blue and white box retrieved from one of the many cabinets in the lab. He did not seem the least bit troubled that the dog had turned out to be a phony and that they had journeyed all the way out to the East Coast for no reason. He pulled out his phone and settled comfortably into reviewing the football scores and feeding Pinky crackers.

Watching Jack scuffling with a pink dog left Nick with a sense of defeat. For the first time in almost two years, he did not know where to go next. There was nothing on his radar, nothing new to explore. He had been chasing shadows since Jaika's disappearance, and he was not any closer to finding her now than he was the day he lost her.

Nick leaned back in his chair and searched his memories for a new plan. Small and thin, his once blonde hair now streaked with dark and a little gray. His weariness could not be hidden beneath his glasses.

"How long have you guys been chasing?" Dr. Rickner asked, dropping his stack of notebooks on the table.

"Huh?" Nick Powell squinted at the old man. "Chasing? What do you mean chasing?"

Dr. Stanley Rickner was one of the college's faculty called in to verify the authenticity of the dog. He was an expert in exobiology and snooping in other people's personal business.

"Especially you. You've got it bad." He studied Nick's gaunt frame and half-shaven face. "I've watched you." Dr. Rickner added some notes to one of his already bulging notebooks. "You're not like the other guys, looking for a rush ... a fire, an explosion, or a little green man. You're looking for someone."

Jack looked up from the football stats on his phone. He and Pinky had shifted to cozy up on a plaid couch in the corner of the station. He didn't really care what the old man thought. Tall, lanky old man with a baseball cap. Shriveled up from smoking and long work days without eating. He probably weighed in at 125 pounds soaking wet.

Nick sighed, and for a moment he was back on that sidewalk, running from Mattie's house, watching Jaika be lifted from the ground by a stranger and carried through a wall of light. A barbarian who surely had killed her by now, if not worse. The scene was as vivid in his thoughts as if it had all happened yesterday. And Nick felt just as powerless to stop it today as he did a year and a half ago. "Yes," he conceded to the old man in front of him. "I lost someone. What about you? How did you end up here?"

Dr. Rickner smiled, just a little. His face crinkled like paper. "I got sucked in when I was young too. My sister disappeared. I never knew what happened to her. Maybe it was just easier to believe it was an alien than a human."

Nick could see the quiet acceptance in the old man's eyes. Not really sadness or anger, just an acceptance that he would never know the truth in this life.

"So, you never found her?" Nick questioned. He was beginning to look a little like the old man. He needed a shave and a good hot shower.

"No," the old man said. "I've chased so many counterfeits." He stiffened and slammed his notebook shut. "But I'm not ready to give up yet. This one was pretty good. They did a number on that poor dog. He really looked like an alien species."

"You gotta admit, he looks pretty cool," Jack quipped from the couch, still scanning sports news. "That whole glowy thing is really nice."

Dr. Rickner chuckled, "I've seen some pretty good ones in my time. They work really hard to fool us. I'm not sure why... maybe they want to be famous or fool the government ... whoever they might be. There was this one time with skinny-legs Howard ..."

"I guess we have to find something new to chase now," Nick interrupted and twisted at the beads he wore around his wrist. "Something new ... something new."

Jack perked up. "You know we could always go to a football game. I know a place about an hour away. It's going to be a great game."

Nick smiled. Jack had been his faithful companion since Jaika had disappeared. Playing football, taking classes, and still taking time to help Nick chase any strange happenings that might lead to answers. The few times he had been stranded or stuck, Jack was always there to pull him out. He could not have asked for a better friend — a friendship he wouldn't have without Jaika. She would have been proud of Jack.

"I've got another week before classes start. I think we should go someplace pretty. What do you think Nick?"

"I could use some sleep."

"And a bath," Jack said, "You smell kinda ripe." He stood and stretched, making Nick look tiny in comparison.

Nick was too tired to laugh.

"I will keep your contact information," Dr. Ricker assured the boys while gathering up his papers. "I just might find something for you to chase. You came highly recommended from the guys at the North station. And they're pretty hard to impress."

Nick had been chasing phenomenon from East Coast to West. Any odd report, strange animal, UFO sighting ... anything that might help him find Jaika. He'd hooked a scholarship with an online school, and worked on classes from cafes and burger joints, any place with a free internet connection. The school work wasn't hard. He just had to get those basic classes out of the way before he could do anything truly interesting. He wanted to build, he wanted to explore, he wanted to learn, but more than all of that, he wanted to find Jaika. He tried hard not to think of what that beast of a man might do to her if she was still alive.

"Where's this football game you want to go to?" Nick ran his fingers through his greasy hair.

"It's a little more than an hour away. Let's head that direction. We'll get us a hotel. You can take a shower. But first I need a burger or some pizza. I'm starving. All this fake football and your pining has worn me out."

"A burger it is," Nick mused. There never seemed to be a moment that Jack wasn't hungry.

"And a shake, a chocolate shake, with whipped cream." Jack grabbed his sweatshirt from off the chair and they headed out to Nick's jeep. Someday he would have to ask Nick to explain how he used stocks to buy a vehicle and plane tickets anytime they needed them. He probably wouldn't understand it, but it would make for a good story. He was pretty sure there was something underhanded in the whole process.

As they climbed into the car, Jack punched Nick in the shoulder. "You need to give yourself a break. You work too hard."

Nick smiled and shifted into reverse. "She would be proud of you ... you know?" His forest-green jeep rumbled beneath him.

Jack smiled and slouched down into the passenger seat. "Yeah, I think she would. I'm a pretty impressive kind of guy." He sighed, and thought for a moment just how differently his life could have turned out. "She's proud of you too."

Nick liked his friend's choice of words. Jack never spoke about Jaika's wellbeing in the past tense. He never doubted for a second that she was alive and that they would find her. In California when the UFO turned out to be a fraud, and the electronic pulses in Arizona that turned out to be a messed-up power plant — not one of these failures had disillusioned Jack in the least.

Nick studied the winding highway and the trees covered in reds and yellows that passed outside his window. Sometimes he forgot to look at the beauty around him. Jack was right, he needed to slow down. The mountains in the distance seemed years away, and he felt much older than nineteen. The jeep's drive shaft rumbled again and he wished he had spent more money and bought a newer version. Maybe he should check his stock portfolio.

A military march sounded from Nick's pocket and he grabbed his phone and handed it to Jack. "It's Rosie. Put it on speaker."

"Hey Rosie! Rosie! Rosie!" Jack did his best gangster imitation. "It's been a long time, girl."

"Hey! Shut up and listen. I don't have much time and I'm not supposed to be calling you."

"Another tip?" Nick questioned.

"Yes, but this is a big one. A *really* big one. There's a company with a research facility. C & J Power. They have had this thing for a while, but I just got the info. They say they have a new species, alien maybe. You need to go ask for work."

"Work?" Jack complained.

"Shut up! They work with grad students. The company researches power stuff. Solar, wind, whatever they can convert to electricity. These guys will hire you if they think they can steal your ideas. Got that?"

"Do we have ideas?" Jack looked confused.

Nick shook his head at Jack, "Do you have a contact there?"

"Yea. I'm on a hard line. And I'm not using my cell for anything, so you got to remember this. Carter Hull, ask for Carter Hull. Tell him Julia sent you. He's ex-military and he owes me a favor."

Jack laughed, "You lie to every guy. Do you ever use your real name?"

"Maybe someday," Rosie sighed. "And this guy was a tall drink of water ... mmm ... Carter will get you a job but I don't know how you will get into the rest of the building. That's your job. And, I don't want to have to visit you in prison. Okay guys?"

"Thanks Rosie. Be safe." Nick knew she took a big chance anytime she called, but she was smart. Rosie would be running the whole military one day, he was certain.

"Can I still have my burger?" Jack whined.

Nick laughed feeling strong again. "Of course. Burger, shower, and a football game. That will give me time on-line to become a grad student."

Jack laughed, "And then more pink dogs. I wonder what will happen to him."

"He'll become famous in the local paper and some kind family will adopt him. The pink will fade and he will become a regular dog."

"It was hard to feel like a regular dog when Jaika was here. Wasn't it?" Jack looked at Nick. "Did you ever tell her how you felt?"

Nick stared out at the road ahead. "It would have messed everything up."

"Me and Rosie knew … it was okay with us," Jack snickered. "You aren't exactly Rosie's type … or mine for that matter."

"What's that supposed to mean?"

"You don't wear camouflage."

"That is true," Nick smiled. "And Rosie does love her camouflage."

"We're lucky, you know. Rosie … in the Marines … she's gotten us lots of information."

"Yeah, she's a good person to have on my side."

"And me too?" Jack snapped.

"Duh … that's why I call you … all the time … that's why you are here now."

Jack put his hands behind his head and slouched a little deeper in the seat. "I know. I just wanted to make sure that you knew. And at least this time I get to eat."

Nick laughed. "This is a special occasion, so don't get used to it."

Carter

Two days later, sports coats, dress slacks, and white button-down shirts — Nick and Jack were cleaned and pressed and ready for a possible interview. They stood in the parking lot of C & J Power studying the massive glass doors and windows that covered the front of the gray building. Steel and metal made it feel more like a warehouse than an office building, except for the stone patio surrounded by perfectly trimmed flower beds and giant pots of red flowers. Three smokestacks stood beyond the main structure. Metal ladders ran along their sides and white smoke poured from the one in the middle. Steel lattice work connected the smokestacks and joined with others to create a maze of walkways that attached to still more metal towers. Further beyond that, two white windmill turbines turned in the sunlight. And scattered, here and there, a dozen storage buildings.

"They look legit," Jack said and tried to look serious. "And I like the mountains. I know we are only at the edge of the mountains, but they look pretty."

"Yes," Nick hadn't even noticed the mountains in the distance. "And that looks like a miniature powerplant in the back of the building. Maybe they really do research power." Nick nodded as a thousand questions ran through his mind. "Their accounts looked clean ... at least the ones I could find online."

"And you look clean," Jack smiled. "You look good in nerd clothes. And I can even see your face with that haircut."

Nick shook his head, "And you look nice too, Jack."

"I do ... don't I?" Jack pulled at the lapel of his jacket. His muscles pushing at the seams of his clothes. "But it's not very comfortable ... and it's white. Does the shirt always have to be white?"

Nick dropped his head. "Just get me in the door and I will send you back to school."

"If we broke in, I could wear something more comfortable." Jack tugged at his collar. "Or maybe we could just ask for the tour?"

Nick started walking, "Sure, I'll just say, we want to see your secret stuff in the back of the building."

"Well, that would be where they would hide an alien." Jack fell in step beside Nick. "Maybe it came to Earth with the pink dog."

"Jack…"

"I wanted to keep the pink dog."

"I know you did…"

"Nobody at school is ever going to believe me … that I rescued a pink dog who glows in the dark."

"I know, Jack … I know. But she needed a home, not a place for people to make fun of her."

"I would have taken good care of her."

"I don't think feeding her chips and soda counts as taking care."

Jack huffed. "Nerd with no faith…"

"Let's just go in. There should be a receptionist at the front desk." Nick was counting on it. A young female receptionist who was especially susceptible to handsome men with big muscles.

Jack opened the massive glass door and whispered, "It would be more fun if we broke in … I'm just saying."

"No worries Jack, no worries."

The inside was just as Nick had expected. The internet information had been sketchy at best and aimed mostly at finding financial donors, so he knew there would be a nice entrance with a place to meet clients. The ceiling was the height of two stories with its metal framework of support beams painted black. Gray, slate floors with white leather couches and chairs filled the waiting room. Even the front counter was made of glass and copper providing a perfect setting for the blonde receptionist behind it. Pencil skirt and stiletto heels, she immediately noticed Jack.

"Can I help you, sir?"

Jack liked being called sir. It made him feel much older than he really was. He smiled and flexed his shoulders, just a little. "I have a whole list of ways you could help me."

Jack was the perfect distraction but Nick couldn't help but think of the angry, chubby grade-school boy he had been when they first met. Everyone was terrified of him, except Jaika. She had seen something no one else could.

"Mindy?"

"Yes," the pretty blonde giggled. "How did you know?"

Jack smiled and decided not to mention her name tag. "I have a gifting."

She giggled again.

"My friend Nick and I would like a tour of your facility. We're grad students."

"We don't give tours," Mindy smiled and looked up at Jack from beneath her eyelashes.

"Well," Nick interrupted. "Perhaps we could speak with Carter Hull?"

"Do you have an appointment?"

"Do we really need one?" Jack leaned in a little closer. "You smell so nice."

"I could call … back there … and see …"

"I would be very grateful." Jack sat his elbow on the counter with his chin in his hand, "Nick and Jack … tell him … Julia sent us."

"Yes … of course."

They took a seat on one of the white leather couches and listened to Mindy on the phone. When Carter Hull walked through the door, the room trembled. A six-foot two-inch lanky frame with a chiseled jaw that lands you a movie contract. Sandy colored hair, tousled just enough to give off that I-don't-have-to-work-too-hard-to-be-handsome look.

"Hello there, chaps," Carter greeted the boys with a handshake.

Nick smiled at the British accent. *Rosie must have fallen head over heels in love with this guy.*

"My darling Mindy tells me you would like a tour."

Nick nodded, "I would really like a job. My dream is to work in research and your company offers some amazing opportunities." It was hard not to snicker. He used the same speech at every place he applied. He never stayed very long. He didn't need the work, just information. So, the interview process was always a breeze, although, this time, he wished he was a few inches taller.

"If you would follow me." Carter turned on his heels with just a touch of swagger and headed to the back offices. He winked at Mindy as they passed the front desk.

"I bet they all fall down at your feet," Nick mumbled. He wasn't sure if Carter had heard his words or not, but either way this guy knew he was charming and just how to use it. Nick disliked him already.

Jack opted to stay behind and get better acquainted with his new friend. That way he would be sure not to say anything stupid.

True to his expectations, the offices held plush carpets and sharp lined furniture. But, the hallway was a different matter. It was as wide as a car and made of a black tile too smooth and unmarked to be slate. There was no echo or creak when they walked. These floors were heavy and reinforced and dark enough to cover smudges or even tire tracks. Nick wondered what kind of heavy machinery might have passed this way.

Two left turns and they were in Carter Hull's office. Carter stepped behind his desk, sat down in a high black leather chair that leaned back against the wall, and then kicked his feet up on top of the desk. "Julia told me a lot about you guys."

"You guys?" Nick stared in amazement as Carter's accent disappeared.

"I get so tired of talking like an Englishman. But it was part of the job. When they hired me, they were looking for a foreign presence in the marketing staff. So, I offered the accent and got the job."

"Well, you had me fooled." Maybe he had been wrong about this guy.

"I am actually from Texas, though my English accent has taken over most of my southern dialect. But I still use an occasional 'gonna' or 'fixin-to.' The worst is when I say 'fixin-to' with a British accent." He slapped his leg and laughed out loud. "I think a few people are on to me, but I refuse to come clean. I have kept my mystery for the last two years."

Carter seemed to be playing a character straight out of a spy movie and that made him less than trustworthy. "So, you have worked here two years?"

"Yes, two years."

"And how long have you known … Julia?" Nick found it difficult not to say Rosie.

"Just a few months. She saved my life. I'm surprised she didn't tell you all about it." Now it was Carter's turn to be suspicious.

"She didn't have enough time for the details."

Carter considered the possibility that this man in front of his desk was a fraud, but he did fit Julia's description. "I was on company business, so I was traveling," Carter sneered, just a little. "There was this girl, a lovely brunette … I took her out for a few drinks. But then lovely's boyfriend showed up. I guess he didn't know they were seeing other people."

Nick nodded and made a mental note to warn Rosie about this guy.

"He pulled a gun … a hand gun … I'm not much for weapons but it was black and pointed at my face. I hadn't even noticed the military crew sitting in the corner, that is, not until Julia was breaking the boyfriend's arm. She took him down and he never fired a shot."

"Impressive," Nick knew that this had simply been a day in the park for Rosie.

"So, after the police and all the questions, I told Julia, whatever she needed, it was hers."

"Did you say all of that with an accent?" Nick wondered how many favors Rosie was going to ask of this poor guy.

"No ... no secrets when someone saves your life," Carter's eyes grew a little misty and Nick knew he was hopelessly hooked. "So, when she called about our alleged discovery and giving you a job, I was ... eager to help."

"Sounds like you didn't have much choice."

"Either way, you're here," Carter was growing impatient with Nick's insinuations. "I work in PR. I meet with donors and possible clients. Maybe I could hire you as my assistant. I could train you ... that would give you flexible hours. I have been swamped lately, so no one will question why you're here. I can easily justify a job working with me, but this thing you want to see ... that's another story. The basement facility is research ... and other things. I don't have codes for that."

"But they are in possession of something, right?" Nick hated wasting time and he didn't want to find another pink dog.

"Maybe … something … violent … aggressive. The men talk in the breakroom sometimes. Maybe its asleep or dead. I'm not even sure why they keep it. It's been down there at least a year."

"That's a long time to be sedated," Nick was beginning to feel that annoying twinge that runs down the back of his neck when things are not what they should be.

"That's part of the mystery. It must have some abilities our guys want to steal or it wouldn't still be there."

Nick shook his head, "So why has it not been reported to … the right people?"

"I can't guarantee it's even there," Carter fidgeted with some papers on his desk and avoided the question, "but I owe it to Julia to help you look."

Nick smiled and twisted the beads around his wrist. "I appreciate your help. If you can get me a legitimate job in this building, I will find my way into the basement."

"You'll need to fill out a non-disclosure and some semi-accurate personal information." Carter rubbed his chin, "You may not get paid."

Nick laughed, "I never do. I will probably be gone before the first pay cycle anyway."

"Free help. Who could ask for more? So … you need a place to stay?"

"I'll find one. I'm just here for the … basement."

My kind of guy, Carter thought, low maintenance. No wonder he and Julia were such good friends. Maybe this would work out after all. He stood and handed Nick a folder with blank forms. "Take care of these, and I will have you a pass-card printed. First names only for security reasons."

"Nick will be fine on the card." Most of his false identities had Nick as his first name. It made it so much easier to maintain the façade.

"It gets you past the front glass doors and the doors to these offices. Beyond that, you're on your own." Carter walked out of the office.

Nick fought the urge to follow him. The pass-card printing station would be a good one to hack, but that could come later. He started filling in the paperwork using one of his many fictitious personas. There were dozens in his repertoire and the details were fixed in his memory but it was hard to focus on such meaningless forms when beneath him could live a creature from another world.

The papers were completed when Carter returned with the pass-card. "This clips to your jacket. You need to wear it while you're in the building."

Nick stood and attached the badge to his lapel.

"The number on your card works as your computer login. You can start Monday, right?"

"Monday sounds great." The weekend would give him time to try and hack their security system.

"The login won't get you very far. So much is encrypted in our system, but Julia says you are a genius."

Nick was childishly pleased that Rosie thought he was smart … Julia … Rosie … whoever. The two men shook hands and walked back to the double doors that led to the lobby where Jack still hovered around the front desk.

"So, tell me more about the basement," Jack looked a little deeper into Mindy's eyes.

"It's all secret," Mindy lowered her voice to a whisper. "I've heard they keep prisoners down there."

"So, what do they do to the prisoners? Is it good stuff?"

Mindy shook her head and stared at Jack's shadow of a beard. "I don't think I would want to be a prisoner even if it was good stuff."

"Well that sort of depends on who you are locked up with, doesn't it?" While Mindy giggled. Jack could see Nick emerge from the glass doors and motion toward the parking lot. "What time do you get off work?"

Nick cleared his throat.

"Well, I guess I have to go," Jack waved a business card in his left hand. "But, I will be giving you a call."

With a wink, he turned and walked out the door with Nick. Once they were in the parking lot, they both started talking at the same time. Jack rambled on about his skill with women while Nick tried to explain the details of his interview.

"I'm glad you got the job," Jack laughed. "I don't think Mindy has the keys to the basement."

Nick raised his eyebrows, "Basement?" The security here must be weak at best. Everyone seems to know the secrets.

"Mindy seems to think there are prisoners in the basement. Maybe that's a good place to start looking."

Nick loved the way Jack saw the world, clear and straight forward.

"Did you tell this Carter Hull your story?"

Nick sighed, "Sure, I told him I was looking for my girlfriend that got sucked into a parallel universe."

"Man, you don't know that. She might be in New York City."

"Well ... Jack ... you are absolutely right. I have no way of knowing where she is. My only reference is the man who took her. He didn't look like the typical New Yorker."

"But you know, people from New York can be weird."

"Have you ever been to New York?"

Jack smirked, "No ... but I watch a lot of TV."

"Of course you do. I am sure there are a lot of half-naked military men hanging out in New York City."

"Yeah, you're right. They probably would have been on the news by now. Okay, so she's not in New York. So where do half-naked military guys hang out?"

"We're going to the car, Jack."

"Car-jack. I think that's illegal, and besides, it's a jeep."

Nick shook his head, "You're getting hungry again, aren't you?"

"Yea, as a matter of fact I am."

After a king-sized pepperoni pizza, they drove back to the hotel. Then they packed and drove an hour to the nearest airport.

Nick always hated seeing his friend go. He sure had an untarnished way of looking at the world. Jack didn't always understand the science or the details of what was going on, but he often saw what Nick could not. His questions often led down a rabbit hole that provided unexpected answers. But he had a scholarship to keep, and that's what Jaika would have wanted. He left Jack with a good-bye wave, and he waited in the lobby until the plane took off. He set an alarm on his phone to signal when the plane had landed. Jack didn't know it, but there was a tracking device on his phone. Nick hadn't exactly asked permission, but his motives were pure. He had lost Jaika, and there was not anything he wouldn't do to keep from losing another friend.

Nick headed back into town to check out a pay-by-the-week hotel he had seen with a small kitchen. It would be homier and cheaper and a nicer place to spend the weekend finishing the reading for his microbiology class and trying to hack C & J Power Company.

As he unlocked the door to room 285, the beads on his wrist rattled and he thought of Jaika. He knew that there could be multiple places Jaika could have been taken. Planets, galaxies, and parallel dimensions were just the beginning. The odds that this creature at C & J Power was from the same world were slim, but he wasn't giving up.

He shook his wrist and the beads slid a little further down his arm. "Don't worry, Jaika. I'll keep looking." Then he chuckled, "Chasing, until I'm old and crinkled like Dr. Stanley Rickner."

Job

The weekend proved less than productive. Nick did skim the assigned reading, but hacking into C & J Power was a different matter. His login was only active while inside the building, and he couldn't risk discovery before he had even had a chance to look around the building. So, using less than legal methods would have to wait. So, he worked on his stock portfolio and made a little money instead.

Monday morning, he greeted Mindy at the front desk. "I'm not sure if you remember me, but I am Nick Paul. I will be working with Carter Hull."

She just batted her long eyelashes and asked about Jack. Nick had hoped for a little more response. He knew he was not a big guy, but he liked to think of himself as the perfect thief. A sort of man-in-black who just used a little magic. Evidently Mindy was not a fan. Nick shook his head and walked to the double doors that separated the lobby from the office hallway, anxious to try his pass-card. He pushed the card into a slit located on a panel beside the door. A beep and a click and the door was open. Nick smiled as he recognized the logo on the side of the security panel. He had already written an algorithm to hack this system and for a moment he was lost in the memory of a storage facility in Boston. A fruitless search that had cost him a night in jail. He would not make the same mistake this time.

He found Carter on the phone using his accent to persuade a client to make a larger investment than last year. He was promising greater power output for less money and something special to be launched at the end of the year. Nick wondered just how much of the story was true.

Carter nodded and pointed to a chair. Instead, Nick chose to prowl around the room looking at pictures and the locking mechanism on the filing cabinets. He noted the brand name of the desktop computer at the edge of Carter's desk. And through the glass wall he could see into the office across the hall where a similar unit sat on that desk as well. The computer towers were small which meant they were newer models and more difficult to hack … but easier to smuggle out of the building … if necessary.

Carter hung up the phone, pulled two folders out of his lap drawer and laid them on his desk.

"So, what's on the agenda for today?" Nick tried to act interested in the company.

"My morning is full of phone calls and emails, so you will have a little time for some exploring. After lunch, we need to drive out to meet a potential donor and discuss a deal."

"Sounds like a good beginning."

"For now, I need to walk down the hall to meet with Steven, so I want you to look over these files. Look for anything odd … out of place."

Carter looked around the room as if someone was watching … or listening. Nick followed his gaze to the security camera that now graced the corner of his room. It was one of those fish-eye bubbles that look more like an alarm than a camera. And it hadn't been there on Friday. Now he would have to be more careful, plus he had another system to hack. That would change his plans. Maybe they could talk about the changes when they left the building at lunch.

Carter left and Nick settled into a chair with a side view of the camera. He didn't want the watchers to have a clear view of anything he was doing. The folder turned out to be somewhat of a disappointment. He had expected results from events that had taken place in the basement, but instead, it was an expense ledger from a company called BRI. All the expenses listed were being paid by C & J Power. The list was supposed to be typical operational costs for power research but this company seemed anything but typical. Four hazmat suits, gasmasks, nitrous oxide, benzodiazepine, and restraining straps … decontamination chemicals and a centrifuge. Nick wondered just what kind of research BRI was doing. The random miscellaneous costs were also troubling. Twelve, twenty, and thirty-five thousand dollars marked simply as miscellaneous. To further deepen the mystery, the folder lacked any contact information. No individual names or addresses.

The second folder held more of the same type of costs for BRI. The problems were obvious, so asking Nick to review them seemed pointless. Carter still had not returned, so it was time to do some exploring. If he remembered correctly, that had been his boss's orders. So, he started walking.

Nick walked down the hall to the right of Carter's office, only to see more offices and two security cameras. Many were empty and those with name plates had their doors closed. He did receive a pleasant wave from a pretty red-head in a black dress. He found the lack of personnel surprising since the company's public financial records indicated a heavy volume of business. He had expected to see more administrative people.

The last door at the end of hallway was marked stairway. And a narrow room directly across the hallway held six monitor screens that displayed the feed from the various security cameras. The one chair in the room was empty which made it a very inviting room for exploration. Four of the monitors showed random offices about the building. Each one displayed for about thirty seconds and then changed to another office. Switching out in a perfect pattern. The other two monitors were dark, indicating that the connecting cameras were not yet in place or at least were not operational. Nick couldn't help but wonder if there were cameras in the basement. The whole system looked half-finished and easy to manipulate. The most important part of the system was the missing part. There was no indication of a storage system. No computer tower or hard drive in place to store the videos from each camera. Perhaps that was to be installed at a later date.

Nick left the security room to check out the doorway to the stairs. There was no second floor, so they must lead down to this mysterious basement he so wanted to see. The door was locked but had the same security panel as the others, complete with a slot for a pass-card. Nick's card caused the panel to produce a low beep and a red light that warned there would be no entry allowed. He turned his back to the camera in the ceiling and pulled a what looked like a credit card from his pocket. The card was thin as paper and transparent, except for the black strip along the edge. He peeled back the clear plastic that protected the magnetic strip along the bottom of the card and rubbed his fingers along the edge. Back and forth with rapid strokes enough to warm the black strip. Then he slowly, carefully, inserted the card into the slot in the center of the security panel. He left it there for thirty seconds which he counted out inside his head. Then he removed the card and replaced the plastic cover. Once it was back in his jacket pocket, he turned and started back down the hallway.

He walked back toward Carter's office and the glass wall into the lobby. This part of the building had the same offices set up except for the large room at the end of the hall. Here he found three rows of computers with a handful of college students huddled together in packs and focused on monitors around the room. Two large television screens displayed rows of numbers and doppler weather radars. Four desks across the back of the room overflowed with papers and blocked the filing cabinets just beyond.

"Are you the guy from the radio station?" asked a girl with pigtails and a baseball cap. "Webber wasn't expecting you until after lunch."

Nick assured them that he wasn't here to do an interview, but they were more than anxious to share their findings. They had been working with the wind turbine behind the building. The generator and the rotor that was turned by the windmill blades had been modified. The students hoped to decrease the heavy *whoom* sound that made them impractical for residential areas. They were excited about the results and played him their video twice before he could escape. It wasn't that their research was boring, it just wasn't getting him any closer to the basement. They were, however, gracious enough to show him the back entrance.

Behind the building, Nick found the transformers and metal towers visible from the parking lot. In front of one of the storage buildings, a man in dark blue coveralls with a name tag that read 'Webber' sat sprawled beside a scattered pile of mechanical parts.

"So, you are in charge of the grad students?" Nick smiled and held out his hand.

Webber stood up, wiped his fingers on his pants leg and shook Nick's hand. "Guilty as charged. Were they talking bad about me in there?" he joked and stuck a screwdriver in his shirt pocket.

Nick used his best new-employee smile. "Something about a radio interview."

Webber nodded, still wiping the grease from his hands. "Oh yeah. The kids are really excited. So, who are you, exactly?"

It was odd to hear Webber call the students kids, when Nick was certain he couldn't be more than twenty-five himself. "I'm Nick Paul ... working under Carter Hull. Just getting to know my way around. Is there going to be an interview?"

"Yes," Webber pointed to the windmills past the metal towers. "They have done some pretty impressive work on that thing. You can barely hear the rotors turn anymore. That could really boost sales."

Nick pointed to the partially complete transformer beside Webber. "Is this part of the Windmill?" He knew it wasn't, but he didn't want to appear too knowledgeable.

Webber shook his head, "I am not only the grad student director, but local repairmen. We have over fifty affiliates that run power with us in some form or another. They bring in faulty systems to be rebuilt." He looked down at the organized chaos of parts beside him. "It's actually my favorite part of the job."

Nick understood just how fulfilling it could be to bring something mechanical back to life. "This can't be the only equipment. I have not seen anything but desk jockeys since I got here. Where does the real work happen?"

"Down below," Webber pointed to a set of metal doors that looked more like a bomb shelter entrance than part of an office building. "All the heavy technology is beneath the building … walls that would withstand any terrorist attack."

Nick could see the security cameras mounted above the doors and the duplicate set of pass-card slots. This basement was definitely the place he wanted to see.

"That computer equipment can remotely regulate all of our subsidiaries. We can reroute power, shut down systems ... we keep clients from being without power." Webber nodded and stood a little straighter.

"Impressive," Nick nodded quietly but inside he wanted to shout at this man to take him through those doors and into the basement right now ... take me to see your secret ... but instead he thanked Webber for the information and made his way back to Carter's office.

His pass-card let him in the back door and he found Carter on another phone call. While he talked, sheets of numbers poured out from the printer. Carter picked them up and packed them in folders in his rolling case. He motioned for Nick not to bother sitting down then quickly said good-bye to the caller.

"Grab your bag," Carter ordered and zipped up his case. "Sorry for the rush, but there has been an accident ... maybe something you would like to see."

Nick watched as Carter switched back and forth from one accent to another. The call had been official business, so he used the accent then. But now, his southern drawl returned. "I hope there are no dead bodies," Nick teased.

Carter rolled his eyes and pulled his case out into the hall. "Well, are you coming?" The accent had returned.

In the parking lot, they climbed into Carter's midnight blue Lexus, which Nick fully enjoyed. He had almost forgotten what it felt like to travel in luxury. Jack would certainly have been impressed.

"So, what happened?" Nick asked, not really caring since it had nothing to do with the basement.

"We have a solar plant about an hour from here that caught on fire. I have insurance adjustors going out, but I want to see what is happening. And I thought you might want to see it too."

"So, what does this have to do with … what I am looking for?"

"Huh," Carter snickered, "absolutely nothing, but while you're here, I thought I might get some work out of you."

Nick didn't really have much choice if he was going to maintain his cover. "Talk to me about BRI."

"Ahh …" Carter used his cheeriest accent. "The folders … those were intriguing accounts. Blue Research Institute … a funny sort of name, don't you think?"

"BRI stands for Blue Research Institute?"

"Yes, but the most interesting part is that I cannot find an address or any contact information. Our financial office is paying the bills but I cannot trace the money. It seems to be within the company. As if we were not paying someone's expenses but only moving the money around." Carter glanced over at Nick. "Which makes me wonder if it has something to do with what you are looking for."

"That would explain the hazmat suits."

"It is reasonable," argued Carter, "to use a hazmat suit for power research. I mean we do have radioactive conditions at times."

"Hazmat suits … maybe … but not retaining straps and nitrous oxide. What are they keeping asleep?"

Carter smiled. He did love a good mystery. "Maybe that is what I hired you to find out."

Nick sighed. In his experience, falsified accounts usually lead to embezzlement instead of any information that might be useful. And he knew as well as anyone how to falsify information. "I am staying late tonight … to see if I can get into the basement."

"Hmmmmm," Carter mocked. "You are the ambitious one. So … if you get caught it was nice working with you."

"I don't usually get caught. Only once or … maybe twice," he lied. It was getting easier and easier.

"Oh, it doesn't matter," Carter assured him. "You have made it so that I am in the clear. I hired you under false records. I will emerge the victim of a swindler. Who knows, I might even make some extra sales … or get time off for mental health reasons."

"It's all about money with you."

"Isn't everything," Carter exaggerated his accent.

They rode in silence the rest of the way to the solar plant. Nick found himself reviewing the BRI accounts. Mentally he floundered between trying to remember everything on the list and planning ways to hack the pass-card system into the basement.

The investigation proved to be nothing remarkable. This station had the same problem as every other solar plant – too much power coming in and no way to store it safely. He had dozens of ideas for improvements, but sharing would only slow him down and get him noticed. So, he smiled and nodded and pointed and drifted his way through the rest of the day with Carter. Lunching at a high-end restaurant and then spending the afternoon with a client. Time went quickly and Nick had a plan in place by the end of the work day.

"Time to head home lad," Carter chided using his best accent.

"Maybe," Nick shot him an impish smile. "I have a little more work to do."

"I see," Carter glanced up at the security camera. "It would be helpful if you continued working on those accounts." He wondered if they could hear the conversation.

Carter pulled a folder from inside his desk and handed it to Nick. "I hope you find what you are looking for." The accent had vanished.

"So do I."

Carter closed his briefcase, shook hands with Nick, and then left the office with the tingle of excitement that comes from doing something you shouldn't.

Nick sat at the desk looking inside the folder for what felt like forever. He tried not to imagine what might be in the basement. Being so close to a discovery always left him jittery and impatient and could lead to mistakes. He listened to voices exchanging good-byes and office doors opening and closing. Lights dimmed here and there until gray shadows lined the hallways. He knew he would have to wait long after the sounds stopped so that no one would see him. His thoughts drifted to Jack and Rosie and his family. His parents were not evil people, just distant, busy, not really interested in what he was doing. He was the quiet kid who never got in trouble, always on time, always making good grades, so they just left him alone. No one ever said it out loud, but underneath their conversations was the hushed implication that he had been an accident. That his parents had never really wanted to have children.

They cared for him, even loved him, but not the way Mattie had loved Jaika. She wasn't even Mattie's real daughter but the way they looked at each other, the way they talked, anyone could see how they felt. He was always a little jealous. Maybe that's why he spent so much time there. Maybe he and Jack both needed a Mattie.

A slamming door jerked him back from dreams of Jaika and their past life. The bobbing of light beyond the doorway meant the security guard was making his rounds. Nick closed the folder and slid beneath the desk gambling that the security room was as empty as it had been earlier in the day. The light flared in the window of the office and then passed by without hesitation. He waited until he heard the glass doors to the lobby open and then headed to the stairway.

The security room was empty as expected, but just for good measure, Nick loosened the electrical cord to shut down the monitors. No one ever checks the plug.

He slipped out the plastic covered card he had used earlier to record the patterns in the card reader beside the stairs. With the plastic removed, it fit perfectly over his own pass-card and the magnetic strips aligned. He glanced down the hallway for the security guard but saw only shadows. A few steps to cross the hall, and he was at the stairway door. His heart pounded and he had to focus to control his breathing. This door might lead to finding Jaika.

The cards slid through the card reader and the light on the panel turned green. Nick heard the click of the door as it released. It floated open, just a thin, dark crack and Nick froze, listening for voices or machines or sounds of an alarm. He took a deep breath, wrapped his sweaty fingers around the doorknob and pulled it open – inside was only a wall, a brick wall, floor to ceiling. The stairway had been sealed with brick and mortar but the security panel never disabled.

Nick ran his fingers through his hair and put the cards in his jacket pocket. He closed the door to the stairway and headed back toward Carter's office, defeated. The computer would show a card used to open the door but it wouldn't be connected to his card. In fact, it would look more like a glitch than a pass-card pattern.

Down the hallway, the security guard opened the double glass doors from the lobby. The two men stood and stared at each other for a moment.

"Dan … right?" Nick tried to sound casual. "Carter told me about you … how much you like racing," he lied. This guy's Facebook had been covered with pictures of NASCAR racers.

The guard's shoulders softened, and Nick knew he was safe. "You must be the new guy. I didn't expect to see you working late on your first day."

"Got to impress the boss, right?" Nick lied again. "But I think I have done enough tonight. In fact, I was looking for you. I don't have a key to lock the office."

Dan smiled, "I can take care of that for you."

He came closer to Nick and they shook hands. Nick fought the urge to scream "Why did they brick the stairway!?" Instead, he smiled and asked who his favorite driver might be. As they walked together to the front door, Dan rattled on about the costs of maintaining a high-quality car and why he loved the business so much. He didn't notice Nick's frustration when they said goodbye, and he certainly would never have understood the dent Nick kicked into the side of his jeep before leaving the parking lot.

#

The next morning at C & J Power, Mindy was at her post as usual, but Nick didn't have the energy for small talk. He even ignored her timid wave as he passed through the double glass doors.

"Don't get comfortable," Carter warned as Nick entered the office. "We have a breakfast meeting, well, really brunch, but we need to leave now to make it on time. And I don't want to be late. This should be a very profitable meeting."

"Good," Nick snapped and shifted his computer bag. "We need to talk."

Carter chuckled and turned on his accent, "Disgruntled already? You have only been here one day?"

Nick just nodded, "First, I need coffee. Then I will wait for you in the parking lot."

Carter smiled.

It was easy to spot Carter's blue Lexus and find a comfortable place to lean against it. The events from last night kept playing over and over in his mind, and he knew that he would have to come back again tonight and do it all again. He would have to break into those outside doors unless there was another entrance dear Carter wasn't sharing.

Carter whistled as he dragged his rollered-black briefcase out to the car.

"You seem happy enough," Nick grumbled.

Carter raised his eyebrows and continued using his annoying accent. "As it were, I did have a lovely evening with an especially delicious brunette." He loaded the case into the car and both men climbed inside.

Nick tossed his bag into the backseat, "No guns? No angry boyfriends?"

"Heavens no. Our dear Julia has taught me to make better choices." Carter started the motor and pulled out of the parking lot.

Nick studied the street signs and made a mental note of their route before he broke the silence. "So ... tell me about the basement."

"Have you been inside, yet?" Carter focused on the road and dropped the fake accent.

"I hacked the security panel to the stairway door at the end of the hall. The door that doesn't lead anywhere. But then, you already knew that, didn't you?"

Carter laughed … just a snicker at first … but soon his eyes watered and the muscles in his side ached. "You thought that was the basement." He pushed back the urge to laugh again. "I can take you down there … to the subfloor, but that won't get you in the basement."

Nick shook his head, "I still don't understand."

"You seemed to know everything that was going on here … the security system, the floor plan … I assumed you knew the basement was one of the detached buildings … not … the actual basement." Carter studied the highway signs and tried to decide where to turn. "The floor beneath my office is mostly computers that monitor power grids for the smaller companies. Lots of expensive equipment. That place is kept colder than the rest of the building and protected by triple thick concrete walls. The only way in or out is a special code on the elevator or the double doors in back."

Nick stared out at the road. "So, the basement is not the basement."

"Exactly."

"When we get back to the office …" Nick was beginning to think he was being sabotaged.

"Yes," Carter understood. "I will show you …"

"Show me what you can," Nick twisted the beads around his wrist. "Why do they call it the basement?"

"It's a nickname. The third building out from the main offices has its own basement. The ground beneath was hollowed out for research. Sealed rooms … clean rooms where the engineers can test the effects of wind sheers on rotor blades, power surges, heat … explosions and even radioactivity. Stuff that kills people."

Nick closed his eyes, leaned back against the headrest, and tried to figure out a way to make the day go by faster.

BRI

At 8:00 p.m. precisely, Nick left his hotel and headed back to C & J Power, hoping that even the engineers had families or friends to see and would be long gone from the office. True to his prediction, there was not a car in sight when he pulled in the parking lot. The twelve-foot light poles in the center of the lot had basic single-angle security cameras that were easily avoided with strategic driving. This meant keeping to the shadows along the edge of the lot. He knew they would eventually figure out who he was, but he saw no reason to make it easy. Nick parked his jeep in the deepest shadows, grabbed his bag of tools and circled around to the back buildings.

The building affectionately, known to the C & J Power employees as the basement, was formerly a storage facility. Its corrugated metal walls looked flimsy and unassuming, not a place to hide secrets. Nick made quick work of the padlock that held the door closed, but he knew this would just be the beginning of the break in.

There had been little information available on the inside of this place. Computer searches revealed several permits for excavation and construction. The facility was not actually under Building 3, but out to the side. This building served only as a façade for the entrance. The ground beyond Building 3 had been dug out to create their testing facility. Fifteen to twenty feet down, soil had been removed and replaced with concrete and shatterproof glass. No clear floor plans had been available, but Nick estimated three or four rooms could fit inside the structure. Based on the permits, the walls were meant to withstand a great deal of pressure, and he was surprised they bothered to file permits at all.

Concrete floors, corrugated metal walls with steel and wood supports created the hollow shell of Building 3. The inside felt dusty, warm, and unused. To the far left stood two round tables, flat-front cabinets, and metal-trim countertops that looked like a kitchen out the 1950's. He could hear the hum of a more modern looking fridge and guessed this place served as the breakroom for the people who worked below. Above the kitchen, at the top of the metal walls, were long transom-style windows that opened with a crank much like an old gymnasium. Two long-dropped ceiling fans could pull air from those windows.

The right back corner of the room was much more interesting. The metal walls of that corner framed out a room no bigger than a closet. The construction of the door matched those inside the main office building with two identical pass-card slots on the right side, which Nick hadn't expected. He mapped out the possible ways not to trigger the alarm. There could be two separate systems and the person entering would have two separate cards to swipe. Or, one card to swipe in both slots. If he chose poorly, he might never see what was behind that door.

Nick looked around the room for cameras. None of the black fish-eye cameras like the ones in Carter's office were in sight. There could always be other hidden devices, but he was probably only going to get one shot at this room anyway. Nick took a small set of binoculars out of his bag that viewed infrared light only. The room seemed clear, so he kept going. As he got closer to the door, he saw a ten-key pad beside the farthest panel. Now he needed a code as well as a card.

After a quick study, he saw that the pass-card slots were not the same. On a whim, he took a small battery-powered screwdriver from his bag. With a few quick twists, the screws that held the far panel were out and it dropped forward to reveal the wiring beyond. Nick held his breath and tried the double pass-card trick he had used on the stairway door on the panel that was still intact. His heart skipped a beat when the light turned green. Then, using an insulated set of wire cutters, he began removing the power to the open panel. The wires were color coded, so he started with the gray and worked his way toward the more dangerous wires. When he cut the red, fireworks flew from the wall and scorched the side of Nick's hand and wrist. He jerked back and almost ripped the panel from the wall.

The lights in the panel flickered and went dark. Nick cradled his hand and listened. There was no beep or light, but he heard the click of the door as it released. What he couldn't hear was the silent alarm that he had triggered on a company cellphone.

Mumbling words his parents had taught him never to say, he pushed the keypad back into place and opened the door. As an afterthought, he took a minute to replace the screws in the panel.

If someone was coming, this should slow them down.

His hands trembled as he opened the door. Then shook again as he listened to the click of the lock as the door closed behind him. There would be no going back. The door led to a platform and an enclosed stairwell. The lights here felt more like those from a generator or the emergency lights after a blackout – hazy red and yellow. Maybe they were on a timer, or maybe he had cut the wire to the primary lights. Nick didn't want to take the time to try and find out.

One step at a time, ten steps down, surrounded by concrete walls, Nick made his way to the next platform. Here, the stairs turned and so did the walls, feeling more like a tunnel with every step. At the bottom, Nick peered out to see two consoles lined with computer monitors and keyboards and switches. The wall next to the stairs was lined with metal cabinets, and each wall beyond the consoles was the beginning of a room. Massive half-glass walls with steel doors that opened into what looked like decontamination chambers. Three rooms controlled from the center consoles.

The rooms were shadowy and dark but a scaled version of a rotor blade was visible through the window of the room to the left. The center room appeared to sink way beyond what he could clearly see. But, the room to the right looked more promising. The lights were dim, but Nick could see the outline of a hospital gurney that held a covered body. His eyes fought the shadows and he stepped out from the stairwell. It was just a hazy shape but it might be just what he was looking for.

Nick sat down at the computer closest to the room and looked for the light controls. Every switch was labeled, some officially printed on the console and others written with black ink on tape. Labels that read 'light', 'door', 'gas', and 'pain'. Nick flipped the switch for the lights, and the room in front of him glowed. Light filtered through the misty air that hovered over the lifeless body on the gurney making the room look like it was on fire.

Even with the lights turned on, Nick couldn't tell what lay on the gurney. What looked like a sheet was draped across the bed and curved and bulged with the creature's silhouette. It didn't appear to be a large creature. A little over five feet long, slender, with no appendages visible. He couldn't even tell if it was breathing.

Nick took a chance and typed in his company login on the computer. Of course, it didn't work, but it was worth a chance. There was no way he was getting out of this place undetected anyway. Hacking the system was always an option, but how could he possibly resist a button labeled 'door' or 'gas'.

The haze in the room could be to slow degradation of the tissue or maybe a modified atmosphere to keep it breathing. Either way, he wanted it gone so he could see. He was either going to kill it or damage the body. Nick flipped the toggles marked gas and light, then listened to the mechanical click of the vents closing. As least that's what he hoped it was.

The outline of the body brightened as the mist began to thin. It didn't cough or convulse or grab at the air to try and bring back the mist. It didn't move at all. As the haze cleared, Nick could see a mop of white hair that covered the creature's head and he hoped it was the back of the head he was seeing, and not the face. He swallowed hard and took deep, soothing breaths to try and calm the heartbeat he could feel in his throat. Then he stood and walked over to the glass to get a better look. The coating on the inside of the glass told him it was a two-way mirror. So, whatever happened inside, the creature would not be able to see him.

Nick studied the door to his left that lead inside this prison of concrete and glass. The door opened into a small, one-man unit that appeared to lead to a second door. A round, white button the size of his palm glowed on the wall beside the door, beckoning Nick to push it, to open the door, to go inside the room. He stared at the button and then back toward the gurney, from button to gurney, trying to make up his mind. This could just be a corpse, just some guy that died on the job. Some accident they were hiding from the investors. Or it could be a monster who would kill him if it woke up. Was it radioactive? Was that why they had ordered hazmat suits? Nick took a deep breath and reached for the button.

And then … it moved.

The creature was covered by a sheet, but the upper body jerked, maybe an arm or a claw or a tentacle. It was hard to tell. Then it rolled toward him to face the ceiling. Nick gasped as an almost transparent wing slid off the gurney to touch the floor. It moaned across the control room which made Nick turn and scan for speakers.

She put her hand up toward the ceiling as if to block out some of the light. *She … yes … that creature was a female.* He reached across the control panel and dimmed the lights hoping it would ease her discomfort. At the change in the light, the creature on the bed sat straight up, pulling her wing from the floor. Then grabbed at the edge of the mattress to keep from falling off. She gripped the bed with her blue arms and looked out at the two-way mirror. Ocean blue eyes in a blue-white face. Blue wings and blue arms, one with a long metal bracelet like that of a gladiator. Her chest was partially covered by a twisted, torn hospital gown. She swayed and shifted her position on the bed, but did not take her eyes off the window. Her breath came in short rapid bursts. She didn't appear to be asphyxiating. There was no coughing or gasping, just her body fighting the effects of the gas.

Nick grew uneasy with her stare and walked over to the far-right side of the window. Her gaze followed every step he took. When he paused at the end of the console, so did she.

She pushed back the sheet and swung her legs sideways off the bed to try and stand. Her feet hit the floor then slid out from beneath her. She grabbed backwards and pushed the gurney sideways. Her lower body was wrapped here and there in what looked like a twisted sheet, just enough to give her some dignity. Nick had expected her to scream or yell but she just sat on the floor still looking at the two-way mirror. She shook her head hard to clear the gas and then closed her eyes. Nick could see the blue wisps of the lifelines that framed her face, one much longer than the other. Her wings twitched and rose a few inches above the floor and then dropped in exhaustion.

Nick moved again, several feet back to the left, shifting his position along the glass. She opened her eyes when he moved and followed just as before. He had been wrong about the two-way mirror. She knew he was watching.

She tried again to stand, grabbing at the gurney, pulling herself upward, feeling it roll to the side and drop her to the floor. She sat there for a moment, angry, frustrated. Then her fingers moved across the wheels next to her leg, feeling the smooth sides and the bolts that connected and turned. Then she slid her hands along the metal pieces that formed the legs of the gurney. The blue girl closed her eyes again, and Nick could almost feel her thoughts, planning, preparing.

Grabbing the base section of the gurney, she pulled her body over onto her hands and knees, then pushed the bed until it stopped against the back wall, spinning it sideways so that the front part of the bed faced the window. Then she extended the claw on her right hand, reached up to dig her nails into the mattress and pull her body up. Standing … leaning against the bed, she turned again to look at the mirror. Her eyes widened and she growled, a low growl that echoed through the speakers and across the control room. Nick was beginning to understand why they had used the gas.

Using her claws to hold to the mattress, she pulled herself around the gurney, legs buckling, arms shaking, edging her way to the back wall. She squeezed between the wall and the bed and then stopped. Her upper body dropped onto the mattress and her claws relaxed. Nick could see her back rising and falling with each breath and her fingers trembling with fatigue. For a moment, he thought she had blacked out. Her body lay so still, twitching, breathing, relaxing against the bed. Then she raised her head and pushed. The bed rolled into the middle of the room and stopped. The blue creature dropped her head back on the mattress, but this time she did not relax. This time her claws tore deep into the fibers of the mattress.

Nick knew exactly what she was doing. She understood the nature of the window in her room. She understood the weight of the bed and the place where it would meet the glass. She wanted to use that bed as a battering ram.

She raised her head and rolled the bed backward, pulling it closer to the wall for another try. Nick couldn't wait any longer. She was going to shatter the window, set off alarms, and maybe even injure herself on the glass. He hit the white button beside the door of her cell and it slid open. The outer metal door slid back into the wall to reveal a closet-like area just big enough for one man. And to the right of the inner door was another white button.

Nick stepped through the door to see a control panel. Red, yellow, and blue lights with switches and knobs. Controls that he was certain would initiate a decontamination sequence that could take forever, time he did not have to waste. Nick hit the white button beside the inner door, but nothing happened. He hit it again and again, pounding it over and over. "Open!" he screamed and shook his fist at the white light, then he stepped backward.

"Think!" he shouted. "The sequence. What does the computer want to happen? Which knob, what happens next." He slowed his breathing and tried to find the next logical step as the sweat dripped from his neck. "The computer wants to run the decontamination sequence. What does it need?"

His eyes narrowed, and he pushed the white button on the inner panel beside the open door. It slid closed to imprison Nick between the two steel doors. "This will work," he whispered. "This will work. This has to work." He hit the final white button and the inner door to the cell slid open.

Ilea sat on the ground beside the gurney, no longer trying to escape. Her wings spilling out around her on the floor. She did not even have the will to scream. She had fought the ground dwellers and the gas for so many suns. Suns she couldn't even see. Maybe this man would kill her and it would be over. She hoped Dodgen was safe … and her mother. At least she would finally know where the mist of life goes … where her father had gone.

Nick took three steps into the room and then realized he didn't know what to do or say. He didn't know if anyone had spent time with her, if she spoke any English. She certainly had no reason to trust him.

He stepped closer to her, watching her eyes. Desperate, pleading eyes, filled with tears of sorrow and fatigue. Nick put his hand on his heart and said "Nick."

Ilea gasped and her body began to shake. She could see the beads on his wrist. The beads that trembled as he spoke. The beads that shimmered ever so slightly with a blue-white light. Ilea reached her hand out toward this man. Those beads were from her home. His lifesong was just like all the others, but the beads were hers.

Nick held his hand out in front of him and studied the glow. "They've never done that before," he said, looking from the girl to the beads and back again. Then held out his hand to her.

Ilea tried to crawl, so Nick moved closer and dropped to his knees still holding out the hand wearing the beads. The glow was getting brighter.

Ilea knew those beads, the patterns on the beads. Those were the patterns she pulled from the stones, torturing them as Dodgen had said. Bringing their songs to the surface, creating random patterns. But those beads, those beads were unique. Those were stones from the deepest parts of the mountain. Stones laced with the strongest crystals. She had chosen those as a gift for a special girl. It had taken her three suns to pull the crystalline songs to the surface.

Ilea whimpered and pushed out her hand closer to this man, "Jaika," she breathed.

Nick gasped. "Yes," he almost shouted, trying to calm his trembling voice. "Yes, these were Jaika's … Jaika gave these to me." He wanted to grab her and yell *where is she*, but instead he scooted forward and took her hand. A delicate blue hand that rested inside his own. Her fingers slid past his to touch the beads. Nick pushed the beads closer to his wrist.

"Jaika," she whispered again, and then said something Nick couldn't understand … something hopeful. Ilea looked up into his face. "Water?" she questioned. It was almost the only word in his language she knew. "Food ... water."

Nick smiled. They had tried to teach her.

Ilea pulled away and opened her claw. She pointed at the glass and hissed, almost like a cat. Nick turned to see his reflection in the glass. A gurney and a blue girl and him sitting on the concrete floor. He had been right. It was a two-way mirror. But she had seen him all the same. So, who was she seeing now?

He turned and put his hands up in surrender. "I won't let them hurt you."

Ilea closed her claws. She didn't understand his words, but she did understand his heart. If he had known Jaika, with such a gentle spirit, she refused to believe he had taken those beads by force. So, he must be her friend. Maybe Jaika had even sent him to save her. Ilea relaxed, her head slipping to the ground to rest on her arm, her wings twitching. Nick reached over to touch the back of her hand, knowing those claws could tear him apart if she were fully awake.

"Nick ... Jaika ... Ilea," she whispered, and her body went limp.

Labcoats

"Young man. Please enter the decontamination chamber?" a voice echoed from the ceiling. The door in the corner slid open.

Nick looked at Ilea on the cold floor of the research chamber. He knew he couldn't stay in here forever. He would eventually have to eat and face whomever was on the other side of that glass. Besides, they could always remove him by force, that wouldn't be fun. He looked back at the two-way mirror to see himself sitting beside Ilea, and he wondered what else she could see through. He stood and walked to the corner of the chamber and entered the tiny room.

"Open the cabinet to your left."

Nick looked at the slick walls of the chamber and the recessed latches he hadn't noticed earlier. He slipped his fingers into the indention and pulled open the cabinet to his left, just like the voice had ordered. The door slid open to reveal three sets of rubber goggles. He slipped one over his head, adjusted the straps, and closed the cabinet.

"Now what?" he asked the voice in the ceiling.

"This will take a few minutes," the faceless voice answered, and the inner door closed.

A white, wet mist sprayed from four tiny hoses in each corner of the ceiling. He hoped it wasn't the same mist they had used on her. "Ilea," he whispered. "Her name is Ilea." *And she knows Jaika*, he smiled. He didn't know how or why or where or when, but they were connected and he had found what he was looking for. The beginning of a trail.

The gas did not make him sleepy but it smelled bad and he tried not to breath. A red light shot out from the sides of the room and scanned across his body in alternating directions. Nick closed his eyes and tried to decide what the gas was based on the smell. A good detective would have known all the possible names. It didn't really matter. Once they were through with the contamination, the outer door would open and he would meet him. Someone ... who would either fire him, arrest him, or help him find Jaika.

The gas began to recede. "Use the white button to open the outer door," the voice came from the ceiling again.

Nick hit the button and the door slid open. Two men stood just beyond the open doorway. Not muscle-bound police or security guards, but tired men with lined faces, graying hair, and white lab coats. Another man, much taller than the other two, was busy making coffee at the back of the room.

Bill offered him a grandfatherly handshake. At least Bill was the name written on his lab coat, right underneath C & J Power. "She spoke to you ... and she didn't try to kill you."

Nick shook his hand, grateful that he was not being arrested.

"Why didn't she try to kill you?"

"Maybe because I'm so good looking."

"At this point, I'll take that as a scientific explanation," said the coffee drinker in the back of the room. "But I *am* better looking than you are ... way better looking."

The small man beside Bill shook his head. "She sees things we don't." Vicente was the name on his lab coat.

"Come on in," the coffee drinker motioned for Nick to sit down in one of the chairs beyond the consoles. "Cream? Sugar? Maybe something a little stronger?"

"All of that sounds great," Nick certainly wasn't going to offend these guys.

"Don't get him drunk, Howard," Vicente warned. "We need to talk to him."

Howard gave Nick a mug filled with milky white coffee and the strong smell of bourbon. "Have a seat. We won't bite, I promise."

Bill and Howard pulled chairs from the consoles and sat down across from Nick. Vicente paced behind them, running his hand through his tousled gray hair.

"Don't worry about him," Howard motioned toward Vicente. "He does that a lot."

"Could you understand her?" Bill was having trouble sitting still.

"No," Nick answered and felt the scorch of the bourbon as he took a sip of coffee. "But her name is Ilea."

"We got that part somewhere along the way," Howard mused. "Not much else. She can fly. She can rip your arms and legs off if she wants to. She can scream really loud ..."

"And she can heal," Vicente added without slowing his pace.

Bill rolled his eyes, "I don't know that we should be discussing all of our findings."

Howard laughed, again. "He's seen everything, what does it matter. He will either go to the police or the military ... or we have to kill him ... or at least lock him up."

Nick shook his head, "I don't want to go to the authorities. I want to stay here with Ilea." He looked over at her cell. "How long as she been here?"

"A long time," Bill shook his head. "A really long time."

"So, why keep her a secret all this time," Nick wanted to know their agenda.

"It's not like she's a pink dog. We can learn so much," Howard bristled.

Nick took a deep drink of coffee, "You wouldn't by chance be skinny-legs Howard, would you?"

Howard chuckled and stretched out his long legs, "I haven't heard that name in a long time. Where did you hear it?"

"Stanley Rickner," Nick was hoping that would win them over.

"He's a young guy. One of my former students."

Nick understood that he was being tested. "No, he's a very old guy. A very scrawny, crusty, old man ... who could use a bath."

Howard laughed, "That's Rickner all right." Then his face grew quiet and his eyes brightened with understanding. "You're a chaser ... just like him." He looked at the cell where Ilea slept. "I guess you both were right after all."

"We kept her to try and harness her gifts," Vicente stopped walking and looked straight at Nick. "When she was brought here, there was extensive damage to her wings and head and leg.

But they seemed to heal almost overnight. Even when she was sedated, she remained healthy and strong. We wanted to know how."

"Our director insisted," Bill lowered his eyes.

"But surely there are facilities better suited to study her," Nick argued.

"Yes, of course there is," Howard stood and stretched again. "But then we would be surrounded by people like you. People who want to question our work … want to test our results." He sat down again and nursed his coffee.

"We took blood samples and tissue samples trying to recreate her abilities," Vicente explained. "If we could find a solution, we did not want it tied up in drug trials, waiting for FDA approval."

Bill nodded, "Our director's wife is quite ill … and Vicente has as daughter … with a tumor."

Nick was beginning to understand why they were keeping her hidden, "Have you been successful?"

"No," Vicente turned away, "nothing has worked."

"But maybe it will now," Howard stared at Nick. "Maybe you are the magic ticket."

"Howard is the only one of us with medical training," Bill pointed at Vicente. "We are both engineers."

"How would you feel about eating and sleeping here for a while?" Howard mused.

It sounded as if they would be keeping him prisoner, but Nick didn't care. He just wanted to work with Ilea. "I can do that," he agreed. "I have some clean clothes at the Sunset Inn."

"Classy," Howard smirked.

"I can give you the keys to my room. Maybe you could bring me a blanket and a pillow?"

Vicente looked at the other scientist. "I think he is worth the risk."

"I know how much your daughter means to you," Bill turned to look at his friend. "I agree. It's worth the risk."

Howard nodded, "We have been working on this for over a year and have little to show for it." He moved to a chair in front of a computer and typed in a password. "You might as well see it all." Files appeared on the monitor with records of their experiments, pictures of her body smashed between the rocks, and some of the damage she had inflicted since her arrival. "Our technicians said she fell from the sky …"

"… through a blue watery light," Nick finished his sentence.

The men stared at him and tried to decide what to say. "Yes," Howard nodded.

"So, we are agreed. Welcome to the team," Vicente Robles smiled for the first time since Nick had been discovered. "You will need another pass-card. I repaired your work to the security panel at the top of the stairs."

"I'm tired and I'm going home. I just don't care anymore," Bill stood and started toward the stairs.

Vicente motioned for Nick to follow him to a set of cabinets and a worn couch nestled to the side of the main room. He opened the cabinet to reveal a pillow and blanket, some water bottles and sodas, a box of crackers, and a jar of peanuts. "Sometimes I stay. If the work seems promising … I stay."

"I lost someone ..." Nick confessed. Vicente deserved to know. "She was taken ... my friend is on the other side of that blue light."

The weariness in Vicente's face softened for a moment, "Then maybe we can help each other."

#

They had ten days together.

Nick quit his not-so-legitimate job with Carter Hull and started spending his nights ... and days in the basement. Vicente's couch looked like something rescued from the curb, but it was better than sleeping on the floor. Nick left the basement only to shower and grab something to eat. The Labcoats, as he came to call his partners, would often bring a burger or leftovers from home.

Their first morning together, Nick awoke to Ilea singing over the speakers. At least he thought it was her. But someone was singing with her. He was certain there were at least three voices mixing together, intertwining the harmonies. The sound washed over him, and he melted under its spell.

Any tension or worry he held … any fear of failure evaporated into the song. Its warmth caressed his skin like the vapors from a cigar. Washing along his face, across his shoulders, and down the middle of his back. Unhindered by his clothing, he could feel it wrapping around his arms and legs, binding him in its euphoria. He could think of no other word to describe what he felt. As if he had taken a drug designed to produce nothing but happiness. He tried to move his legs, but he didn't want to leave the song. So instead, he waited for it to change or shift from this feeling of perfect peace.

A computer alarm beeped the time, and Ilea grew quiet.

Nick stretched and yawned and ran his fingers through his greasy hair. All the stiffness he should have felt from sleeping on Vicente's couch was missing. He shook his head to better clear his thoughts and then grabbed some snacks from Vicente's closet. Ilea was sitting cross legged in the middle of the floor and smiled as he passed the window to her room. He hit the white button for each door and skipped the decontamination.

Ilea watched him as the inner door slid open and flexed her wings behind her. "Food … water," she said.

Nick nodded and wondered if she thought it meant hello. He held up a package of crackers and said, "food."

She made no motion to move from the floor, so Nick sat down beside her. Ilea's eyes were bright and wide like a child expecting a birthday present. It was hard not to stare at her blue skin and white hair that seemed to move like water. Her wings were folded back, but their lower edges trialed along the ground, and he desperately wanted to see her fly.

Instead, he opened the crackers and took a bite then handed one to her. It was an odd sensation for Ilea. She couldn't remember the last time she had eaten solid food, and her stomach twisted. In fact, she had trouble remembering the last time anything had happened except for this room and that mist, and Dodgen, and the prison and the flowers. Everything blurred together.

"Cracker," Nick said pointing to the bag and back to the cracker in his hand.

Ilea understood. "Cracker," she said, and held out her hand so that he could give her a few more. Then she pointed to the soda can and said, "Water."

"Oh no," Nick laughed and picked up the water bottle. "This is water." Then he raised the soda can and popped it open with a *shhhhttt*. "This is soda." He took a sip and handed the can to Ilea.

Ilea raised the can to eye level, feeling the bubbles within. She took a long drink and then started to cough … and even burped.

They laughed together, then Nick handed her the bottle. "Maybe we should just stick with the water." He twisted off the lid and handed her the bottle.

She had a vague memory of another bottle like this, maybe here in this room with the white lights. Water that tasted of metal. Together they finished the crackers and the water. After they ate, Nick tried words for everything: door, floor, light, bed, and girl. Once they ran out of room topics, he grabbed a tablet and pencil from the console in the control room. They drew trees and clouds and grass and people.

It was difficult not being able to ask her about Jaika. He wasn't even sure how to ask her about her home. On a whim, he pulled out his cell phone and brought up a space view of Earth. Ilea had never seen a planet from the sky or a cell phone, so she didn't know what she was seeing.

To help her understand, Nick flipped the phone and took a picture of her sitting on the floor. When he turned the phone around, Ilea could see her own face staring back at her.

Nick expected her to jump or run or at least be a little surprised. But Ilea could see more than the picture. She could see the tiny dots of light that came together to create the shapes. She could see the bits of energy inside the phone that kept it alive, much like her bracelet. And she could see the waves of power that came and went from the phone to the boxes and the wires inside the walls.

So she just said, "Ilea" and looked at Nick as if he should have known.

He shook his head and he pulled up a picture of the house where his parents lived. "Home. Nick home," he said and pointed to the picture.

It looked a little like the gray house of the glassmaker and the homes the other ground dwellers built in Palon. Nick was a ground dweller, so Nick should have a ground dweller house. Ilea nodded and said, "Home."

She caught her breath for a moment and looked toward the mirror. Nick watched her open the claws on her right hand and drum them against the floor. "They won't hurt you," he said, knowing that at least one of the Labcoats had arrived. "I won't let them."

Ilea retracted her claws, but continued to watch the mirror. Nick showed her random pictures on his phone to distract her and try to figure out where she came from. He started with a picture of a grassy meadow, but Ilea just shook her head. That was not any place she had ever seen before. Then he showed her a picture of the ocean.

"Oooooooo," Ilea marveled. Could there ever be so much water in one place? "Nick home?"

Nick wasn't sure what to say. He didn't live in the ocean, but if she meant Earth as his home the answer would have to be yes. Ilea reached out to touch the picture, and it changed. Again and again she touched the screen and the images transformed. Then she leaned back, relaxed her shoulders, and took a deep, heavy breath. Nick laid the phone on the ground in front of him and watched the images continue to change. Ilea no longer touched the phone or the screen but the images changed none-the-less. Buildings and people and animals that she had never seen.

Nick swallowed hard and stared at Ilea, watching her control the phone.

"Home," Ilea said and looked up to meet his eyes. The images stopped changing to display a picture of a mountain – a rocky, craggy looking mountain. It wasn't her mountain. She knew it wasn't her mountain, but maybe it would make him understand. "Home," she said again, then pointed to the image.

"Mountains," Nick murmured. "Well that makes sense. You can fly so you can live any place you want. Shoot, you could live in Disneyland and no one would notice."

He reached down to pick up the phone and for the first time, Ilea noticed the burn marks on the side of his hand and arm. Nick raised his hand and tried to think of simple words to explain. "Hurt … pain … wound."

Three words for the same thing, she thought. There must be many great battles fought here to need so many words to describe a simple injury. Ilea held out her hand, palm up, and wiggled her fingers. Nick moved his burned hand forward and laid it in her hand.

"Mmmmm," she cooed, just a little. Then she reached over with her other hand and laid it on the wound.

Nick could feel the warmth of her skin, and a tingling sensation where each finger touched. His hand started to itch and crawl …then to sting …and then to burn. Nick grunted and jerked it away.

Ilea gasped and shrunk back … like a child in trouble. She had not meant to cause him such pain, but his lifesong was different than she had expected. Maybe he was not from Palon after all.

Nick studied his hand and saw the pink places where his skin had healed. He flexed his hand, opening and closing his fingers without stiffness or pain. Slowly he began to understand what was happening. Then he held out his hand toward Ilea and said, "Please."

Ilea scooted forward and covered his hand with both of hers. She moved her fingers over his burn and cooed, just a little, just like before. But this time, she moved with painstaking caution, watching his eyes for pain. Her fingers wandered along his hand and up his arm almost to the elbow. Nick watched as the charred pieces of flesh brightened and faded. Not even a scar was left.

"Thank you," Nick said, as she let go of his hand. He wanted to make sure Ilea understood, so he put his hands together as if in prayer, placed them on his lips, and bowed his head.

Ilea copied his movements and bowed toward him as well.

They worked some more on her English. She taught him words from her own language as well. Tal words for light and sky and thank you. Nick found it hard to stop thinking about his hand. It was if the wound had never even been there.

Howard had been watching from behind the mirror and decided to come into Ilea's cell. "Well, I guess we are not going to die from bacteria." He pointed to the open doors. "Because I know you completed the full decontamination process ...right?"

"Sorry," Nick lied.

"Doesn't matter. I think it is time for a change." He looked at Ilea, "If she won't kill me, I think we should let her out of this room. Maybe a tour of the facilities ... underground, of course."

Ilea watched the two men, feeling the quiet happiness between them. Nick stood and held out his hand to Ilea. She stood beside him and gave her wings a good shake.

"I don't think I could ever get used to seeing that," Howard said in his gruff, bourboned voice.

"It is ... amazing," Nick agreed and held back all those save-for-later questions such as how high can you fly? How fast? Are you the only one?

Taking small, timid steps, Ilea followed Nick through the doors of her cell and into the control room. Chairs, floors, lights ... things she knew and some she didn't. But most importantly, there was still no sky. She missed the sky ... and the red moon.

The men pointed and handed out words that she did not understand. Table, chair, computer, couch. She listened closely and tried to repeat each word, but the stairs behind the wall at the side of the room were much more interesting.

Nick and Howard took turns sitting and laying on the couch to demonstrate its uses. Ilea tried to mimic their movements, but her wings kept catching on the back pillows. Finally, she lay on her stomach with her wings draped over the back of the couch and spilling onto the concrete floor. She knew they wanted her to be comfortable, to rest, but she wanted to scream and run and fly. Her body ached for the open sky.

"I want to see your hand," Howard motioned sideways while Ilea bounced around on the sofa.

"You were watching?" Nick faced Howard and lifted the hand Ilea had healed. He flexed his fingers and turned his hand over and back.

"So, we didn't need her blood or her tissue, we just needed to ask," Howard mused. "I wonder if we could bring Vicente's daughter down here."

Nick nodded, watching Ilea move the pillows onto the floor.

Alone

At the end of the second week, everything changed.

Howard, Bill, and Nick sat with Ilea on the floor of the control room as they had for the last eight days. They used a tablet and flashcards to practice her English. Bill took notes on the Tal words that Ilea supplied. He was creating a simple database to translate English and Tal, and he hoped to eventually create an app for Ilea.

They heard the door slam and Vicente shouting as he ran down the stairs to the lab. "They're coming!" he shouted. "They will take her!"

Ilea rose to a crouching position, her wings stretched out, and her claws open. Then she growled.

Nick put his hand out toward Ilea. "It's okay. It's just Vicente." But she did not relax.

Vicente emerged from the stairwell followed by a serious man in a three-piece suit. Vicente went straight to the metal cabinets on the back wall and began taking out vials. "We must destroy everything."

"Dr. Warren … who is coming?" Howard looked annoyed and not the least bit surprised to see the other man. "Nick, this is Dr. James Warren, the director of C & J Power."

"My source tells me a strike force is about ten minutes out," Dr. Warren said, hanging his head in disappointment. "I'm not sure how they found out."

"Too many loose ends," Nick shrugged. "It was inevitable."

Vicente started emptying the vials on top of the computers. The heavy smell of fuel began to burn the inside of his nose. "We have a plan, but you have to get her out."

Dr. Warren held out his hand to Nick. "They told me how much progress you've made. I had … such hopes."

Nick shook the doctor's hand and stared in disbelief. Over … *this man is saying it's over … that we have to stop working with Ilea.* A knot formed in the pit of his stomach as he realized he was not going to find Jaika.

"We knew this might happen." Howard looked at Nick. "We have a plan."

"Yes," Bill nodded. "We know just what to say."

Nick knew there was a slim possibility they could make it to his jeep. Or he could drive away and she could meet him later. But there were just too many variables. They would catch him sooner or later and then they would find her. Where could they go that they couldn't be tracked, no phone, no credit cards. He wasn't ready for this. They might even kill her. It was just too risky.

Nick grabbed his computer bag from one of the chairs behind the console and made his way back to Vicente's snack cabinet. He removed the computer from his bag and stuffed it behind a case of sodas. Then he pulled out four water bottles, a jar of peanuts and a box of crackers. Not exactly survival gear, but at least it would give Ilea a fighting chance. And he wasn't sure just how much she could carry.

He finished packing the bag with a UV blocking, tin-foil looking tarp that Vicente had stored in the base of the cabinet. It wasn't much protection, but it might keep her dry.

"Come with me," Nick ordered Ilea as he made his way to the stairs. "Come … now."

Ilea didn't understand what was happening, but she knew those stairs were the way out of here … maybe to the sky.

Howard grabbed Nick's arm as they moved toward the stairs. "There's a back door. Just beyond the fridge. It's hard to see unless you are looking for it."

Nick nodded, gripped Howard by the shoulder, and shook him just a little, with an it's-been-nice-to-know-you kind of shake. After all, there was the possibility they would all end up in jail.

Ilea followed Nick up the stairs, two steps at a time. At the top, he opened the door just a crack and peered out into the empty warehouse. The soldiers were not there yet. He could feel his heart pounding in his ears.

He reached back for Ilea and pulled her with him out the door. Together they ran toward the kitchen and the refrigerator. The door was to the right, just as Howard had said. The same wood and metal as the framing, so it almost disappeared into the wall. Nick lifted the latch and pushed it open.

The sunlight was blinding. Ilea had been without it so long that she stood just inside the door taking in every ray. Then her stomach twisted as she realized that this tiny sun in the sky was not her own. Ilea stepped outside the door and looked across the sky, above the building and over the metal skeletons of the transformers. Where was the red moon? Where had they brought her that she could not see the red moon? Was there even such a place? The people here were just like any other ground dwellers. Nick said she was on Earth, but was that not a place still under the red moon? Something was terribly wrong.

"You have to go," Nick pleaded, trying to make her understand. "There are people coming to take you … to take you away. So that I can't help you anymore."

Ilea stared into his clouded eyes and felt the frantic rhythms of his lifesong.

Nick handed her his computer bag and opened the flap. "I put in some water and some food." He pointed to the packages of peanuts and crackers that he had taken from the break room. "And a blanket." Nick pulled out part of the silver heat shield he had stolen from the testing room.

Ilea tried to look brave, but she was terrified. This world was not her own. It could have monsters and dangers she had never seen before. She couldn't understand why Nick was sending her away. Couldn't he come with her?

On a whim, Nick pulled his wallet from his jacket pocket and took out one of his many business cards. "This is me … my name … my phone number. If you need me … if you need a friend." He knew everything he was saying sounded stupid. Even if she did understand the words, Ilea didn't know how to use a phone. He wished desperately that there was another way, another plan. If there had just been more time. If he took her with him, they would find her. They would catch her and lock her away from everything and everyone. At least in the sky, she had a fighting chance.

Nick stuck the card into the side pocket of his computer bag and slipped the strap around her neck and shoulder. "Now go," he commanded. "Fly as fast as you can. Get away from here."

"Come," Ilea pleaded, but knew in her heart that she could never carry him very far. Maybe if she had a harness …

Nick shoved her away from the building. "Fly!" He tried again to make her leave. He hated himself and the tears he saw welling in her eyes.

Ilea felt the shift in the road leading up to the building. More ground dwellers were coming. Great wagons carrying four, five, or maybe six men. Each traveling at such speeds no saktar could keep up. Soldiers with metal guns like the men Kaleus sent into battle.

Ilea stepped away from Nick and tried not to cry. He was saving her from the soldiers. Somehow, he knew they were coming and for some reason he couldn't take her from this place. She hoped the soldiers would not kill …

Ilea ran. Unfurling her wings as she moved. She had not flown since her imprisonment, and her legs and shoulders ached with every movement. The sun burned her eyes. The air smelled of dirt and plants, but it was a good smell, the smell of freedom.

Her wings caught the air, and she reveled in that familiar popping sound that comes as they fill. As she rose above the hard ground and scattered trees, a lonely, empty feeling settled in the pit of her stomach. That tiny sun was not her sun. And she was without the red moon. The moon that watched over all of Regar.

Nick held his breath as her wings lifted her from the ground. The green bag fell only to be caught by the claw of her foot. He watched until she was only a tiny speck in the blue-white sky and prayed that Jaika was safe somewhere. The Labcoats and Dr. Warren walked out of the building behind him followed by the heavy smell of smoke.

"We have to go." Vicente gripped Nick by the shoulder.

Nick nodded, feeling numb and empty. He removed a lanyard from around his neck and handed it to Vicente. It held a flash drive at the end. "I made it for you ... for you and your daughter. There are multiple files, but the one you want is labeled hope."

"Thank you." Vicente smiled, then turned to listen to the sound of distant sirens. The police and the firemen would be here soon. "What better way to stop the secrets of the government than to put them in the public eye?"

Nick understood the plan now. The fire would destroy the evidence and force the gunmen out in the open. Together they hurried out to the parking lot. Smoke was already pouring out of the lab and the rumble of a small explosion shook the ground.

"Nick, you can leave, you know," Bill smirked. "You never really existed anyway. Your employee records were falsified … remember?"

Dr. Warren looked at Bill and then shook his head. There were more secrets to investigate.

Nick saluted the three men in white lab coats standing at the edge of the parking lot, then climbed into his jeep and drove away. He could hear the sirens in the distance and see the black SUVs pulling into the front of the building. Black body-armored soldiers ran for the lab as a plume of black smoke erupted from inside. He knew they would be okay … his Labcoats. The fire would destroy the evidence. The whole thing would look like a research accident. He could almost hear the Labcoats saying their lines to the police. *Something spilled … something overheated … something was out of control.* Vincente would have planned every word.

In his rearview mirror, Nick could see black smoke billowing above what was once the basement. His car window rattled, as something exploded under the ground. He would have to change his license plates incase his jeep was on any of the security videos. It would take a few minutes to square up his bill at the Sunset Inn. Then maybe he would go visit an old friend. He wondered just how difficult it would be to find Dr. Stanley Rickner.

#

At first there was no sign of any other ground dwellers. Ilea could see grass and trees but not people ... no life below her. She flew toward the clouds to disappear from the men in the prison and the soldiers with guns so that those on the ground would see her as only a Breen. No matter how high she flew, her bracelet would keep her body warm.

She understood what clouds were ... and rain. She had seen clouds twice before in her lifetime, and felt the water fall from the sky. The thunder still echoed in her memories, the water washing over the land, rushing forward, carrying with it whatever lay in its path. It felt strange to be in a sky filled with so many white, wispy clouds and such a white, sad, tiny moon. It felt even stranger to be free from the lights and slick walls of her prison. There, Nick made sure she had water and food, but out here, she had no friends. She was free but she was completely alone.

There were mountains in the distance … not her mountains. But maybe there would be people there, people like her. Maybe this place was like in the stories that the elders told. The stories of men traveling so far away that they couldn't see the red moon. She held on to that hope as she flew, over flat ground and rocks and trees … over homes here and there … flying until her wings ached, flying until she was over the water. Not a channel of water like the great river beyond Palon, but a massive pool of quiet, still water. More water than she had ever seen. Ilea forgot to be afraid and dropped low to drag her toes on its glassy surface, leaving a trail behind her in the water. And below her, below the water's surface, there was life. Wiggly, squirmy life that found breath in the water. Tiny, thin darts of life and slow-moving wanderers that swam at the bottom. Patterns and lifesongs she had never seen before.

Beyond the water were rows and rows of trees. Trees that did not grow near Luz. Perfect lines of trees that were too straight to have grown without a ground dweller's help. At the edge of the tree rows were two homes, one much smaller than the other. Ilea circled low but did not see any ground dwellers. So she tucked her wings and dropped to the ground at the edge of the tree line.

The sun was on the edge of the land. Even with her bracelet, she could feel the temperature dropping and her stomach begging for something to eat. She walked beneath the trees and studied the round, red fruit that hung from the branches. Every tree was the same, its lifesong, its fruit, all the same. Nick had brought her one of these red orbs. He had cut it into pieces to remove the hard center. Ilea dropped her coat and satchel and hooked her claws into the side of the tree, then climbed high enough to grab several pieces of the fruit. Using her wings, she dropped back to the ground and took a bite.

Ilea settled on the ground, leaned back against the rough bark, and found peace under the trees. Maybe this would be a safe place to spend the night. She didn't know what lived here, what crawled on the ground or flew in the air. She didn't even know what to be afraid of. Her wings ached from the journey and her eyes felt heavy. The fruit tasted sharper than the one Nick had given her.

She missed him and the old men in the white coats.

#

The sunlight filtered through the branches to wash across her face. A flirtatious animal scratch-scratched in the leaves above her. Ilea shook the sleep from her eyes and stretched out her wings and arms then flexed her claws. She wriggled her fingers then swung her neck from side to side to relax the knotted muscles. Her wings quivered as though shaking off water. The white, shiny prison seemed so very far away. She wondered what Nick might be doing, if the men with guns were still there or if he had been taken to a prison like hers.

Ilea opened the green bag then drank from one of Nick's bottles. She also added four of the red orbs to her food collection. With her bag in hand, she walked out from under the trees to look for the mountains. Their jagged tops rose above the tree line and scattered homes on the landscape. She would be there today. She would find a new home today.

Three steps forward and she rose above the ground. Slow, strong thrusts of her wings brought her skyward. She was in no hurry. The mountains were not going anywhere. This morning, there were others in the sky. Much smaller than the Breen, but just as skilled at flight. One of those pestering Breen would have been a welcome sight today. Silly Breen, always following the Tal, begging for a chase.

She thought of her family as she flew toward the mountains. Dodgen would be fine. He was a trickster who could take care of himself. She smiled at the memory of all his pranks. Her heart ached most of all for her mother, and how lonely she would be without her father. The tears burned her eyes, and she pushed the thoughts away and focused on the landscape of the mountains instead. The rocks were taller in the center but there seemed to be more outcroppings off to the left. That side would have more flat places to land and cover to hide.

Ilea flew above the scattered homes and the rocks and the trees. The land seemed to go on forever without change. So much green, and there did not seem to be any sand in this place. Some of the homes were small while others seemed built for multiple families ... or legions of soldiers.

Pathways connected the homes. Long stretches of pathways covered in dark, melted rock. Wagons drove the pathways. Loud, lifeless machines in all colors and sizes.

Then she heard that same roar in the sky. The sound was coming closer, unyielding and strong. Ilea pulled in her wings and dropped toward the land to feel the rush and heat of the monster as it passed overhead. It had been lifeless, like the wagons, and unafraid, carrying ground dwellers in its belly. She scolded herself for growing complacent and not feeling the giant before it came so close. She must never forget that this was not home.

The mountains were closer now and the trees blocked out the land. There was water winding through the trees like the great river beyond Palon, but this water cut away at the ground to leave a deep, winding gully. There was no sand here like the sand that surrounded the cliffs of Luz, and she could feel no crystals except for the one in her bracelet that hummed as she flew. Yet this place was green and lush and filled with water like the places on Regar where the crystals were thickest.

Dropping lower, she saw two homes that stood on the top of two towers that rose above the trees. Half-built homes with open sides. One of the towers held a ground dweller and she wondered what kind of monster might send him to such heights.

She flew on past the towers and into the cliffs. The stones felt like home with soft, steady lifesongs that did not move but protected bits of life scattered across the mountain. Deeper into the cliffs, Ilea found a flat place where she could land and rest and look for a home. She settled on the plateau and lay out flat on her back, feeling her muscles relax. There, beneath the glow of the setting sun, she dozed for a moment, enjoying the safety of being higher up than most of this strange place. Loneliness crept into her bones, and Ilea battled the emptiness that painted the inside of her chest. She tried to image what her mother might say at this moment. She was always practical and without fear or hesitation. *There is no time for sadness* ... yes ... those would be the first words from Seela ... *we need to focus on the task at hand.* Ilea smiled at the thought of her mother bossing everyone around.

She stretched and pulled open her green bag to drink from one of the clear bottles. Then she ate one of the red orbs she had stolen from the line of trees and began to study the rock that surrounded her. She needed a home, some kind of protection from the weather and whatever creatures might visit. Craggy, towering fingers of rock edged the plateau with smooth ruts cut in-between where water had run. So, if the weather turned bad, Ilea knew this place could become a river. She studied the roughness of the rocks and the smoother surfaces to find the places protected from the wind. This mountain was quieter than her home. This mountain had not shifted and splintered in a very long time, so many of the exposed surfaces were worn smooth. Unlike the sheer cliffs in Luz with their jagged edges that jutted up out of the ground as if pushed by a hidden monster.

Claws and feet and hands, she climbed the crags to find the few splits in the rock where the mountain had once moved and left holes and deep drops between the stone. Places that were rough and unbeaten by the wind and water. Homes deep in the chasms like the homes in Luz.

She spotted several deep niches in the rock where two men could easily sleep, but too small for a home. That would have to work for tonight. Her strength and the sun were sinking fast. Ilea retrieved her green bag and climbed down the mountain to the most comfortable looking niche.

A few tiny lifesongs worked quietly spinning webs in the back of the hole, but she would not bother them. Ilea would rest here tonight and tomorrow she would make a plan. She pulled out the silver crinkly blanket from the bag and tucked it around her shoulders and legs. *I need to rest*, she said to herself. *I need my strength to find a new home.* Ilea pulled the blanket tight against her body. *I need to find more food.* She wiped at the tears that dripped from her lashes. *I need to be brave. I just want to go home.*

Tower

The shadow of the morning sun caught the edge of the rocks and flickered just enough to wake Ilea. Her back was sore and her arm was numb from cradling her head. With the green bag draped around her neck, she climbed from her cave and scaled the cliff back to the open plateau.

She ate and drank and stared up at the sun's rays jutting between the rocks and tried not to miss her family. If Dodgen had been here, things would have been different. He would have already led them on some crazy adventure chasing shadows and mysterious creatures. Ilea tightened her jaw and decided that she could make her own adventure. Today she would look for the man in the tower. The man who watched for soldiers or monsters or something else very exciting. This was her first real day of freedom. It was time for an adventure.

From the tallest part of the cliffs, Ilea could see one of the strange houses built on top of a tower. It rose above the trees and the sides were half open. She was almost certain no one lived there all the time. It must get cold inside with little protection from wind and weather. So, the only reasonable explanation for the tower was to watch for something.

She was certain there had been a person inside this tower-home the day she arrived in the mountain. He was obviously a ground dweller. If he could fly, he wouldn't need a tower. Tal did not have towers, only ground dwellers, and they were watching for soldiers. Armies of soldiers that came to their cities and attacked their people … killed their people … and sometimes worse. So, what or who was this tower made for watching?

Ilea piled rocks on top of her green bag then climbed to the top of the cliffs and jumped. Falling forward, arms spread wide, the air burned her eyes and filled her lungs until her wings swept outward to slow her down. She circled above the trees looking and feeling for any ground dwellers. Thirty, forty, fifty people wandered here and there not far from the water. The winding, rhythmic, moving water that cut a path through the trees and the ground to make a swirling, thrashing mess as it hit the rocks along the way. But closer to the tower, there was no one.

Ilea spun sideways and dropped toward the trees. But the foliage was too thick to land without tearing her wings. So she turned back toward the mountain and landed closer to the rocks. She would walk through the forest and take her chances with whatever terrified the man in the tower.

There were no trails or paths in this part of the forest and the vines and brush pulled at her legs. After she walked for a while, Ilea dug her claws into the side of a dying, leafless tree and climbed to the top to get a better sense of direction. The tower was close. She could even see its empty insides. She rested for a moment, clinging to the bark, painfully aware that her blue skin did not blend well with the trees. She was glad she could fly back home ... not home ... that was the wrong word. It was more like ... a hideout ... yes ... that is what it should be called. From the tower, she could fly back to her hideout.

Back down on the ground, she continued until she could see the bottom of the tower. The base was made of dark metal much like a soldier's weapon, with a ladder attached for a ground dweller. If there was a ladder, then this must be the way inside. Ilea clung to the ladder, wrapping her claws around each step. Ten, eleven … twenty rungs and she was at the top and beneath the door. She stopped and felt for lifesongs. There were tiny creatures that flew and some that crawled around the room above her. She could feel the dust and water in the air, but no people. No ground dwellers. No dangers she would have to fight. But just to be sure, she held to the ladder with her feet and shoved both hands against the door. The door flew open and slammed against the floor of the tower making the walls shake. Ilea held her breath and waited for a growl or a scream or a yell. But nothing came. So she peered up from beneath the floor.

As expected, the room was empty. There were cabinets with locks and two metal chairs, but no ground dwellers. The ceiling was much taller than she expected. A man twice her size could easily stand inside without hitting his head, and she wondered if there were giants in this place.

Ilea pushed from the top rung of the ladder and climbed into this tower home. She walked to the side of the room and hung her head out from one of the half-walls of the tower and tried to decide what the ground dwellers might be watching for. The trees were thick enough to hide any soldier, so they must be looking for something that would rise above the forest. The thought of a giant monster coming this way sent a shiver along her back. But such a creature would surely leave a path of destruction behind it, so whatever they watched for had not been here in a very long time. Ilea puffed … *unless it could fly.*

From the back of the tower she could see a building. The trees had been cut and a ground dweller had built a home only a short flight away. Ilea leaned on the half-wall of the tower and studied the little brown house with a shiny, slick metal roof. She propped her elbows on the ledge, settled her chin in her hands, and decided that this roof was not at all a good place for a Tal to land. Just beyond the home was a short fence and another much smaller house, much like the one she had seen at the home by the trees that grew the red fruit. One man could live in such a tiny house, but it could also be a place to store weapons or supplies or even food. She watched the little house until her back ached and her arms tingled. Then she stood and stretched and wiggled her wings.

"This will be my adventure," she said to the air, wishing with all her heart that Dodgen could hear. "I will come back … tonight … under that

305

sad, tiny, white moon and find out exactly what is inside."

Ilea climbed on the ledge of the half-wall and swung her legs over the side. The closeness of the tower would make it easy to find this house in the dark. She let herself think of Dodgen one more time and then swung her feet backward to push off from the tower. Her wings caught the air as she dropped toward the pointed tops of the trees then carried her toward the clouds. She circled and spun and flew back toward her hideout. There she would spend the day exploring the mountain and looking for a better place to stay … not a home, just a better hideout.

#

By night fall, Ilea had traded her first hideout for a much larger, much higher cave. It was further up the mountain and had a crooked view of the forest, so she didn't feel so isolated. The sun rays could filter through the doorway in the evenings, so it wouldn't be dark all the time. The darkness was heavier in this place without the red moon. Even with the spindly-legged creatures that spun and the long stringy crawlers, she still felt alone without its red glow.

Ilea emptied her green bag and piled rocks on top of the crackers and red-orb fruit just in case there was something important to carry back from her adventure. With the bag around her neck, she climbed to the top of the cliffs and dove. The clouds were gone and the sky blazed with stars that helped to fill the void left by the missing red moon. But the little moon was trying. Tonight, it was low and full and shone with an orangey color. Ilea nodded her approval as if the moon could see.

Her wings carried her over the tree tops toward the tower silhouetted in the moonlight. Ilea felt no ground dweller's lifesongs as she passed over. She circled low and wide, tilting her shoulders to make the turns. The small home was empty, just like the tower, but the larger home held two ground dwellers who might hear strange sounds like a door being forced open ... so she would have to be careful.

A dingy black-brown, short-furred, four-legged animal lay on the ground close to the small house. His eyes sparkled red in the shadows. Ilea landed behind the building and listened to it making growling sounds. A ground dweller came out of the larger home and spoke with it.

"Whatsa matter, Diesel? Are there monsters out here?"

He was a thick man who looked older than her father and carried a heavy sadness that shook his bones. He sat on the ground beside the growler to stroke its fur and study the trees for danger. Eventually he went back inside and the strange animal followed him. She could see lights shining here and there through the glass windows of the house. Windows just like the gray house in Palon. The trees and the animals were different here, the land and the water … more water than she had ever seen … but someone here knew how to melt the sand and make the clear parts of the wall. Someone here could find the sand and maybe a way back to Luz.

She edged her way around the sides of the small house to its door. She could feel the heavy latch and the square box that looped through the latch to hold it closed. Ilea smiled and thought of Dodgen as she whispered to the metal and pulled out the impurities in the loop. Once the metal dissolved, she pulled the loop from the hooks on the latch, and the door swung open with a loud squeal. She braced herself for another squeak and pulled it open, just wide enough to shimmy through the crack. The sound echoed into the trees and against the house. Ilea held her breath and waited for the man or the growling animal … but no one came. She took several deep breaths to quiet her shaky hands, then tightened her wings to squeeze between the door and the frame and into the shadows of the little house. Three walls were covered in shelves that held tools and boxes and things with little or no lifesong. Deep in the shadows, she could feel more spindly-legged crawlers and some hard-back bugs with antennae. Tucked away in the farthest corner was a long, ropey animal coiled and sleeping in the dirt. Ilea could feel the darkness in his jaws and knew there would be poison in his bite.

There were baskets on one shelf with the red orbs just like she had taken from the line of trees. And brown, rough shaped, dirty roots in the other basket. She placed several of the red orbs and one of the roots in her bag, then added a metal knife from one of the other shelves. It had a cover and would not take up too much space in her bag.

The coiled animal in the corner raised its head and flicked its tongue into the air. It began to unwind and slither toward Ilea's leg. Poison could be tricky. Healing a wound was not the same as stopping poison. So, Ilea clutched her bag against her chest and stepped back toward the door, slowly, one step at a time. The animal bowed its head and began to coil and twist and prepare to strike. Using her back, she pushed open the door, stepped backward, and felt the hot lifesong of a ground dweller.

"Hey!" he yelled, pointing at Ilea. "What are you doing there?"

Ilea gasped and darted toward the trees. Her green bag fell as her wings lifted her from the ground. She caught the straps with her foot, but it slipped away as the flap came open. The bag and the fruit and the knife spilled out on the ground while Ilea grabbed at the air. She didn't stop or even slow down. She just flew, back to the mountains, back to her hideout, fighting to quiet her heart.

Her wings closed as she landed in the flat, open area toward the top of the mountain. Her breath came in choppy gasps and her body quivered. She paced the flat rock, scolding herself for her fear. She had been so afraid of the coiled creature that she had not felt the ground dweller. And even worse, the green bag was gone.

Ilea settled among the rocks to focus on her breathing. As her heart quieted, she thought about the man outside the tiny house. The ground dweller did not fire a weapon or swing a sword. He had not even tried to grab her. Maybe she would go back again and look for her green bag. It was easier to believe that he was not an evil man. Maybe this was the man who worked in the tower to watch for the beast. At least her supplies were here, under the rocks. But without the green bag, it would be more difficult to return to the line of trees for fruit and water, and her supplies would not last forever. So she vowed to brave the ground dweller and go back to look for the bag.

Mig

Seventy-five feet in the air, Miguel Hernandez felt like a giant as he looked out over the forest. It had been a good season. There had not been a fire in almost a year. The rain had been consistent enough to keep the brush moist and the chances of fire almost nonexistent. The summer was still hot, but Miguel welcomed the uneventful days and the hours spent alone in the watch tower. He used his binoculars to study the mountains and speculate about his guest from the night before … and convince himself that he really did see a girl fly. He had not been drinking or sleep walking, so his vision should have been clear. The green bag she had left behind proved she was real. The apples and the potato and the knife that had fallen to the ground were evidence that someone had been there. But a flying girl … that seemed impossible. Real or not, tonight he would sit and wait for her to return.

Still, the excitement of a burglar was a welcome distraction from worrying about his son. Andy had been in the burn ward at St. Luke's Children's Hospital for the last six months. His mother, Lori, had been by his side for most of that time hoping and praying that one day he would walk and talk and eat and do those things that a ten-year-old boy should do. This was not the kind of life they wanted for their son.

He pulled out his radio and called down to the ranger station below, "This is Mig, call sign alpha twelve reporting."

In the station, George answered in a snarky voice, "Is it all clear up there, Mr. Fairy Chaser?"

Mig wished he had not shared his story about the break-in last night. George had worked here for fifteen years and knew most of the rangers in this area, and he couldn't keep a secret. They would never let him forget it, especially if he did not find any real proof.

"Yes," said Mig. "It's all clear. How about the camp sites?"

"Clear down here too," George laughed. "They are packed in … idiots … you would think this heat would chase them away."

"You think anything over fifty degrees is hot," Miguel mused, his voice crackling on the radio. "This is a good time for a vacation."

"Lots of hikers down in the canyon. Idiots," George repeated. "It's really a stupid time of year to go hiking, but they are doing it anyway."

"Well, you keep watch over those hikers and I will just sit up here and relax."

"And look for fairies," George could not resist another chance to tease. "George clear."

"Yeah, yeah … Mig clear." Mig opened his backpack and pulled out a cold bottle of water. "Best birthday present ever," he smiled at the memory of Lori and the cake and the insulated backpack.

He took a drink and then went back to his binoculars and the mountains, scanning the shadowy places. It seemed the most logical place for a flying girl to live. "That's where I would live," he said to himself. "If I could fly … I'd live somewhere high up so I could see." He envisioned a gargoyle perched on a rock glaring down at the forest.

She was just looking for something to eat, he thought. Apples and potatoes, that was all she took. Except the knife … *my hunting knife* … he would have taken that too. He didn't really get a great look at the fairy … or whatever it was. The shed was dark and it moved erratically like a scared kid not at all like a trained hunter. Still, it did fly away, he was sure of it.

Around lunch time, Mig gave up and climbed down to the ranger station to trade places with George. They pulled out their brought-from-home lunches and ate and talked about the campgrounds and the crowded park and the crazy tourists.

"I saw car plates from Michigan," George shook his head. "Michigan for crying out loud. Idiots."

Mig just smiled, "Maybe they are trying to find some warmth."

"Lots of people from Texas," mused George. "Now those I understand. If I lived in Texas I would come to the mountains too."

"They would probably send you to the mountains." It was Mig's turn to tease.

"Me and the missus drove out to the orchard this weekend ... got us some more apples. But I think it's a little hot out there. I think I will bring them inside."

Mig thought about the fairy. "Maybe we could leave them for one more night?"

George slammed his hand against the tabletop. "You think your fairy's coming back, don't you?"

Mig tried to think of another logical answer. "You never know what might happen."

"Who would have thought to bait a trap for a fairy with an apple," George continued. "I thought they ate pixie dust or dragon breath."

Mig rubbed his forehead. "She can have the whole bucket of apples if she will just come back and show you guys she's real."

"Either way, she'll be faster than you, old man."

Mig nodded. He was older than most of the rangers. Much too old to be a father. He had served twenty years as a military medic before he retired and married Lori and found a place to hide as a park ranger. He liked the peace and quiet, no bombs or grenades, just crazy campers … once in a while. It helped with the dreams and the shakes that never seemed to go away. They had moved to this place to be close to the burn center. Lori worked in the school and spent the rest of her time with his son. Andy was lucky, the doctors had said, he might have died. Mig didn't think living through the house fire was lucky at all, and he hated himself for feeling that way.

"I'll leave your apples," George said, "and the potatoes … and there's onions out there too, you know."

"She didn't take any of your smelly onions."

"You did scare her away. Maybe she was here just to get some of my onions."

Mig stood and cleared away his lunch, shaking his head, snickering at his friend. "She's coming back … just you wait."

#

As the last of the sun's rays sparkled across the mountain, Mig filled the green satchel with the sheathed hunting knife and extra apples and potatoes and hung it on the shed door. Then he walked back up to the ranger station and found a comfortable spot just inside the doorway so he could watch the shed and still listen for the radio. A folding chair, his binoculars, and Diesel curled up between his feet, he waited for the fairy.

The full moon brightened the night, but nothing moved in the trees and it was lonely with only a dog to talk to. Mig was dozing in the chair when he heard the dog growl. He wasn't really his dog, he just hung around the station looking for food and a friendly ear rub. Mig jerked upright and searched the shadows around the shed. The satchel had not moved.

He stood in the doorway then stepped out into the moonlight with his hands thrown out wide in a welcoming gesture. Four more steps toward the shed and he held his breath. A shadow moved beside the shed.

"My name is Mig," he said. "It's just me out here. No one is going to hurt you. Sorry I scared you in the shed last night. I put your bag on the door. It's waiting for you ... apples, potatoes, everything you need."

The dog turned and looked at Mig as if he was crazy. But he had stopped growling. He whimpered softly and trotted over to the shed. Mig watched as he paused at the corner of the building and a hand began to scratch behind his ears.

"He likes you," Mig encouraged.

Ilea stepped out from behind the shed. Her blue eyes glowed in the moonlight and her skin merged with the blue-gray of the shadows. The dog sat down beside her and rubbed his head against her leg. She could feel the gentleness in both the man and the animal.

Ilea knelt to the ground and held out her hand to the dog. Once again, she stroked the back of his head. Beyond him, the satchel hung from the door of the shed.

"His name is Diesel. He doesn't have a family, so he stays with us."

Ilea just kept petting the dog.

Mig reached his hand up to pat his chest. "My name is Mig." Then he walked over to sit down on a half-stone fence that served as a water break between the trees and the station.

The dog began to prance and jump and beg to play. Ilea could feel the joy shaking his shaggy-unkept body. She stood and removed the satchel from the door, never taking her eyes off the man on the fence. The flap was open so she could see the red fruit and the knife. Ilea pulled it close then walked over to the fence. She sat on the rocks more than twice an arm's length from the stranger.

Miguel started to ramble. "My name is Miguel, but my friends call me Mig. I always thought it was cool because a Mig is a really fast airplane. It's a small jet that flies super-fast, and I always wanted to fly."

He paused and smiled at Ilea. He knew he should be afraid or shocked, but after all the death and pain and sorry that had filled his life for so long, a little magic was a beautiful thing.

He wondered if she could understand any of what he was saying. For a moment, he tried to imagine what it would feel like to fly without a machine beneath him – open air, clear sky, wind in your face. He wondered how much weight she could carry when she was flying, and if she was average size for a blue girl. Maybe she was the smallest or maybe she towered over all her friends. And did all of them have the same wispy lines down the edge of their face?

He caught her looking at his right hand and tried to explain how a chainsaw had cut off his pinkie and part of his ring finger. He made a cutting motion with his left hand over the missing fingers to mimic a saw. He told her how the elk had fallen into the river and was tangled in a web of debris. How the current had pinned him against the rocks and no one had been strong enough to untangle the mess and set him free. How his friend, Sampson, had crawled across the rocks and used a chainsaw to cut him loose. But there was no way to explain the terror he had felt when the buck panicked at the noise of the chainsaw, and Sampson had slipped and swung sideways. The blood, the pain, the screaming … that was a story for another day.

Ilea tried to listen. Some of the words were familiar, and some sounded more like a Breen chattering for more food. She knew it must have been painful when those fingers were cut. The scars along his hand reminded her of Dodgen and the wing that he hated so much. She thought of the suns and suns she had spent trying to heal that wing. The nights she had sung outside his room or slept at the foot of his bed to try and bring him some relief. Mig's fingers would be no different. Old scars do not sing. They can never sing.

Mig and Ilea sat quietly on the fence. She didn't know what to say and neither did he. There were just too many questions and not enough words. She wished Nick could be here. He would have like this ground dweller.

Ilea stood quietly and walked back toward the small building Mig had called a shed. "Shed," she whispered.

Claw and hand and foot, she swung her body upward to the top of the shed. Miguel stood and stared, wide-eyed. Even more speechless than the night before. He watched as Ilea unfurled her wings against the moonlight then lifted gently from the shed to the air. She nodded in a thankful sort of way and flew out into the darkness. He watched until her shadow disappeared. She was here for a reason, Mig was sure of it. Something good was about to happen ... something good.

\#

The next evening, Ilea returned to the shed. Diesel came running out of the trees, catching his foot on a branch and rolling across the dirt. Mig was sitting on the fence waiting and watching Ilea flutter to the ground, the sound of canvas caught in the wind. He wore the same brown uniform as the night before. The sun was not quite gone, so he could see the true watery-blue color of her skin and the white of her hair, three ponytails tied in back. Her face was young and innocent and curious. This time she sat beside him on the fence.

"Ilea," she said, pointing at her chest. Then she pointed at him and then the dog. "Mig … Diesel." She continued with almost every word Nick had taught her, "Shed, rock, sky, sun, moon, tree …" until she ran out of words.

Mig laughed, "Well … Ilea, I'm glad we got that out of the way." It was clear she wanted to learn more, so he would try to oblige. Besides, he didn't know what else to say.

The ranger station had more to offer than apples and potatoes, so Mig had brought a grocery bag with samples. He picked up a banana then peeled the skin down. Ilea's eyes grew wide. This food was yellow like the ganda fruit from her home, except it looked and smelled different. It was longer and skinnier and squishier and not much like a ganda after all. But for a moment, it was like having something from home. Mig broke off a piece and held it toward the girl. Ilea was careful to keep her claws concealed as she took the food. Her skin was tough, but ground dwellers were easily scratched and easily frightened.

"Banana," Mig said.

"Bana," Ilea repeated, squishing the fruit against her teeth with her tongue. It wasn't ganda, but it was a nice change from red orbs and crackers. So, she held out her hand for more.

They finished the banana together and then Mig began to unload his bag. He took out a package of potato chips, a slice of cold pizza, a left-over chicken sandwich, and six chocolate chip cookies. He would say the name and she would repeat it, then each of them would take a bite. Sometimes even Diesel got a piece. They followed this routine until the bag was empty. After tasting one of the cookies, Ilea picked up the container and put the whole package in her green bag, watching Mig for a reprimand.

"So now I know your weakness, right?" Mig smiled even though he knew she didn't understand.

Suddenly, Ilea stood and backed away from the fence. It took a moment for Mig to catch up, but eventually he heard the car coming down the gravel road. It would be George coming to trade shifts.

Ilea

"You have to go," Mig commanded. He wanted the others to see her. He wanted to show them he wasn't crazy, but Ilea wasn't ready for that. And George would not be so understanding. "Go," he said and waved her away.

Ilea understood the anxiousness in his voice and the tension in his life-song. Whoever was coming was not her friend. "Hide," she whispered.

Mig turned away to watch for the car and heard the curtain ruffle of her wings as she left. He closed his eyes and burned that sound deep in his memory. A sound he never wanted to forget.

Roller Coaster

The park rangers changed schedules and Ilea began to visit during the day. Mig set up a signal using a bandana as a warning that he was not alone. They practiced words, both from English and the language of Luz. He showed her old paper maps of the area and talked about his life as a soldier. He taught her about the campers prowling along the edges of the water, who set up makeshift homes and cooked strange food on open fires that smelled of smoke and grease and made her mouth water. Somewhere between the words and the pictures and the emotions, they found a way to communicate.

Today when they met, something was wrong. Mig's lifesong was whirling and dark. He was afraid.

Ilea held up her hands in surrender. "No Mig," she announced.

He wasn't quite sure what she meant. He was standing right in front of her, but she always had a way of knowing how he felt. "I have three missing hikers in the canyon," he held up three fingers as he spoke. "On this side of the water. If you keep following the water, the land gets deep, like a hole. Three young men went hiking in that direction. They have been gone since yesterday morning. I have men out searching." He kept rambling about helicopters and search parties, and how he should teach her more English.

Ilea understood only a few of his words. She did know that he was worried and scared.

On a whim, he brought out his cell phone and pulled up an aerial view of the forest. He zoomed in on the ranger station. "Mig," he pointed.

Ilea understood completely. Nick had one of these machines and this picture was from the sky. Most of what she knew of this place, she had seen from the sky. Things were much clearer that way. He squeezed his fingers together to make the image broader to include the canyon. "Canyon," he said and ran his finger along the dark brown area.

Ilea could see the change in color and the foliage. This image did not show the lifesongs and patterns that ran through the trees and rocks and water, but she understood the places he showed her. "Canyon," she repeated.

Then Mig made the image larger to make sure she understood.

"Caaaaanyon," Ilea's eyes brightened.

"Three," Mig again held up three fingers as he spoke. Then, on his phone, he brought up the picture of the three hikers the family had given him. They had their arms around each other. The boys had taken this picture just before leaving on their hike. "Three ... canyon."

Ilea understood that Mig was afraid for these three ground dwellers. She did not know if they were dead or hurt or lost, but she knew that she could find them much more quickly than he could. "Ilea ... canyon," she patted her chest. "Three ... canyon."

She listened to his lifesong to be sure he knew what she meant. Then she stood to leave for the canyon.

"Wait ... wait." he pushed out both hands asking her to stop.

Ilea sat back down on the stone fence and watched Mig run back inside his home.

In the station, Mig picked up one of the drones used for reconnaissance. The motor was damaged, but the camera worked just fine. And better yet, it was battery operated. The camera had its own power source. More importantly, this camera was already set up to send images to the monitor in the station. He could even pick it up on his phone. He also grabbed one of the radios the rangers used. He turned the dial to change the station to number three. This was a station none of the other searchers would use, so they wouldn't hear Ilea. Then he changed his personal radio to station three as well.

He came back outside with the camera and the radio. He handed the equipment to Ilea and then unbuckled his belt and slipped it off. She held the camera as he fed the belt through the hooks on its back. Once Mig was finished, Ilea held her hands up like a child waiting to be dressed. Mig buckled the camera around her waist and tried to show her how the buttons worked on the radio. He wasn't sure if she would be able to talk to him, but at least she could listen to his words.

He practiced directions with her, turning his body and using hand motions. "Forward ... back ... left ... right."

Ilea copied his movements and repeated the commands. "Left ... right ... back."

They drilled for a few minutes and then turned on the camera. Mig held up three fingers and pointed out past the trees. "Ilea ... canyon ... three."

She smiled all over. It was deliciously exciting to be needed. Maybe she could help Mig with these young boys. Ilea shook her wings and then ran past Mig, three steps and she lifted off in the direction of the canyon.

He opened the app on his phone and the feed from the canyon appeared. He could see the land spreading out beneath her. The tree tops, high and low on the way to the canyon.

Ilea flew so low he could almost count the needles on the pines. The view was partially blocked here, but in the canyon, she would be able to see everything.

The radio crackled at her waist and Mig's voice said, "Canyon ... canyon."

She knew he was just testing the machine. The button on the side would answer him, but right now she needed to focus on the boys.

Mig watched the screen as she almost brushed the top of the trees and then fell straight down into the canyon. It was like a carnival ride pitching forward. The camera dropped endlessly, then jerked sideways as she spun. Ilea turned her body toward the sides of the cliff and began to search. She flew back and forth in a methodical, grid-like pattern. Slow, rhythmic motions that followed the formations in the rock. Mig watched for anything unusual, but the camera feed was often hazy and too far away for a good look. So, he would have to trust Ilea to find the boys.

She flew almost two hours before she paused. The feed on the camera slowed and hovered. Mig studied the canyon wall, but the camera was shaking so much the image was a blur. Little by little she moved closer to the cliffs causing the camera to rush forward with each push of her wings. Eventually, Mig could see a path through the rocks and the brush where the boys may have walked … or climbed. Then he saw the body. One boy, lying on the trail, motionless and silent.

Ilea had not planned for such an injury. She knew she couldn't carry him without a harness. She hovered lower and lower over the boy. His lifesong was weak but he was alive. There was an injury on the side of his head where the skin had been ripped back the blood dripped warm and fresh, and along his back were four cracked bones. The other boys were not here. Maybe they thought he was dead, or maybe they had just abandoned him.

Her wings tilted and she dropped away from the cliff, then began the same crisscross search pattern above and below the body. As she came to the top of the cliffs, Mig could see the marker and the picnic tables. Site 43, that was where they were.

Suddenly, Ilea dropped hard and fast toward the bottom of the canyon, and closer to the water. Mig had that same roller coaster-ride sensation as before. Then the camera spun and dropped again, and Mig could see the red tent at the bottom of the trail. Ilea wasn't sure if this was what they were looking for. She hovered above it and hoped that Mig was watching.

"Ok," Mig's voice crackled on the radio. "I'm sending help. You need to hide."

There was that word again. *Hide* … even here in the sky, she was not safe. Hide, she thought. I need a harness to carry that boy, not a place to hide. Ilea spun and flew up the cliff to hook her claws into the rocks and land beside the unconscious boy.

Mig's voice crackled again. "The chopper is coming. You need to go."

She leaned out across the boy to study his head and back. She could feel the swelling in his skull and the tears in the muscles that held the shattered pieces of his spine. In her heart, she knew that when the ground dwellers came and carried him from this place, the pieces of his back would splinter completely and he would never walk again. She reached out her hand and pressed her fingers just above his ear where the blood oozed red and began to sing. Her claws digging into the rocks. Her wings twitching and jerking to keep her balanced and Mig watching through the camera. He could hear the gentle sounds of her voice, the cooing and singing. He watched as her fingers caressed the boy's scalp. Blood gushed from inside his head, then the swelling receded. The skin began to stretch and grow and the wound sealed leaving only dried blood on his face.

Then she laid her arms across the boy's chest. From her elbows to her fingers she lay across him, blocking the camera. She pushed all her strength into those tiny bones in his back that protected the fluid filled cord that controlled his arms and legs. She could hear the flying machine in the distance and the voices of the ground dwellers above her at the top of the cliff. There wasn't much time, so scarring couldn't be helped. The pieces must be held in place. Two of the bones were crushed and scattered out into his body, so she had to fuse the pieces that were still intact. This strange configuration of the bones might be uncomfortable at times and might even hurt when the weather was cold, but he would walk. This boy was young and strong and his body would adapt. If she only had more time ... more time.

Mig couldn't see the bones meshing together inside the boy, but he could hear her song, her chant, her plea to the wounded boy. "Hide, Ilea," Mig begged. "They won't understand."

Something hot ricocheted off the rock beside her, and the crack of a gun echoed across the canyon.

"Get out of there!" Mig commanded. "Fly Ilea, fly!"

Ilea pushed away from the cliff. Her wings pulled her backward and she fell toward the bottom of the canyon, away from the man with the gun.

Mig's stomach dropped as he watched the video fall from the cliff. "More with the roller coaster," he moaned and looked away. He didn't know who was in the tent below, but she had saved the boy on the cliff. He had watched her do it.

Ilea stopped further down the canyon on a rock out in the river hoping the blue of her skin would look more like the blue of the water and no one would notice. She wanted to see the boy taken.

The flying machine came over the top of the cliff. Ilea took the radio from her belt and turned the buttons until she could hear voices. The men in the machine talked to the men on the ground. Mig's voice came across the speaker telling someone where to find the boy.

Two men hooked ropes into the rock and began to lower themselves down to the body. Other men lowered a basket-bed from the top that they guided along the rocks. Once they stopped, she saw ropes and straps and pieces of cloth moving around the boy. Then the flying machine came closer. It could not hover like a Tal. It rose and fell and wavered back and forth to keep its place. Finally, a man swung from beneath it to hook cords to the bed. Then as the machine rose, the bed followed.

One of the boys came out from the tent at the base of the cliff. He waved and motioned for the others to come and help. She knew there would be more straps and harnesses and another basket-bed for the third ground dweller.

As the men worked, through the static, she could hear the voices talking on the radio. "Good job ... now lower the harness. We need more rope. Good job finding the boys, Mig. Steph, fly a little higher. Good job with the bed. ... good job."

Ilea pressed the button on the side of the radio and said, "Good job. Good job."

She could hear the men chattering. "Who the heck was that? Is there someone using this channel? If you are not part of the rescue operation, you need to clear this channel. This is for emergency use only."

Mig smiled because he knew without that strange woman on the radio, there would have been no rescue.

Ilea waited until the ground dwellers left and then flew along the river, dragging her toes and feeling gloriously alive. She would have so many stories to tell Dodgen when she got home.

The next morning, Mrs. Jackson called Mig to say thank you for finding her son. He had been the one on the cliff. The one who did not move. The doctor's said he was going to be fine. He had a head injury that was healing quickly and massive bruising on his back. The odd thing was that they found extensive damage to the spine, but it looked old and already healed. She wondered if he had fallen in football or some other time and just not told her about it.

Mig listened and nodded and knew Mrs. Jackson was wrong. He knew that her son had broken his back only yesterday and that the only reason he was walking was because of Ilea.

Andy

When Ilea came the next day dragging her green bag, Mig brought out a package of chocolate chip cookies and tried to explain about the grateful parents and her amazing job at finding the lost hikers. She just smiled and ate one of the cookies.

After he finished his story, most of which Ilea did not understand, she opened her bag and pulled out the drone camera and the radio. "Good job," she said.

"Thank you for bringing these back," Mig took the camera, but put the radio back in her bag. "You might need this."

Then they sat there for a while, in silence, on the stone fence, while Ilea ate cookies and rubbed Diesel's ears, and Mig tried to decide how to ask her for help. She fidgeted and shook her wings now and then.

"I have a son," he started, watching Ilea to see if she understood. "My son is sick." Mig laid the box of cookies on the fence then stood and began to pace. Walking up and down the fence line, he tried to find the simplest words to explain that his son needed her to heal him just like the hiker. But he couldn't find them. He didn't know how to tell her about the burns and the hospital, the pain and the weariness.

Ilea reached for another cookie and watched him worry and pace and ramble. When he paused, she pointed to the cell phone clipped to his belt. Mig looked down at his phone and realized what he needed was pictures. Using his phone, he accessed the video from the drone camera. With a swipe of his finger, he sped through the tedious images of rocks and mountains and trees to stop at the motionless boy on the cliff. The video slowed to show Ilea touching the boy's face and the wounds above his ear closing.

"Help," Mig said, "You healed this boy."

"Help," Ilea repeated and nodded. Help didn't seem like the right word to use, but Mig was happy.

Next, his finger slid across his phone to find a picture of Andy standing beside him on a fishing boat. Holding the phone close to Ilea, he pointed and said, "Andy ... help Andy."

Ilea shrugged and reached for another one of the cookies on the fence. This boy didn't look like he needed any help. He seemed ... happy.

Mig could tell by her disinterest that she didn't understand. How could she possibly understand without seeing Andy now? There were pictures on his phone of Andy in the hospital not long after the accident. Pictures he used to show the doctors. Pictures that helped with his millions of questions. Pictures that filled his heart with anger and hate. He opened one and passed the phone to Ilea.

She studied the burns on his face and down his arms, and the hard, black spots across his stomach. In places, the burns were so deep that his skin barely held his body together.

"Help Andy," Mig whispered, the tears welling in his eyes.

Her face brightened and she stood. "Help
… help Andy." She grabbed Mig's arm and pulled
him toward the truck.

Mig motioned for her to stop.
"Tomorrow," he said, "new sun." He talked like
he was in an old western movie. "If we go to the
hospital, you need to hide."

Ilea twisted the hair in one of her ponytails.
She knew that word … hide ... but not hospital.
Mig would have to teach her that one. "Sun," she
said and backed away. She kept nodding and
hoped that Mig understood that she would return
with the new sun. Her body twisted and she ran
and opened her wings to catch the air. As she rose
above the trees, her thoughts filled with the images
of the young boy in the bed and the burns that ran
the length of this body. Her heart ached for the
places that would have scarred and died and lost
their song by now. Ilea knew that the new sun may
bring only failure.

#

Ilea pulled the heavy, brown coat tight
around her shoulders and the hood low across her

face as she walked into the hospital. Her feet slid across the floor to keep the rain boots from coming off, or worse yet, tangling in the coat. Her heart pounded in her chest and her hands felt sticky beneath the cotton gloves. If anyone saw her face, she knew there would be chaos. These ground dwellers would be afraid of her, just like the men at the prison before Nick came. And when people are afraid, they can do horrible things.

From the first moment they entered the building, the pain was deafening. Ilea had never felt so much pain in one place before. Layer after layer of agony. She could feel young lifesongs vibrating and fighting against the agony. Others seemed to be dreaming, drifting in and out of consciousness, feeling only pieces of the pain. Mig had said this was a place of healing. The ground dwellers could not heal the way she did so they used medicine and knives. Up and down the hallways, she could feel the cold places where the scars closed across old wounds and freshly stitched cuts. But the sadness was even stronger than the pain. Waves and waves of sadness that bellowed from sick and well alike.

"Uuuuu," Ilea gasped in horror and crumpled to her knees.

Mig put his arm around her waist and helped her to stand. "I know these clothes are heavy. But don't worry, I will help you walk."

He had misunderstood the reason for her weakness. Just like her father, he could not understand the depth of what she could feel. Ilea stood and tried to close her thoughts and her own lifesong to those around her, just so she could walk.

Two women in loose-fitting clothes spotted with flowers greeted them as they entered. "Good morning, Mr. Hernandez. Andy is doing well today."

Mig knew they would never say anything different, even if it wasn't true. "Glad to hear it. I … I brought my friend. Remember the friend we talked about?"

"Yes, Mr. Hernandez, don't worry about it. You go on in the room."

Ilea didn't know that Mig had called earlier in the day to speak with the nurses and the doctor about his friend who had been burned just like his son. His friend who wore heavy clothes to conceal her scars and disfigured limbs. His friend who wanted to come and sing and pray for his son. So not one person asked any questions about the oddly dressed woman that he led into his son's room.

A young man in a white coat with a black cord draped around his neck greeted them as they walked down the slick, white hallway. "Hello, Mig."

Mig paused and gripped Ilea's shoulders a little tighter. "Dr. Bennett … good morning … this is my friend, Ilea."

Ilea could feel his pity.

"This is Andy's doctor," Mig explained, but Ilea was not sure what that meant.

"I'll come by and check on Andy later," Dr. Bennett said, studying her heavy coat.

"Thank you," Mig pushed Ilea past the doctor.

As they entered the room, Ilea could see a woman sitting in a chair by the bed. Worn and disheveled as a soldier might be after battle. She smiled despite the dark circles under her eyes.

"Ilea, this is my wife, Lori." Mig fidgeted with his keys in his pocket.

Ilea wondered if this woman knew that beneath this heavy coat was not a ground dweller at all, but a blue-skinned Tal.

Lori nodded and stood and then backed up against the wall as though she was trying not to get in the way.

Mig motioned to the bed where a small boy lay hooked to wires and lights and tubes. A clear mask covered his face and his breath came in short, raspy bursts. A shiny white box beside the bed displayed jagged lines and beeped a slow rhythm. Ilea could feel his hazy lifesong floating from agony to dreams with each passing moment.

"This is my son, Andrew," Mig almost choked on the words.

Lori watched as the faceless coat nodded and waddled further into the room. Mig helped Ilea sit down in an overstuffed recliner, then pulled her trench coat up around her legs. He motioned to Lori and she followed him out into the hallway. Ilea felt the weight of fear and worry as she passed. Any good mother would be concerned about leaving their helpless child with a faceless stranger.

Once they left, Ilea could relax. She was glad they were out of the room. It would be easier to focus on the boy if they were gone. She wriggled her arms out of the sleeves of the coat so that she could put them in her lap. She slipped out of her boots and pulled her feet up underneath the coat and sat crisscrossed in the recliner. Then Ilea closed her eyes and reached out for the boy … just the surface of his light. She wanted to know his song well before she tried to join. To embrace all his pain at once would be too much, even for a healer. The fact that this tiny boy could bear it at all was astounding.

Ilea took a deep breath and began to sing, soft, humming and cooing sounds. Andy's skin had formed hard crusty shells over the top of his open wounds, and she knew she would have to reach deeper to find the light beneath them. Gently Ilea wove her light into his scars and the burns inside him that still wept. Coaxing and calling, she brought their song alongside her own. And together, their songs floated along the boy's arms and chest and the thin skin across his face. Much like stroking the soft fur of an animal, her light soothed and caressed.

The songs deep within him raged against her light and cried out to Ilea for peace. The lining of his throat and mouth and the skin within his lungs that should have been wet had lost their songs and now only trembled with pain.

She felt Mig peek inside the doorway, but she pushed his song aside and focused only on the boy. Piece by piece, rhythm by rhythm, she released her strength into his lungs and coated them like mother's milk. They did not have the ability to heal yet, but at least their pain could be soothed.

She searched for the layers beneath the wounds that were still intact and pushed them to heal so that one day they could rise to the surface. If she pushed too hard, his body would be filled with scars and too many places that could never sing again.

Ilea was growing weaker, so she guided the last of her strength into the flesh around his neck and face. The tissue was thinner there and would heal more quickly. His eyes must have been covered when he was hurt because they were untouched, but his cheeks quivered with her song. As the skin meshed along his cheekbones and neck, Ilea sighed a heart-wrenching heavy sign, content that his face would be smoother by morning. The dead flesh would crumble and fall away.

Ilea slipped her feet back into her boots and her hands into the sleeves of that monstrous coat. She stood and stretched and tried not to think of anything. Her boots clunked as she stumbled out into the hallway. Mig caught her and gave her balance.

"I ... come back," she said, "tomorrow and tomorrow ... suns and suns."

Mig knew she did not have all the words she needed to explain, but he understood. Making Andy better was not going to happen overnight. Mig held her by the shoulders and guided her back to the front desk. She felt Lori rush past them both to be with her son. Ilea knew she would not be able to see a difference. She would not know that he swallowed with less pain and that his lungs no longer burned with every breath.

Mig led Ilea out the front door, past the nurses' station and the watchful eyes of Dr. Bennett, and back to his old truck. She could feel the eyes of the ground dwellers watching them as they passed. He backed out of the parking lot and started down the road to the station. Before he could ask what happened in the hospital room, Ilea began to pull off the pieces of her costume.

"Please ... stop," Ilea begged and slipped out of the coat. "Please ..." The tears burned her eyes. More than anything she needed the sky and the sun ... and to fly.

Mig pulled the truck to the side of the road and watched Ilea remove her gloves and boots. "Don't worry," she said, feeling his anxiousness. "I know the way."

Without waiting for an answer, Ilea opened the truck door and ran, not caring who might see. She ran and lifted off from the ground. Her wings popping like canvas sails and Mig could hear the *vhoom* as they carried her away. She spun in the sky and then flew straight into the sun, drinking in its warmth and life, rising higher and higher, leaving this horrible world behind — and then — she screamed — screeching, howling like an animal caught in a trap. She screamed at the sun and the air. She screamed for her father and for Kayz and Dodgen … and for the children in the hospital who could not scream. She shrieked and flew into the sun, higher and higher, until she could no longer breathe. Then she folded her wings and fell. Her head spinning, her heart breaking, she relished the emptiness of the sky until she felt the air pound against her ears, and rush into her lungs. Then Ilea forced her wings open and spiraled and leveled and flew back toward the mountains.

Mig stood outside the truck and watched her fly. He listened to her scream and tried desperately not hear those of his son's … those piercing shrieks that burned in his memories. His heart ached for his wife and his son and when he could bear it no longer, he closed his eyes, shook his fists to the sky … and screamed with them.

#

The next day was much the same. Mig helped Ilea into the worn wool coat and gloves and the heavy rubber boots, and then drove her to St. Luke's Children's Hospital. Together they walked into the cold, strong-smelling building and down the hallway to Andy's room. The women all wore pink today, and Ilea found it easier to be brave. She already knew the building and the people and the young boy she must help. Again, Mig and Lori stepped out into the hallway to wait and hope. And again, Ilea was left to work.

She was more comfortable, more confident today. She quickly wriggled out of her coat and boots and sat crisscrossed in that black, leather chair. Then closed her eyes and surrendered to Andy's lifesong. This time, Mig and Lori could hear her song wafting out into the hallway, drifting under the door and around the edges. They could hear the cooing and the high pitches that rolled into low, gravelly tones. And for a while, they lost their own weariness. Their spirits lightened and they relaxed. Mig slipped his arm around his wife's shoulders and they leaned back against the wall behind the orange painted bench. They closed their eyes and listened to Ilea's song.

Time seemed to stand still, and before they knew it, two hours had passed. Ilea stood and stretched, then shuffled her clunky boots, out into the hallway. She pulled her hood low on her face as she walked. She had forgotten her gloves, and one of her white-blue hands hung out from the sleeve of her coat. Mig reached down and tugged at the cuff of her sleeve to pull it down over her hand. Ilea turned her back to them and dug the gloves out of her pocket. She slipped them on and chided herself for being so careless. It was much too easy to lose herself while she worked and forget to stay hidden.

Lori thanked her, telling her how grateful they were that she had come to help Andy. Ilea just nodded and did not explain that it was what she did. It was her gift to life. Mig lead Ilea back to the door and out to the truck.

As they pulled out of the parking lot, she slipped out of the coat. "Better," she said and pulled off her gloves. "Better, better, better."

Mig wasn't sure if she meant Andy was better or if she felt better with the situation. Either way it was progress, it was hope.

Inside the hospital, one of the nurses stopped by Andy's room to check his vitals. "Hello, Mrs. Hernandez," the nurse interrupted softly.

"Jasmine," Lori smiled at the woman in pink. "I'm glad you are here. Just listen to that beautiful sound."

Jasmine stood frozen and listened to the monitor beep and the respirator breathe. Up and down, wossshhhhhhh pop, wossshhhhhhh pop.

"Mmmm … isn't that a beautiful sound?" Lori sighed with contentment.

"I don't understand," Jasmine said.

"His breathing, can't you hear it?" Lori shook her head. "There is no more rattle or rasp. No more wheezing. He's just breathing. Can't you hear it?"

Jasmine listened again, wossshhhhhhh pop, wossshhhhhhh pop. All she could hear was the respirator.

"He's getting better," Lori nodded.

Jasmine walked over to the monitor and began to read the information. She pulled Andy's records up on her tablet and compared the numbers. Back and forth her eyes scanned the screens, from the monitor to the tablet. "He *is* breathing better. The numbers … the numbers are so much better. It looks as if …" Jasmine turned to look at Lori, "As if he might be able to breathe on his own. I need to talk to Dr. Bennett."

Lori just nodded … and listened … and smiled.

#

Today, Ilea chose to sit on the floor. It reminded her of Luz and the times spent singing for the city. Andy was growing stronger, but there was so much damage, so many levels of pain, it would take suns and suns to make him whole.

Lori had grown accustomed to the song of healing. She would often pace the hallway or sit in Andy's room to listen. Ilea would sometimes alter her song to strengthen Lori and take away some of the sadness.

Today she sat down beside Ilea on the floor and let the vibrations of the song wash over her skin. Ilea felt Lori's spirit tugging at her own so she quieted her song and waited for Lori to speak.

"Thank you," she whispered to Ilea. "Thank you for what you've done."

"Welcome," Ilea said in her best English and listened to Lori's restlessness to do more. Andy's mother had never seen the face of a Tal, and Ilea wondered if she would feel the same if she could see the claws and wings that hid beneath the brown-gray coat. "You can … help."

Lori looked at her dark hood and the bright blue eyes shining from beneath. "I don't understand. I am doing all I can."

Ilea smiled beneath the hood. "Sing with me," she whispered.

Her words were so simple and yet they felt like an insurmountable task. Lori knew her song was not going to help Andy, but maybe Ilea needed to hear it … or maybe Andy needed to hear it. Anything was possible. A month ago, Andy had little chance of ever recovering, but Ilea had changed all of that. At this moment, she could believe in almost anything.

"Teach me," Lori said to the faceless coat.

Mig leaned against the doorway watching as Ilea slipped off her glove to reveal a delicate blue hand. She turned it palm up and held it out to Lori. "I will show you."

Lori took her hand, expecting her skin to feel different. Because of its color, it should feel cold or rough, but she could feel only the warmth of another life pulsing beneath her grip.

"Push out." Ilea lifted her gloved hand to touch her forehead. "In here, everything away."

Lori held her hand a little tighter and tried to understand.

Ilea tapped her forehead again. "Only Andy ... only love ... only peace ... only good."

Lori nodded even though she didn't completely understand all that Ilea was saying.

Ilea passed her hand over Lori's face, forcing her to close her eyes. Then the daughter of Adolphus quieted her heartbeat and began to sing. Just a hum, a hint of a song.

"Try," she whispered to Lori, "try."

Lori's face turned red, and Ilea felt the warmth of her embarrassment flash across her body. "Shhhh," Ilea corrected sweetly. "Only good." Again, she raised her hand to her head. "Give good to Andy." She did not have the words to make Lori understand that the richness of her thoughts would cover any failure in her skill.

Ilea quieted herself and began again. A soft hum of a song, a single pitch held long and low and delicate against the air.

Lori closed her eyes and thought about her son. She thought about Andy walking and running and playing. She thought about him moving his body without pain. She thought about him growing up and going to school. So many good things she wished for Andy. And then she matched Ilea's hum … a single tone.

Once Ilea felt their songs join, she raised the pitch … ever so slightly, and Lori followed. Then one more step upward with Lori beside her. A few more tones, up and down. The song wrapped itself around Andy and pulled them both with it. Ilea wanted his mother to see her son's lifesong, to see all that was inside him, good and bad. She wanted Lori to feel it all, so that she might find it again if Ilea was gone. Ilea knew she could not stay here forever.

Lori gripped Ilea's hand and followed the song, rising and falling like a carnival ride. Rising and falling with Andy's pain. She felt the stiffness in his skin and the heat that still lingered inside his legs … the scars in his lungs and the places worn smooth from Ilea's song. She held on until she could bear it no longer.

Lori jerked her hand free, trembling, breathing hard. Ilea turned to Lori and slipped her hood from her face. Lori had never seen such a creature. Her eyes, her cheeks, the blue of her skin and the feathery wisps that curved so unevenly in front of her ears. Ilea smiled softly and nodded to Lori as if she understood everything in the whole world.

Lori wanted to hug her, to wrap her arms around her and give her all the goodness she felt inside. Ilea drew a small, trembling gasp as she felt the joy within Lori become her own. And she knew that when she was gone, Lori would be able to help Andy. Not the way she did, not healing every piece and moment in the body, but help him to grow stronger and heal himself.

Mig found himself smiling in the doorway, not understanding everything that had just happened, but knowing that Andy was going to be fine.

#

Andy grew stronger, and in time, they developed a routine. Mig would bring her to the hospital and she would work. People would stop at the nurses' station at the end of the hallway just to listen. Her song was seldom rhythmic. It was not music to sing with or clap or dance to, but there was no denying its charm. She wove her music up and down the hallways of the hospital, wrapping it around the people in the building, just like when she sang for Luz. Her song stayed longer in some places and skittered past others. She missed Tori and Zaharra and Argia and the strength they could bring to her song.

Ilea began to spend more and more time in the hallway, sometimes walking up and down the stairs to the other floors and the other lifesongs. She could feel the people watching as she passed, especially Dr. Bennett. He studied her with distrust and anger and hated the way the others accepted her. She had become almost a permanent fixture in the hallways of St. Luke's Children's Hospital. No one minded her bulky clothes or her clunky boots. Everyone felt better when she was there, and that made Dr. Bennett even more suspicious.

It was nice to have purpose again, even if only in this world, this far-away place. Ilea knew there was a chance she would never go home, but at least for this moment, she felt like she belonged. This was the reason the creator had made her. She was exhausted each time they left the hospital, but a warm sun bath and a trip across the sky left her strong and ready to work again.

Today they were taking out the tube that kept Andy fed. The respirator had long since been removed and his breathing was relaxed. But today, he was going to get to eat something called Jell-O. Ilea was not sure she understood why they were so excited, but she knew it was a good thing. She asked not to go into the room with them today. She asked to sit outside in the hallway and sing for the others. Mig didn't see any reason why not, so she made herself comfortable on the floor beside the orange bench. One of the nurses, wearing blue today, brought her a blanket. Ilea just nodded with her faceless coat and thought about the hard ground of the landing in Luz. The open place where she and Tori had met to sing for the city. Her boots clunked as she scooted over to sit on the blanket. As usual, she slipped out of her boots and sleeves and nestled beneath her gray-brown coat. She pulled the hood low to cover her face and gave herself to the lifesongs.

When her song grew tired and her body stiff, she left to roam the halls of St. Luke's. She headed to the blue hall of the hospital, one of the back areas that held only a few children. These children had a different kind of pain. Mig called it cancer. It was not a wound to be repaired. It was a malfunction of their song. These children were difficult to help. Ilea would sing to the pieces of their bodies, and they would heal. But then the cancer would grow again. It was frustrating, and she kept trying to find the song to make it right. She remembered the shackles of Kaleus's prison and how Dodgen had helped her to see the weakness. But even destroying the cancer, like she destroyed the shackles, only seemed to make it stronger.

So instead of healing, she had begun teaching. She was teaching the pieces of each child to sing away the cancer. Turning servant songs into warriors was not an easy task. Each part of the body was designed with a particular skill, so they rebelled against Ilea's lessons. But she did not give up. This would take time, time she gratefully spent working instead of being afraid.

She sang for Jonas and Kyle and Juaquin until she could sing no more. And when her song was exhausted, she made her way back to the front of the hospital to find Mig. Her boots dragged, and she ran her gloved hand along the wall as she walked down the long hallways, studying the numbers and names beside each door. The numbers and the names that she couldn't read. She didn't notice the hook on the door handle. The hook on door 153 for hanging signs of encouragement and love. The hook that caught at her coat, that caught at the belt that swung loose between the loops that held it in place. Her coat jerked sideways and pulled the hood from her face. Ilea grabbed at the coat and spun to see Dr. Bennett standing in the hallway, watching, always watching. His eyes wide with surprise. She could feel the fear coursing through his limbs and his heart pounding in his chest. Ilea saw the same hatred in this man that she had seen in the soldiers on Regar. She would never be able to come back here again.

Ilea freed the belt from the hook and stepped backward, the coat hanging half off her shoulders. He could see her white hair and blue skin and the feathery lifelines along her cheeks. She held her hands out toward Dr. Bennett, and he stepped back even further. A gray-haired man and a woman with three children entered the hallway behind him. The woman started yelling and pointing. Ilea pulled the hood up over her face and started toward the opposite end of the hallway. If she could make it to the stairs, they would never catch her. The hood slipped as she walked and two nurses in blue gasped as she passed the adjacent hallway. The boots dragged and slowed her down, so she slipped them off, one by one, leaving a trail as she moved. Dr. Bennett followed behind and could see her blue feet sticking out from beneath the coat. Twisted feet with a claw on the side for climbing. It was almost a thumb and arched her foot above the ground. But it didn't matter anymore. It didn't matter what he saw.

With the boots gone, she started running, and Dr. Bennett ran after her. His fear had given way to rage. He wanted to know why this creature was in his hospital and what she had planned. Ilea burst through the double doors at the end of the hallway and frightened a man with a rolling bed. Ten more steps, and she was in the stairwell. She climbed, taking them two at a time. The coat slithered from her back and dropped on the landing of the second floor. Three young girls screamed as they passed on the stairs. Still she kept going, passing each level until she reached the last.

When she opened the final door, she was free. Out in the sun on the roof, she was safe. She stood on a flat roof with a two-brick high edging on all sides. Waist-high, metal, mechanical boxes were scattered across the surface and connected by wires that lead away from the building. From here she could see other parts of the city and the ground dwellers who walked here and there along the roads.

As she peeled off her gloves, she heard the door to the roof open. Ilea ducked behind one of the metal units and waited for him to leave.

"Ilea," Dr. Bennett pleaded. "I'm sorry I was afraid. I just was … surprised. I didn't know what to say or do. Forgive me for being afraid. Are you still here?"

He walked across the gravel covered roof and looked behind each of the metal casings. His voice was calm, but Ilea could still feel the anger stirring beneath. She knew she must be careful, and she shouldn't stay any longer. She peered out from behind the case, and then stood to face Dr. Bennett. Fear, worry, surprise, Ilea could feel him trying to decide what to do.

"I don't know what you are," he said, staring in disbelief. "You're the reason Andy is getting better … and the others. I knew something was going on."

Ilea stepped back toward the edge of the roof not knowing what to do. This man with his lab coat looked like the three men who had worked in the slick-white prison. The men who had helped Nick teach her words.

"Be careful," Dr. Bennett pleaded. "You'll fall. It's four stories up."

Ilea kept moving backwards not seeming to care about the edge.

"Please," Dr. Bennett pleaded.

Ilea didn't know what to think. She didn't know if he was her friend or her enemy. She didn't know if he would call the men from the prison … the men with guns who would come and take her away. She hated him for exposing her and keeping her away from the children. Jonas would surely die without her.

With a final glance at Dr. Bennett, Ilea turned and ran to the edge. Practiced and smooth, she gripped the brick ledge with one foot. Then, her body arched, and she dove from the building.

"No!" Dr. Bennett screamed and ran to the edge of the roof.

As he fell to his knees, Ilea rose before him. Her wings opened wide and gently twitching to hold her steady at the level of the rooftop. There was a part of her that wanted him to know she was Tal, that she was not like him, that she was different, that she was special. Keeping this secret had been frustrating and sometimes painful, but she understood. With her secret exposed, the dangers increased.

Their eyes met as she hovered there, just above the roofline, his face ashen and cold. And then she flew … straight for the sun.

"Ilea!" he called after her, watching the impossible, watching a woman with blue skin fly as easy as any bird. It was difficult to make himself believe he had really seen such a thing. He watched her until she was only a tiny dot in the sky. Then he gathered his wits and went to find Mig. He was the one responsible. He would have answers.

Water

Ilea hid among the trees at the ranger station. Pacing in the shadows, climbing, jumping, shaking her wings to pass the time … and calm the tremors in her stomach. Diesel whined and paced beside her. When the waiting overtook her, she flew, circling the station, watching the road from the hospital, rising then diving, but always waiting.

Eventually, Mig did return. He found Ilea on the half-stone fence, watching as he climbed out of the truck, watching with the sullen eyes of a child prepared to face the scolding of an angry parent. Lori was beside him holding Nick's tattered green satchel and the heavy brown coat.

Mig didn't need to explain. Ilea was smart enough to understand the consequences. The doctor had been furious, calling her an animal and a wild creature. He had called hospital security and the police and any other important figure he could think of. Mig had tried to calm the situation, explaining that it was his son's life after all. This wild creature, as the doctor labeled her, was helping everyone, especially Andy. But it didn't matter. Her lovely blue face would be on the security cameras, and Ilea would never be safe here again.

Mig and Lori sat down beside her on the fence.

Ilea bowed her head. "Sorry," she whispered, "sorry."

Diesel licked her toes.

"My dear sweet child," Lori's heart ached with her sadness. "You have no reason to be sorry." With one finger, she lifted her face. Lori studied the blue of her eyes and the feathery lifelines in front of each ear. "Look at all you have done. My Andy is going to be okay thanks to you … everyone in that hospital is better off because of you. There is no reason to be sorry … I will always be grateful."

Ilea brightened with the sound of her words and the love that rippled through her lifesong.

"But … you are not safe here … do you understand?" Mig was grateful too, but the scene at the hospital had changed everything. She was in danger now, and it was his fault. "You cannot stay here."

Ilea nodded. She understood all too well. She could stay in her hideout but eventually the flying machines would come and the men with guns. She would have to start over again … somewhere else.

"Hide," she whispered.

Mig shook his head and chuckled. "I don't suppose you have a friend I can call?"

"Friend," Ilea smiled as she thought about the men at the shiny prison. The hours they had spent teaching her their language. The pictures and the drawings and the writings. The men with guns and the green bag. She could still see Nick's face as he took her out that metal door and told her to leave. And his words, his words she didn't understand — "if you need a friend."

Ilea jumped up from the fence almost dancing with excitement. "Friend … yes … friend." She rambled on and on about her idea using words from the city of Luz, words that no one else could understand. Then she reached for the green bag in Lori's hand. "Friend," she almost shouted, "call a friend." Ilea squatted down to open the bag. From the zippered pocket on the side, she took out a tiny white card, and handed it to Mig.

"You have a business card?" Lori tried to hide her disbelief.

Mig read the card, "Nick Powell, Stock Broker and Financial Consultant." He looked at his wife. "She has a financial advisor?"

"Financial," Ilea repeated.

Lori tried not to laugh. "I don't think so."

Mig took out his phone and dialed the number on the card only to get an answering machine. "This is Nick. Leave a message."

"My name is Miguel Hernandez. I am a park ranger. I know this is going to sound crazy, but Ilea is here … with me … and she is in trouble. I need to get her to you … if possible. Can you come get her … or meet her somewhere?" Then he hung up the phone.

Ilea squinted. "Nick?" She didn't understand.

"He'll call you back," Lori tried to explain. "He's your friend. He'll call you back."

"Call you back," Ilea repeated, looking even more lost than before.

Before either of them could decide what to say, the phone rang. Mig switched it to speaker so that Ilea could listen.

"This is Nick. I got a call from you about a friend of mine."

"Nick … food … water … friend … Nick," Ilea tied to use some of the words he had taught her.

A muffled laugh from the speaker helped to ease the tension and Mig's concern that he was sending Ilea into a trap. "Yes, Ilea is here."

"So, you are in Colorado?" Nick had already tracked the call.

Lori passed her husband a worried look. How could he have known where they were?

"That sounded a little creepy," Nick didn't want to explain that he had a makeshift and probably illegal device to track cell phones. He paused to think of some way to prove his honesty.

"Tell Ilea that my hand is much better … the one I burned … the one she healed."

Mig took a deep breath to calm his nerves. "How do we do this?"

"I am too far out," the phone buzzed with Nick's muttering and planning. "Wait … wait … I have a friend who can meet her. Jack is close … at the university. I can send you the directions."

"A map would be great. I can pull it up on my phone to show her."

Nick chuckled again, "You taught her to read a map?"

Mig smiled, "Maps were easy. A bird's eye view …"

"Of course. I should have thought of that."

Lori caressed her husband's arm. Since their son's injury, she had lost sight of just how strong Mig could be.

"I am going to hang up and text you the site. There is a practice field toward the back of the campus. It should be empty … at least I hope it will be," Nick tried not to think about what kind of trouble Ilea might be in, or who might be after her, or what the college students would do if they saw her. "Jack will know where to go. She has to find Jack."

"Ok," Mig responded and swiped the off key.

Within moments, his phone buzzed and pictures and maps appeared. Mig showed Ilea the way to the university … to the place Jack would meet her. He enlarged each image to show her the landmarks and the significant buildings. He talked about direction and the sun and what to look for. He pointed at the mountains and the ranger station and tried to make her understand. With satellite images, they looked at the cities, just the way she would see them. Great stretches of forest and farmland and the gorge she would see in the distance, but most importantly the practice field at the edge of the school.

Mig reached into her bag and pulled out the radio. The button clicked and the static crackled. "It will shut off on its own, so the battery lasts for days and days. And you can charge with the sun." He didn't tell her there was a tracking signal from the radio that would make it possible for him to find her, to watch her journey. "You can call me … call a friend."

Ilea smiled. She had two friends now to call.

Lori folded the ugly brown coat and put it inside the green bag beside the radio.

"You have to go, now. Jack will be waiting for you." Mig swallowed hard. "Hide if you need to. Don't let them find you."

Ilea wasn't smiling anymore. *Hide* was such a horrible word. Danger and fear and hatred were never far behind. She hugged Mig and Lori and fought at the sadness that covered each of them, sadness as heavy as those shackles in the stone prison. She half-nodded and stiffened her back with a facade of strength.

Ilea put her hands on Mig's shoulders and stood on her tiptoes to kiss him quickly on the check. She picked up the green bag, and stopped to rub Diesel's ears one more time. She waved at her two friends then turned and ran. Three steps and her wings carried her over the trees, past the tower that watched for the beast that never came, and over the canyon. As she passed the river and the campsites, she could feel the terror rising above the land. People shouting and crying. Something was wrong. She knew she had to get to Jack but the fear was so strong it came in waves across the tops of the forest.

Ilea tucked her wings and found a clearing to land. Close to the water, a woman shouted. Ilea tiptoed close to the campsites to listen to their excited voices always making sure to stay unnoticed in the shadows. The ground dwellers had gathered along the water's edge, pacing, yelling, waving … afraid. Their lifesongs were dark and full of wrinkles. Ilea climbed one of the thicker trees, hand and foot, keeping her wings tight against her back. She slithered in and out of the branches until she could see beyond the ground dwellers.

One woman kneeled on the ground with her face in her hands, weeping, desperate, losing hope. The fading in her lifesong was unmistakable. Two men who wore dark brown uniforms like Mig fought the water with a rope. One man waded into the river holding onto a line tangled in the debris. Broken trees and branches piled and wedged themselves against the rocks … sharp, craggy rocks that lined the river on the other side and jutted out of the center part of the water. That's where she saw the yellow shirt of the dying boy. He clung to life, wedged among those same rocks and broken trees. He was not dead yet, but no one could reach him and his lifesong was growing weak. His skin was almost as blue as hers. The fading glow of his lifesong was slipping away and she couldn't help but think of her father. She remembered watching his body fail, and dreading the whisper of mist to come as his lifesong disappeared. The soldiers took her before she could save him. There had been a chance … he might have lived.

"No," she whispered, "this must not happen."

Even if they tried to hurt her, she would not stop. Ilea climbed higher in the tree until the upper branches leaned from her weigh. She hung her green bag on the tip of a branch, and then she jumped. She caught the branch of the tree beside her and pushed off again. Her wings unfurled, and she rose above the trees. The pop of her wings was buried beneath the rumble of the water. She rose above the trees and dove … down toward the water and the yellow-shirted boy.

The people on the land began to scream for her to stop. They couldn't know why she was there. She flew along the water's surface to grab at the boy as she passed. But the water and the debris held him fast. Her hands skidded across his body and she missed her grip. Still the people shouted and threatened.

Ilea spun sideways and rolled in the sky, diving back toward the boy to land on the largest branch in the pile. The branch that pinned him against the rocks. Her claws dug deep into the wood and she leveraged her weight to stay balanced. Crouching on the log, she reached for the boy. Her hands hooked beneath his arms and pulled. As his weight shifted, the log rolled forward, and the debris pile collapsed, dragging Ilea and the boy with them. The current pushed them under, rolling, tossing, driving them forward.

Ilea struggled against the current, opening her wings to fight against its strength. Still holding on to the boy, straining, choking, her foot-claws scraped against the rocks and forced them upward. Their bodies rose from the water. Ilea's wings thrashing against the spray, short powerful wing thrusts flinging water and dragging their bodies into the air. The yellow-shirted boy slid from her grasp and Ilea thrust her foot claw through the top of his shoulder.

They flew away from the people to find an open place to land. She needed time with him alone. Time to strengthen his lifesong. As they landed, she laid his body on the ground, limp, with eyes that stared but did not see. His shoulder bled from her claw, but he was dying from the cold and the beating of the rocks. Ilea leaned across his body, rubbing her hands across his chest and calling to his lifesong, singing almost as frantically as when she had held her father. She sang to his body pieces, for his heart to beat strong, for his muscles to give him warmth. The wound on his shoulder began to close, and the cracks in his leg bones sealed tight. She knew he would be alright.

The others were coming. Their angry voices shook the trees. It was time to go. Maybe, someday, these people would understand that she had saved his life, but not today. It wasn't safe for her to stay. It didn't seem to be safe anywhere. Ilea needed to find Nick … to find Jack. Three steps and her wings lifted her from the ground. Her shoulders tilted and she spun and dove and her left foot grabbed the tattered green satchel that still hung from the tree top. Her wings carried her to the clouds leaving behind the canyon and the boy and Mig and Lori … and Andy.

Doorway

"Yes, it's her. I know it's her," Nick assured his friend.

"So, I am supposed to walk out into the middle of our practice field and wait for a bird?" Jack already knew about Ilea and her special abilities. He wasn't the least bit surprised that Nick had found her … again, but he was so easy to tease.

"Jack, I need you to do this for me. Head south. I sent you some directions. I will meet you somewhere in the middle."

"Okay, I will cancel all my plans and go out to the practice field, but if she turns out to be just another pink dog … well … I …"

Nick laughed. "You are going to love her."

Jack stuffed his phone in his pocket and started walking. He was already on the university campus, so it wouldn't take long to reach the practice field. Since there was no rush, he headed to the stadium by way of the Student Union Building where he picked up a couple of hamburgers and a milkshake. He sat next to a redhead while he finished his burgers and part of her fries. Then slurped on the shake as he sauntered toward the back of the campus. Halfway there, he decided he might need his truck, so walked back to the main parking lot, stopping at a sorority bake sale to pick up a few chocolate chip cookies.

He parked outside the main gates of the stadium. Concrete and metal, with bleachers and heavy gates that blocked the tunnels into the stands. The beginning of the mountains loomed just beyond the visitor's side making it feel safe and protected. The gates would be locked and the playing field empty. But that was not a problem. Jack had charmed the cute little blonde who ran the concession stands when there actually was an event here. After a few smiles and some casual conversation, she had given him a key. Just one week into the semester, he had the keys to the kingdom.

Jack unlocked the gates, listening to the keys rattle and chime. His footsteps echoed along the corridor that lead him out in the grassy field. He found a comfortable place in the end zone and sat down on a giant capital 'N' to eat his cookies and watch the sky.

The light was growing dusky and Jack was hungry again when he finally saw, what was too big to be a bird, land in the hillside rocks beyond the stadium. He stood and walked out into the center of the playing field, holding his arms open wide, trying to make her feel welcome. His eyes strained against the shadows in the rocks, but he knew the spot where she had landed. He knew where to watch. When her wings opened and she rose from the cliff, it took his breath away.

"You are so much better than a pink dog," Jack mumbled to himself as she floated from the rocks to the field. She landed about ten feet away clutching a green bag and pushing her wings closed behind her. Jack stared at her ocean-blue skin and her eyes that glowed in the dusky light with almost the same color blue. Her hair was marshmallow white and pulled back in three ponytails, one high and two low. Feathery wisps edged her face like swirling tattoos with one side being much longer and darker than the other — a little lopsided. Even though she appeared like a fairy from the sky, Jack had this funny feeling that she was just somebody's little sister.

"Ilea?" he asked and then immediately felt stupid — as if there might be another blue girl. "I'm Jack. Nick's friend."

She listened to his rambling ... his arms still open wide.

"I know you are not sure that I'm Jack, but just how many crazy people do you think would be standing out here in the middle of the field?"

He motioned for her to follow, then walked back toward the metal gates where his truck waited, glancing over his shoulder now and then. There was still a good distance between them, but she was following. When he reached the gate, he pulled out the keys and pointed. "That's my truck out there. We are headed south to meet Nick."

Ilea stopped and opened her green computer bag to drag out that horrible brown coat she had worn at the hospital. She slipped her arms inside and pulled the hood up over her face. "Hide," she whispered, but not loud enough for Jack to hear.

"Nice," Jack said. "I see you are prepared. I was just going to run for it, but I think the coat is a nice touch.

He smiled at her blue feet sticking out from beneath the heavy coat, then turned and unlocked the gate. From beneath her hood, Ilea watched this stranger, feeling the goodness in his lifesong … the child-like excitement pulsing in his chest. She should be able to trust him. This man was Nick's friend. She stiffened her back, raised her chin, and walked toward the gate, staying close to the corridor wall and out of Jack's reach.

"I get it," Jack said. "It's kind of a scary place. You're lucky you've got Nick." His eyes hazed over with memories. "Sometimes he's all you need."

He walked out to the truck and opened the passenger side door. When Ilea came close, he reached out, spun her around, and lifted her into the truck. "There ya go," he said, unaware of the pounding in Ilea's heart and the claws open on her left hand. She quieted her lifesong with the knowledge that she could climb in and out of the truck with just her foot claws if needed.

Jack climbed in behind the wheel then unzipped an ice chest shoved between the front seats. "I got snacks," he smiled. "Beef jerky, peanuts, chips, crackers, peanut butter … I have a spoon for that." Next, he pointed to several sweaty water bottles. "Guess I should put some ice in here," he laughed, poking a mushy quart of ice cream. "It's really not too bad that way. I could drink ice cream … depending on how hungry I am."

He watched Ilea sniffing the beef jerky package, then started the ignition. "We are headed south. Nick's gonna meet us halfway. He'll let me know where … eventually. I know which road. That's enough. He'll have a plan when we get there. He always has a plan."

Ilea slipped off the hood of her coat, but Jack motioned for her to stop. "I would feel better if you waited until we get out of town. It will be dark soon … and we will hit the highway … then it won't matter anymore."

"Hide," she said with her teeth clamped together. Then she pulled her hood back over her head, and slid down into the seat. Jack could hear the crinkling of the beef jerky wrapper beneath the coat.

The sky grew dark as they cleared the city and merged onto the interstate. Ilea's crinkling and chewing grew quiet. Her body slumped against the door. Jack could hear the rhythmic, peaceful sounds of her breathing and decided to leave her coat exactly where it was. He fumbled with his phone and finally plugged it into the stereo. Then connected a set of headphones before reaching down into the ice chest to pull out a package of red taffy. Chewing, twisting, pulling, smacking ... he silently mouthed the words to some unheard song and settled in for the ride.

He thought about Nick, and he thought about Jaika. He wished she was here to see all of this. College and jobs and a life she had made possible. He wondered where she was and tried not to think about what might be happening to her ... that giant of a man who had carried her away ... through the wall of light. It still seemed like a dream. But Nick, Nick had tried to find the science behind it ... the solution to the doorway ... the way to bring her back. He had never lost hope. He would search a million years if necessary to find her. And of course, now there was Ilea to think about. Jaika would have liked Ilea.

He sang and snacked and counted the miles until finally, a little more than three hours later, he pulled into a small town in New Mexico. The mountains were only in the distance now. The land was flat, mostly, with scrubby bush-size trees and scattered dirty-white rocks mixed with red-clay. The main street was lined with flat roofed, adobe style buildings. A few had paper-sack looking luminaries that glowed along the walkways to the front doors. They looked almost eerie beneath a moonless sky.

"Nick's message says there is an old church at the edge of town, but I need something to eat first," Jack whined.

Ilea squirmed beside him then sat up, blinking her eyes and turning her head to try and see where they were. Jack reached across the ice chest to pull Ilea's coat across her body.

"We'll use the drive-through window. No one will see you."

It was late on a weekday in a small town, so not many restaurants were open. He did find a little hamburger grill. "I had hamburgers for lunch," he mumbled. "Why couldn't there be a pizza place open … yeah … with lots of pasta."

Jack ordered them both a burger with tiny packaged condiments. He wasn't sure if Ilea was a mustard or ketchup kind of girl. She might not even like burgers, so he added a giant order of fries, just in case. Jack's time spent flirting with the waitress slowed down the order but paid off with an extra order of fries, at no charge of course.

As they drove away, Ilea stuck her hand in the sack and pulled out a fistful of French fries. "Fries ... fries," she almost chanted, not caring that her coat had fallen to the floorboard.

"French fries, huh? Nick can't teach you about his fabulous best friend Jack, but he can teach you about French fries."

He handed Ilea a burger to go along with her fries then pulled back onto the main road to look for the church. Out of the corner of his eye, he watched his pseudo-kid sister unwrap the burger as if she thought it might explode. Gently peeling back the paper and sniffing the meat. The ride in the truck, the flight across the mountains, the hiding, the fear ... it was all too much. Ilea decided it was worth the risk of poison and took a deep bite.

"Never had one of those before, huh?"

Ilea glanced up at her new friend as the grease dribbled down her chin.

"Mmmmmmmmm," Jack mumbled. "Good stuff."

"Good stuff," Ilea repeated with a mouth full of food. "Good stuff … fries."

Jack shook his head. Someday, he would have to explain to Nick that Ilea thought a hamburger was called good stuff, which, of course, it was."

He guided his truck onto a small road barely big enough for one car. Nick's directions were taking them to a different part of town. Closer to the edge of the city where faded mobile homes and piles of discarded furniture and trash were the norm. There were no glowing luminaries here.

The paved road gave way to dirt and Jack switched on the four-wheel drive. The dusty path ended at an old mission style church. The walls were stone and dried mud and worn smooth with age and wind. The windows were closed off with crisscrossed planks. Jack could almost hear the ghosts wailing from the shadows. He drove to the back of the building, as far as the road would allow. Beyond the church was the same dead-grass desert peppered with rocks and scrub brush that he had seen along the highway. In the darkness, he could just make out the mountains watching over them in the distance.

Jack took out his phone and typed a quick text to Nick just to let him know they had arrived. Then he leaned his seat back to stretch out his legs and wait for an answer. I am in the car with a flying girl, he thought to himself. There can't be another man on the planet that can say that … and I can't even tell anybody.

"I could be famous," he mused. "Maybe I could write a book … my adventures with Ilea." He glanced over at the shadowy figure beside him eating French fries. "Driving across a few towns in a truck is not much of an adventure. But I could make up some stuff. I could have you rescuing people from tall buildings or fighting off bad guys. Maybe I could make you bulletproof. Are you bulletproof?"

Ilea smiled and ate another French fry. Jack's ramblings reminded her of the times she had spent with Mig, listening to him chatter about his family and his past. A world she didn't understand, and stories full of words she didn't understand, but it was nice. It brought peace to Mig's lifesong.

"You really can't understand what I am saying, can you?" Jack nodded. "But you are really good at making that face that makes people think you are listening."

They both shuddered as the rearview mirror flashed with distant headlights.

Jack started the motor. "If that's not Nick's jeep, we are out of here. I got a shotgun behind the seat. Don't tell anybody. I don't think it's legal here."

Ilea felt the tension rising in Jack. She reached down in the floor and shoved her brown coat into the green bag, just in case they had to move quickly. They sat frozen, waiting, until Nick's green jeep pulled in behind them. Jack took a deep breath and each man got out of his car.

"It's good to see you," Jack smiled and slapped his friend on the shoulder.

Ilea climbed out of the truck dragging the tattered computer bag and a half-eaten sack of fries. "And it's good to see you," Nick answered, but he wasn't looking at Jack.

"Yeah," Jack smirked, "good to see you Jack. Thanks for taking care of my new friend and driving her through two states to bring her here."

Ilea stepped closer to Nick, her fingers still clutching the bag. She could feel his lifesong warming. Nick reached out to touch her face. His fingers traced the swirling lifelines that framed her cheeks. Her eyes glowed with the blue light of the summer sky. And then he swept her into his arms, almost crushing her against his chest.

"I thought I had lost you," he whispered. "I thought I would never see you again."

Ilea wriggled from his grasp, trying to breath.

"Who's that?" Jack pointed to multiple sets of distant headlights. "Who would be coming out here?"

"They couldn't be following me. My cell phone, the GPS, everything was blocked."

"Don't look at me," Jack shrugged. "I have every security app turned on, just like you told me … just like you set it up."

"The truck?"

"I haven't done anything to my truck. No new parts … nothing … I've been a little short on cash."

Ilea felt the nervousness in the two men. She looked out at the lights at the far end of the dirt road, then pulled her heavy brown coat from the computer bag. "Hide," she announced, swinging the coat around her shoulders. They all turned at the clunk of the radio falling to the ground.

Jack picked it. "Colorado Parks … and Wildlife," he read from the back.

Nick huffed, "They are following her. This has to have a tracking device." Nick started walking toward the church. "The man who called me was a park ranger. It's his radio," he mumbled. "I should have seen this coming." He pushed the radio between two of the planks that covered one of the windows. They listened as the plastic cover thudded on the dirt floor inside the church. "Now … we have to go."

Nick turned and looked at his friends. "Leave my jeep here so they will search inside the church … that might slow them down… but we have to go … now."

Ilea could hear the machines now, the machines that came closer and closer as they talked. She growled low and pushed Nick toward the truck. He squeezed into what was almost a backseat. A ledge that flipped down from the side wall of the inside of the truck. The others climbed inside while Nick held his jacket over the dome light desperately trying to stay as invisible as possible.

"No head lights," Nick ordered. "You can drive in the dark, right? Slow, no dust for now."

"What if I said no," Jack snapped as he started the motor. Then he smiled. They were going off-road. "Do you know where we are going?"

"I have a plan," Nick assured him, but it sounded more like a question.

"I am sure you do." Jack shook his head.

"Head toward the mountains … just … head toward the mountains."

Jack drove his truck out into the brush, desperately fighting the urge to speed. The truck would tilt and lurch as it ran over a rock or bush or something he hoped wasn't alive. Swaying back and forth they crept across the wilderness.

Ilea didn't need the sunlight to see. The land was alive with song. The trees, the bushes, the animals that ran and flew and slept in between them all. She raised her hand close to Jack's face then pointed to the right side of the truck. They were approaching a tree stump that could easily blow out a tire or split an axle. Jack steered right and then stared, wide-eyed, at the shoulder-high stump that passed just outside his window.

"Keep going," Jack cheered. "I'll follow you."

Ilea watched and guided, moving her hand left then right. Some things were impossible to miss, so the truck would pitch to the side, tossing its passengers back and forth.

Nick leaned over the front seat. "There should be a road out here that leads to the mine."

"The mine?" Jack complained. "We are going to hide in a mine?"

"If the entrance is not boarded up, we can pull the truck straight in. They will never find us."

"Ooookay … oooooookay … in a mine. I am going to drive into a mine," He shook his head in disbelief and then reached down to retrieve a warm bottle of root beer from the ice chest. "I'm glad I brought my snacks." He hooked the bottle top on the edge of the radio and pulled. The cap went flying.

Nick rolled his eyes noting the multiple bottle-cap notches dug into the front of the radio.

Ilea pulled her legs beneath her in the seat to raise her line of sight then started pointing to the right. She repeated some of the good words she could remember, "fries, friend, sky … good stuff …"

"Maybe she found the road," Nick mused.

"I'm glad someone knows where we are going." Jack veered the truck to the right, following Ilea's directions.

The truck began to level and the tires fell into the ruts of the dirt road.

"So, she can see in the dark. Is there anything else I should know?" Jack rambled as he squinted out the windshield trying to see the road. "Can she shoot lasers out of her eyes or tear down buildings?"

Nick thought about his hand where the burn was healed and the stories the Labcoats had told him. "She just might be able to do all of that."

Ilea settled in the seat. "I guess it's all clear now," Jack said, then belched … a root beer burp.

Ilea giggled and watched out the window of the truck. She could feel the mountains growling closer, the heaviness and groaning of their song, and the whisper of the night crawlers in between. But the ground off to her right felt different. The earth there carried burns and scars from weapons.

The ground was full of holes and caverns and rubble left by ground dwellers.

Suddenly, she understood. "Hide!" she yelled and held her hands up for Jack to stop.

He hit the brake, and she opened her door. The dome light blinded them as Nick grabbed for his jacket. The ding ding ding warning from the truck followed her outside. She closed the door and then ran, lifting off from the ground. Jack and Nick heard the pop of her wings.

"She left us," Jack groaned to the ceiling.

"Maybe it's better that way," Nick mumbled tearing strips from a roll of duct tape he had found under the seat.

"Better for her … maybe … I think we should run. I have a test next week."

"I'll take it for you," Nick muttered then stuck a piece of the tape across the dome light.

"No, no that's not how it works. Jaika wouldn't want that."

Nick caught his breath. He had not even thought about her since Mig had called. "Jaika," he whispered. "You're right. She wouldn't want us to do it that way."

"And she wouldn't want you to tape up my dome light."

The truck shook with the thud of Ilea landing on the hood. Her face appeared, pressed against the glass. Her wings wide behind her. "Hide, hide," she chanted.

Jack put the truck in gear and let it move forward. "I miss my headlights."

Ilea pulled in her wings and scooted to the edge of the hood almost like an ornament perched on the top. Then she extended the claws on her left hand and dug them into the metal of the hood.

"She has claws?" Jack almost shouted. "I'm glad she likes us. She likes us? Right?"

"Don't make her mad, Jack." Nick wondered what that would look like.

Jack kept the truck moving along the dirt road until Ilea turned and waved toward the right. He turned the steering wheel and followed her motions until she stopped them in front of a faded wooden sign almost as tall as the truck. Jack backed the truck in behind it.

When they opened the doors to get out, the silver tape glowed over the ceiling light in the truck. "You are such a nerd," Jack snickered.

Together, they followed Ilea toward the massive rocks beyond the sign. With her wings twitching outward and her eyes glowing blue, she made an almost terrifying shadow in the darkness, but Jack and Nick followed. Stumbling in the night until they stood before a brush covered hill with wooden framing that outlined a door. Rotting planks crisscrossed the opening. Basketball size rocks were stacked in piles around both side of the entrance.

"Is this supposed to be a mine?" Jack's voice seemed to shake the planks. "This doesn't look like a mine," he whispered this time.

Ilea opened her claws on both hands then dug them into one of the planks. Slashing and prying, it fell to the ground in splinters. Nick pointed to the two boards closest to the ground, so Ilea opened her claws once again. Each time she struck the planks, she could feel the mine quiver. She could see rows of wooden slates that lined the ceiling within to keep the mine from collapsing. But the quiver did not come from the wood. It came from the thousand heartbeats that clung to the frames. Tiny creatures, no bigger than her fist.

hung by their feet. Their wings tucked around their bodies just like hers. Not Breen ... and yet ...

Her claws tore into the bottom most plank. Nick yelled something but the roar of the wings within the mine covered his words. Nick stood to the side, but Ilea and Jack hit the ground as the bats exploded from the hillside. The wall of bats spiraled and twisted and rose into the sky like a black cloud. A cloud with wings and teeth and claws. Ilea watched their lifesongs as they tore into the night sky, and they left her heart aching for home. She got up and finished removing the bottom plank, then ducked her head and walked inside.

Jack looked at Nick. "Are you sure this is a good idea?"

He shook his head, "We can't fight them in the open ... and I am running out of ideas. At least in here the passageways will narrow. We can fight them one at a time."

Jack dusted off his pants, then huffed and walked into the mine, "Men with guns ... one at a time is so much better."

Nick knew he was failing his friends. He knew he should tell Ilea to fly away, but he couldn't bring himself to let her go, just yet. He walked into the mine behind his friends. Both boys turned on the flashlight that came with their cell phones. The light danced along the rocky walls of the mine. Twenty-five steps into the cave the ground gave way to an open shaft, straight down. Rusted pulleys and cables hung from the ceiling and draped into the hole like giant snakes. Ilea and Jack stood at the edge and peered down into the abyss. Jack's cell phone glowed white in the darkness.

Nick studied the rusty motor to the side of the hole. "It must have been an elevator."

"Hellooooooooo," Jack's voice echoed inside the hole. "That's a looooong way dooooooooooo …" The rocks crumbled beneath his feet. Slipping, fighting, grabbing, Jack disappeared into the hole.

Ilea dropped into the shaft behind him. With her wings closed around her body, she rocketed past Jack into the darkness. Her body twisted as she opened her wings, scrapping the jagged edges of the cables. Ilea cried out in pain as she pinned Jack to the wall. Her claws digging into the stones. Jack flailed and wrapped his arms around Ilea, sliding from her shoulders to her waist. There he stopped, holding on for his life.

Ilea started climbing. Hand and foot and claw, she climbed up the rocky walls dragging Jack as she moved. Nick waved his phone at the top of the shaft, thankful they were both alive. Ilea growled as she willed her body upward. Hand, foot, and claw, she felt the muscles in her back tearing with Jack's added weight. Her wings opened, flinging blood onto the cables. She thrust them backwards to push her closer to the top of the shaft.

Nick watched as Ilea climbed like a spider money, scraping Jack's spine against the stones. As they reached the top, Nick grabbed Jack by the collar and pulled. Ilea climbed up over the edge, and together they pulled Jack to safety.

"Holy cow," Jack mumbled. His eyes rolled back in his head. "That was scary. Man … am I gonna write a great book."

Ilea lay trembling on the ground beside him. Her muscles burning and her wings screaming with pain. She closed her eyes to focus on the torn muscle in her back …then she felt the machines. The heavy, black machines that carried the men with weapons.

"Hide," she cried. "Hide." She kept repeating the word until Nick seemed to understand.

"They're coming, aren't they?" Nick stared at Ilea in the white glow of his phone. "They found us."

He tugged at Jack to help him to stand. "We need to go deeper into the mine. There are so many tunnels, they might not find us."

Ilea stood and leaned against Jack as they made their way into the mine.

"Go around the hole this time," Nick warned.

"Yea … yea … at least they wouldn't find us in there." Jack was in too much pain to laugh. "I hope she can see where to go."

Ilea could feel the fear crawling inside the two men. She had never felt either of them so afraid. The men in the black machines must be horrible indeed. Just like the men who had killed her father. For a heartbeat, she considered running to the open end of the tunnel. She could be in the sky and gone before the other men arrived. Instead, she twitched her wings and tried to hold her head high. Today, she would die protecting her friends.

The tunnels twisted and turned and narrowed as they walked. Ilea searched the stone for places that were weak and could fall, and for places they could hide. She guided them deeper into the mine. Jack's cell phone was beginning to dim.

"If you hear them, you need to turn that off," Nick patted his friend on the shoulder.

"I know," Jack muttered. "I'm really not having fun anymore."

The ceiling dropped so they had to duck to keep going. Stooping and staggering they followed the curve of the passage. Nick ran his hand along the ceiling to keep his bearings. Without warning, the tunnel turned sharply and the ceiling disappeared. Nick, Jack, and Ilea stepped out into a room the size of a small house. A room dripping with stalactites and white frothy stone and a small pool of crystal clear water.

Ilea gasped and began to whimper. She ran to the far wall of the room and pushed against it. How could she have been so wrong? This wall should be another tunnel. Why could she not feel the stone?

Jack and Nick shined their phones across the ceiling and the ridges along the side walls. The light sparkled when it touched the foamy white rock close to the water. Ilea wilted to the ground beneath the knowledge that she had led her friends to a dead end. There was no escape. The men with weapons would be here soon.

"It's not your fault, Ilea," Nick stared at her on the ground, helpless and lost. She could have easily escaped without him. "It's my fault. I led us here. It's my fault that we will be …"

"Thanks for worrying about me," Jack chuckled, then leaned against the wall by the entrance to try and boost his phone light.

Nick turned to his friend, "I'm sorry." He knew they would kill them both and take Ilea with them. They would die here and no one would ever know. "I'm truly sorry."

"Don't worry about it. It's been a fun ride. Better than I ever thought would happen."

Nick walked over to sit down on the ground beside Ilea. He reached out and took her hand, then began to stroke her knuckles and her palm and ran his fingers along her bracelet. "This doesn't have magic powers, does it?"

Ilea didn't understand. But it didn't matter. The soldiers were coming. She could feel their heartbeats and almost hear their voices. Her heart ached for her friends, and she knew she could not sit and do nothing. Ilea stood and walked closer to the entrance of the room. She would meet the warriors as they came through. She would protect her friends.

Her voice quivered at first, but the chant of her morning prayers was etched into her bones and its rhythm overcame her fear. She closed her eyes and thought of home. The landing where she sang to her city almost every day. She thought of her mother and Dodgen and the people she would never see again. Her prayer was gentle at first. A prayer of hope and peace and joy. But it grew in strength, pushing outward into the tunnels of the mine. She threw open her arms and sang to the soldiers, showering them with warmth and peace and the desire to sleep. Tears began to stream from her eyes. The soldiers were not slowing. Her song was not working. She didn't want to die here. She missed her family and her city. But no matter the cost, she would not fail her friends as she had failed her father.

"Ilea," Nick whispered and stepped beside her. He gripped her arm just above the wrist, wrapping his fingers around her bracelet. "We will face them together."

Ilea felt the hum of the crystal in her bracelet as Nick joined his lifesong with hers, and her singing moved beyond the tunnels, beyond the mine and out to the sky. The soldiers and the ground and the black machines shook against the force.

"You have to stop," Jack pleaded. "You're going to bring down the mine."

Ilea twisted and wrapped her fingers around Nick's wrist, around the beads he wore to remember Jaika, around the beads that she had cut from the crystals of Luz. … and the beads began to glow. White-blue light split the air. Nick cried out in pain as its heat burned against his skin. He jerked and tried to pull away, but Ilea opened her claws and dug into his wrist, spattering blood across his shirt. He grabbed at her claws with his free hand and pulled her closer as he dragged her toward the back wall, trying to escape her grasp.

Her eyes rolled upward and her head dropped back. The stone in the back of the cave, the rock she could not feel, became a wall of watery-blue light.

"She opened a portal!" Jack yelled. "It's a door ... it's Jaika's door!"

Jack didn't wait for an answer. He wrapped his arms around his two friends and pushed them toward the light.

Nick cried out, "What if she's not there? What if Jaika is not there?"

Jack nodded and held his friends even tighter. "Then we will just have to open another door!" Then he walked forward through the doorway of light, carrying, his friends with him.

Ilea gasped and sputtered as Jack dropped her and Nick into the sand. The doorway behind them vanished. She closed her eyes to make everything stop spinning. Then she pulled her knees to her chest to sit up. There, on the horizon, she saw it — her red moon. She knew every shadow and every mountain. It was her moon, but only a piece. It sat low in the sky and most of it was hidden by the sand. Way too low and too far to the right, but she was home. That was her moon.

"Did we make it?" Nick sputtered, unable to stand. Blood oozed out of his arm onto the sand.

"Yes," Jack whined, pointing in the opposite direction of the moon. "But I think we chose the wrong door."

"Why …" Nick closed his eyes and let his body go limp.

Jack shook his head. "Because … I see a dragon."

Epilogue

Wearing his favorite tweed jacket with the leather patches on the elbows, Vicente Robles walked in the intensive care unit of White Hall Hospital as he had done so many times before. He wouldn't be wearing his lab coat again for quite a while. C & J Power had made sure of that.

It was late and only one nurse sat at the station where he got off the elevator. His step was a little quicker than usual, and his eyes a little brighter. Maybe the nurse could see it.

He paused at the door of room 211, watching his daughter breath, watching the light on the monitor flash on and off, and wishing she did not have to use that long tube just to eat.

It had been some time since she had spoken or even moved. It was getting harder to remember her voice. He missed her like water and air and sunlight and all the other things that a man needs to live.

Vicente sat down in the stuffed chair beside the bed, the one they use for family members who come to visit. "My lovely Vanessa. My beautiful child. I have brought you a gift."

He pushed his glasses a little higher on his nose and pulled out a cell phone from his jacket pocket. "You must listen, my child. You must listen with every part of you ... every part."

The phone lit up when he hit the side. A few more taps and the file he needed displayed on the screen. "Remember ... you must listen."

Vicente hit the button and Ilea's voice began to sing, blended harmonies full of morning prayers that only the Tal understood. Her voice warmed the air and painted the walls with hope. He laid the phone beside his daughter's hand then leaned back in the chair to listen with her. The song echoed across the room, weaving its spell through the air.

There were so many wires, and that horrible feeding tube, but Ilea's voice covered them all. Vicente studied his daughter's face, the curve of her jaw, the fading color of her skin. It could have been the light ... or the shadows ... or even the wind — but he was certain — Vanessa smiled.

Acknowledgements

I would like to offer a special thank you to those who make my books possible. My amazing editors Brenda and Betty. My cover designer Peggy and my consultants Casey, Brit, Terrie, and Rachel. I am grateful for their time and support and willingness to answer my endless questions. But most of all, I want to thank you, dear reader. I hope you have enjoyed the journey. I would love to hear from you:

FREE BONUS CHAPTER
Visit my website
https://alexraebooks.wordpress.com/
explore other books in the *Children of Regar* series and receive a
FREE BONUS CHAPTER

Watch for upcoming stories on
Facebook @AlexRaeBooks
or email me at AlexRaeBooks@gmail.com

Pronunciation of Regarian Names

Adolphus (ə `däl fəs)

Argia (är `jē ə)

Dodgen (`däd jen)

Galimar (`gal ə mär)

Genoa (`jen ō ə)

Harea (hə `rā ə)

Ilea (ī `lē ə)

Jaika (`jā kə)

Kaleus (`kā ləs)

Kayz (kāz)

Merith (`mer iTH)

Oberon (`ō bər än)

Regar (`rā gär)

Seela (`sē lə)

Torri (`tôr ē)

Zaharra (`zär ə)

ā=a in age, ä=a in are, ē=e in eat,
ə=a in about, ī=i in kite,
ō= o in pole, ô=a in walk

411

www.ingramcontent.com/pod-product-compliance
Lightning Source LLC
Chambersburg PA
CBHW071149250626

47159CB00001B/28